STRIKE THREE:
YOU'RE IN LOVE

To request permissions, contact Our Corner Publishing at info@ourcornerpublishing.com

First Edition

Design by Arka WR | ttakooo21@gmail.com

ISBN 979-8-9863336-9-4

www.ourcornerpublishing.com

www.annadenisch.com

This book contains mature and sexually explicit content.

If you are not of legal age to view such content in your country, please put this book down.

Viewer/reader discretion is advised.

Table of Contents

Team Rosters

Gardeners of Eden

Coach: Lawrence – He/Him
Pitcher: Michelle – She/Her
Catcher: El – He/Him
First: Amy – She/Her
Second: Charlie – They/Them
Shortstop: Valerie – She/Her
Third: Louie – He/Him
Left: Blake – He/Him
Center: Derek – He/Him
Right: Rosie – She/Her

Shades of Infernal

Coach: Briney – They/Them
Pitcher: Lily – She/Her
Catcher: Sam – He/Him
First: Rich – He/Him
Second: Jean – He/Him
Shortstop: Farrow – He/Him
Third: Faye – She/Her
Left: Cyrus – They/Them
Center: Anwar – She/Her
Right: Altan – He/Him
Designated Hitter: Cody – He/Him

Chapter One
Meet-Cute(butt)

Cody didn't even want to play baseball in the first place. And if he was going to put himself through the dredge of standing around waiting for something to do, he certainly wasn't going to do that on the weekend for *work*. His job kept him so busy during the week that the weekends were the only time he had to do anything actually worth doing. Instead of playing this dumb game he could be grocery shopping, or cooking, or cleaning (god, he really needed to clean). But no. He was here. In the sun. With bugs buzzing around his ear. Holding a bat and staring down at the cold gaze of the opposing pitcher. All because Cyrus had found out Cody used to be play little league.

If the team wasn't already down by two runs, Cody might have just gotten himself struck out and moved on with his life. But while Cody didn't subscribe to 'corporate loyalty' or whatever, he still liked winning. And he figured he owed Cyrus for getting that promotion over them. Not that he felt he had particularly earned that promotion.

Cody stepped up to the plate and readied his bat.

"Good luck," the catcher said in a light and airy voice.

"I don't need luck," Cody said.

The pitcher wound up and tossed the ball. Cody tracked it expertly and swung at just the right moment, sending it sailing into right field. He tossed the bat and made a run for it, making it around to second with plenty of time to spare.

Cody heard the "Safe!" and smirked, looking back at the catcher. That'll teach him to wish Cody 'good luck'.

El didn't particularly enjoy sports, as a whole. They made fine background noise when he was doing errands or chores, sure, but he hardly cared for them. He had only joined this league because he had been new to the company and thought it would help him make the connections he needed to succeed. But now he was a few years in and completely stuck. While he did take pride and joy in being the best catcher in the league, not just the team, he did wish he could step away without letting everyone else down.

El's boss and team manager had tried to argue against the designated hitter that the Shades of Infernal (brilliant name for a fashion house, he always thought) team had decided to bring on a few games into the league. But any argument against Rafael was almost a guaranteed loss. Rafael made an obvious choice as umpire, being a freelance photographer that worked for almost all of the companies in the city these days. And, true, he knew his game inside and out. But he wasn't exactly consistent in his judgements. And so, the late comer had been allowed.

El would mind, on principle, if the new guy didn't look so good in his uniform.

By the time the new batter was up again, his team had pulled ahead by three runs. Which meant El's team needed to step up their game. The hitter walked up to the plate, a challenging glean in his eyes as he shot El a look.

It should have made El angry, he figured, but it only intrigued him. And as the batter got into position, El couldn't help but comment.

"You have a very nice butt," he said.

The hitter stalled and missed the first throw completely.

"STRIKE!" Rafael called. A little too loud, El thought.

The batter turned his scowl back to him. "Did you hear what he said to me?"

Rafael shrugged. "Yeah? So?"

The batter huffed in exasperation. "He can't say stuff like that."

"Nothing against it in the rules," El said.

"It's a compliment," Rafael agreed.

The hitter grumbled and knocked the dirt from his shoes. "Exactly who's side are you on here?"

"Oh, whichever side gets the most veins to pop out of the most heads," Rafael said with a laugh. El wasn't too big to admit that he didn't fight Rafael much on most things, as he did let El get away with quite a lot.

Although, in this case, he hadn't even been trying to get away with anything. He just genuinely thought this guy had a nice butt.

The batter shook his head and took a calming breath before readying again. His hit was just a few inches off, the ball sailing right under him.

"Strike two!" Rafael announced.

"Yeah, no shit."

"Hey, don't make me red flag you," Rafael said.

"That's soccer," El said.

"I'm the ump. If I wanna red flag someone, I'll red flag them."

El chuckled softly and got ready for the next pitch. He could see the hitter's eyes squint, his body tightening up as he prepared. He was clearly riled up, which might serve well for El's team, at least.

Michelle made the next pitch, a curveball to the left, that the hitter swung at expertly. Unfortunately, his expert swing didn't make a connection. The batter growled and glared down at the ball in El's mitt. El could see him practically start to fume when Rafael yelled, "Strike three, you're out!"

"Good try," El said. Because it had been a really good swing. And then the batter turned his glare to El before he walked back to the dugout.

The rest of the game was pretty uneventful and boring. That's why Cody hated this sport so much. It was always so boring, even while playing it. The other team, *The Gardeners of Eden* (which he assumed did something with plants?), ended up winning in the last inning by one run. Which you'd think would be exciting, but was just a lackluster walk-in.

Once the game was officially over, Cody started to leave. But Altan, one of the triplets that played outfield with Cyrus and Anwar, blocked his path.

"You did really great today, Cody," he said, chattering excitedly. "This is the closest we've gotten to winning in a while now."

"Yeah, but we still lost," Cody said. Not that he cared for any real reason, just personal pride. He had come in and did his best. He couldn't be expected to carry the whole weight of a losing team just because he felt a *little* guilty about the job he didn't even want.

"You're probably just rusty," Cyrus said, joining their brother in blocking Cody's path. "We'll get 'em next time."

"Yep, sure."

Cody turned around to leave the other way and let out a surprised yelp when he nearly smacked into Anwar.

"You are coming to the next game, right?" she asked.

Cody sighed and placed his hands on his hips. "If I say yes, do you go away?"

All three of them nodded.

"Fine. I'll show."

They let out a small cheer and then finally dispersed, patting Cody on the back as they left. Cody grabbed his bag and figured they must be pretty desperate to get a win. Briney might have mentioned something about a years-long losing streak. He may not like the company, but he liked most of his coworkers enough. So, he at least wouldn't actively lose on purpose.

As Cody trudged back to his car, he spotted the catcher from the opposite team walking along the sidewalk with a bit of a dance to his step. The actual parking lot was in the opposite direction, so Cody figured he must live nearby.

"Hey," Cody called out, jogging up to him.

The catcher turned around, and Cody's breath stuck in his throat for a minute. The guy had one of the brightest, most cheerful faces you could ever imagine. And when he smiled at Cody, it was like the sun itself was smiling at him. The number one problem with baseball now was that it hid that beauty behind a mask.

"Oh, hello," the catcher said in that light voice of his. "Good game."

He held out a hand and Cody shook it. "Uh, yeah, sure." He cleared his throat. He *was* going to give this guy a piece of his mind, but he couldn't bring himself to yell about something as stupid as a baseball game at that face. "Uhm, just wanted to congratulate you," he said instead.

"Well, thank you, but it was a team effort."

"Nah, I meant your weird butt comment."

"Sorry?"

Cody hated to admit it, but it was a pretty solid strategy. "It's the most creative distraction I think anyone's ever come up with."

"It wasn't meant to be a distraction," the catcher said. "I just thought you had a nice butt." Then he smiled a bit and looked away briefly. "But it is good to know it has that effect as well. I'll have to remember that one."

Cody stared at him, trying to figure out if he was adorably clueless or just ruthlessly conniving. Either way, Cody was interested. "What's your name?"

"El." El held his hand back out.

"Cody." He shook it again, holding on a little longer than probably acceptable. "Say, El, can I give you a ride?"

El looked around a little, his cheeks reddening a bit. "Yes, I think you could. That's very nice of you. Thank you."

Cody smiled and started leading El to his car. Maybe something worthwhile would come out of this whole baseball nonsense after all.

Chapter Two
The Flustering of Cody

The next day at work, Cyrus still kept coming by Cody's cubicle every five minutes. Only now they were doing so to congratulate him on his stellar performance that weekend.

"I already agreed to go," Cody reminded them. "You don't have to keep pestering me. In fact, the more you keep pestering me, the less likely I am to actually show up."

"Right, got it."

Cyrus scrambled away and Cody tried to go back to his work. But he couldn't stop thinking about that damn game. Well, more specifically, that damn catcher. Cody still couldn't get a read on El. Nearly the entire car ride home, El spent the time discussing (and praising) Cody's plays, while giving very last-minute instructions on how to get to his place. It was just four blocks away, but they had almost gotten lost twice. Cody had dropped him off, and then sat there in his car for a solid ten minutes trying to figure out what to think.

And all this time later he still had no idea what to make of El.

"Mail call," Anwar announced, dropping the stack of envelopes on Cody's desk.

From the next cubicle over, Cody heard Rich groan. Cody stood up and peeked over the edge.

"S'amatter?" he asked. "Another memo about color swatches?"

"No," Rich responded. He picked up an envelope that had something sticky on the front of it. "Got this attached to my mail."

Cody snaked around the wall dividing them and took the letter. It was addressed to the Gardeners of Eden. They were in the same mailing code of the city, sure, but their offices were still far enough away that this was weird. Or fate.

Cody had always been a fan of fate.

He raised an eyebrow at the mystery envelope. "You wanna burn it in a ritualistic cleanse?" he offered.

Rich let out a smoky huff of a laugh. "Doubt it would work. I'll just send it back."

He reached for the envelope again, but Cody pulled it out of reach. "Actually, know what? I'm gonna be heading down that way for lunch. I can just drop it off for them."

"Why would you do that?" Jean asked, his head popping up on the other side of the cubicle.

"To be neighborly," Cody said. Which earned him some well-deserved looks of disgust. It still boggled his mind how two companies that didn't even remotely work in the same industry could have such a gripe over *baseball*.

But then Jean's eyes lit up, and he nodded in understanding. "I get it. You're going to go spy on them," he said with a dark smile.

Cody was not going to go spy on them. "You got me," he said. "What's a good day without a little corporate espionage?"

Rich mimicked Jean's smile. "Just remember, if you get caught-"

"I know nothing and no one," Cody finished. Then he gave them a mini salute and returned to his desk, letter held tightly in hand.

El had loved his job, once. He still loved parts of his job, sure. He enjoyed most of his coworkers. He liked having a nice big office that he could decorate however he saw fit, usually full of his overflow of books from home. And he enjoyed getting to travel to the plant nurseries he was in charge of and meet with the local owners who so passionately cared for their businesses.

But he did not enjoy having to crush most of their passions under the corporate rulings.

But El tried not to think about it too much. He was just going to keep doing his job and getting paid and saving up for...well, something.

El picked up a packet on his desk and started going through the request coming in about a nursery just outside of the city that wanted to move to a bigger location. The phone rang before he could get too far into it.

"Hello?"

"Good afternoon, Mr. El," Valerie greeted. El had grown accustomed to the bright and cheery voice of their receptionist. He wasn't sure he'd ever get used to anyone else running the downstairs. "You have a guest here."

El hummed and double-checked his planner. "I'm not expecting anyone. Who is it?"

"A Mr. Cody?" Valerie said. El's heart beat a little harder. "Says he has something to give you?"

El nearly choked on his own spit. *Get your head out of the gutter. For goodness sakes, you're at work!* "Ah, yes. Go ahead and send him up. Thank you."

El stood up and walked around the side of his desk to stand before the elevator. But he didn't want to look too eager, right? With a slight cough, El turned around and pretended to look at the papers on his desk. But now it looked like he was actively trying to ignore Cody. Which he didn't want to do.

Thankfully, El worked on the 13th floor, so he had plenty of time to 'look casual' by leaning against his desk, one piece of paper in hand, as he waited patiently for Cody to arrive.

Cody knocked on the half-closed door and then slid into the office.

"Cody," El greeted with a bright smile. The last time he saw Cody, his hair had been all stuck down from sweat. Now, however, it was styled, laying in soft red-orange layers that accentuated the golden-brown of his eyes. And if El thought Cody looked good in a baseball uniform, it was nothing compared to the well-tailored suit he wore now. "Nice to see you again," El said, before his thoughts started to wander. "Did I leave something in your car?"

"Er, no," Cody said. He shook his head softly, his hair moving just a bit. "I just, uh, we got this stuck in our mail." He pulled a letter out from his inner pocket. "Just thought I'd drop it off for you. Quicker that way, you know."

"Oh. Thank you." That hadn't been what El was expecting, of course. But he had been known to get his hopes up in the past. El took the envelope and furrowed his eyebrows at it. "Uhm, this isn't addressed to me." He turned the envelope around to Cody. "It's for the accounting department. Down on seven."

"Yeah, I know that," Cody said, his voice pitched a bit in offense. "I just, uh," his voice trailed a bit as his attention wandered. El pulled the envelope back and smiled, feeling a little hint of warmth on his cheeks. Maybe his hopes had been right after all. "I wanted to make sure it got to someone responsible, and trustworthy," Cody offered. "Clearly can't trust the mailmen, so...yeah."

"Well, I'm glad to know you think I can be trusted." El turned around and placed the envelope in a pile on his desk. "I'll be sure this gets to the right department."

"Should I not think you can be trusted?" Cody asked. He had that challenging glint in his eye from the game. The one that made El's stomach do a little flip.

"Well, we did only meet a few days ago," El said. "So, it seems like a bit hasty of a judgment."

Cody shrugged. "Well...you just seem like a trustworthy guy." Then he grimaced a little, and El almost laughed at how adorable he was.

"I appreciate the compliment. Thank you." El smiled at him again. He could see the hesitation in Cody, like he was trying to decide on something. El didn't have lunch plans. But then the phone on El's desk rang. He sighed at his high hopes. "Sorry, I should probably get that."

"No worries," Cody said, a forced smile on his lips. "I should get back to work myself. Salt won't mine itself, eh?"

El nodded at him and Cody spun on his heels and left. El smiled to himself as he took the call. Cody certainly liked to put on an air of confidence, but he also seemed very easy to fluster. And it wasn't El's fault that Cody looked so cute when he was flustered. And it certainly wasn't El's fault that the baseball games left plenty of opportunities to do some flustering.

Chapter Three
A Little Rain Never Hurt

It was cloudy for their next game against the Gardeners, which Cody much preferred. Without the sun, there was less chance of a glare, which meant he had better odds of showing off his skills and proving he was better than El. Good enough for El? He couldn't make up his mind exactly what he wanted to prove, but he was going to prove it!

As they were getting ready, Cody looked out to the other team's dugout and made eye contact with El. El smiled and waved before covering his beautiful face with his helmet. Cody gave him a small wave back.

"What are you doing?" Briney asked.

"It's called waving," Cody informed them. "It's this newfangled way to say hi to someone."

Briney rolled their eyes and looked half an inch away from murdering him. Although, to be fair, they always looked half an inch away from murdering someone. Which made them a pretty effective team coach. And a pretty effective budget manager, come to think of it.

"Well, stop waving and start warming up. We need you on your A-game today."

"Oh, you don't need to worry about little ol' me."

Cody slipped on his gloves and glared over at El. He wouldn't admit it out loud, but he spent a few nights that week down at the batting cages, getting more than just a warmup. It was a little silly to get so invested in a company game, but batting did help alleviate the stress of his job, so Cody just considered it an after-work relaxation move. Even if it put him even further behind on his housekeeping chores. At this point, he figured it'd be easier to buy a new set of dishes than try to clean the ones sitting in the sink.

"Alright, Lily," Briney said as the Gardener's took their place around the field. "You're up first. Remember, Michelle curves hard to the left, so make sure you don't go swinging at any balls."

"Aren't we supposed to swing at balls?" Altan whispered to his siblings on the bench.

"I think they meant like, ball-balls," Anwar replied.

"Like not in the strike zone," Cyrus agreed.

"Oh, that makes more sense," Altan said.

Cody chuckled at the triplets and shook his head. It was a good thing one of them wasn't leading the team. It also wasn't all that surprising that even someone like him had beat someone like Cyrus for the job.

Cody leaned against the fence and watched Lily step up to bat. He knew he probably should be paying attention to the pitcher and how their throw style was today. But he couldn't tear his attention away from El. He moved with surprising ease and grace, pivoting expertly to the side whenever a curve ball got away from the play. And as Cody watched El's leg spread out, pretty far, he noted, he felt a heat rising to his face.

The hard hit of the bat on the ball broke him out of his stupor and he watched Lily rush down to first. But one of the outfielders made the catch, putting her right back in the dugout.

"Good show," Briney commented as the grumbling Lily took her seat. "Jean, you're up."

Jean stood up and made a show of stretching his neck before he walked out there. He was a bit fast and loose with his swings, so if anyone needed reminding of when not to strike, it was him. But he managed a nice drive down the center line and made it to first with no problem.

"Mackinson," Briney said. "Get up there."

All three triplets stood up. "Er, which one?" Anwar asked.

"I don't care," Briney said.

The three turned to a small huddle, and Cody watched as they played a quick game of rock-paper-scissors. The loser, Altan, walked up to the plate. No wonder they needed Cody's help to win.

Altan, unsurprisingly, struck out pretty quickly. And he looked a little relieved when he came back.

Briney growled. "Alright, Cody. Go show 'em."

"Oh, I'll show 'em alright," Cody said, swinging the bat over his shoulder as he walked up to El.

"You look very dashing in your uniform today," El said.

Cody shook his head and didn't bother looking at him. "Not gonna work this time, sorry."

"If you say so," El whispered.

And *that* did work. Cody was so busy trying to figure out where El got the nerve or confidence to say that, that he missed the first pitch.

"Strike!" Rafael announced, ever so helpfully.

"I guess it did work after all," El said. And when Cody looked back, he had a little smirk, half concealed by his face guard.

That's it, Cody thought as he shook his mind loose and readied the bat. *I'll show him.* Instead of trying to ignore the things El said, Cody decided to let it fuel his anger. He always did work best when he was all riled up.

The next pitch came right at him, a clean drive, and he swung with all the spiteful power he could muster. The contact of the bat on the ball even sent a little sting up his arms, but it was worth it to watch with a satisfied grin as the ball sailed out and over the back fence.

"See?" Cody said, gently dropping the bat. "Didn't work."

"A very nice hit indeed," El agreed, beaming up at him. "Good job!"

Cody grimaced and started his victory lap, all the while still trying to decide whether El was nice or evil.

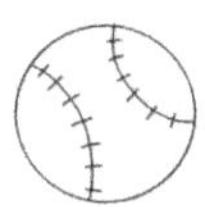

They won by two points, and the celebration in the dugout was loud, boisterous, and fitting. Cody had come into the games a few weeks after the league officially started, and he assumed this losing streak of theirs had been quite extensive. So, he decided he'd relish in the cheers and comradery. After all, he was pretty instrumental in their victory. And a little praise for something he was actually good at was always nice.

After about half an hour of excitement, Cody managed to worm his way out of the dugout without getting immediately dragged back in. He slung his bag over his shoulder and made a quick getaway to the parking lot. He raised his eyebrows in surprise when he saw El standing next to his car, gear bag in hand, just waiting, with a small smile on his face.

"Looks like rain," El said, pointing to the darkening clouds.

Cody stared at him for a moment. El really didn't live that far away. In the time it took for Cody to escape, El probably could have walked there and back again. Which meant he was looking for a ride for a different reason.

On the one hand, Cody didn't want El to just get away with assuming he would give him a ride (even though he would) and kind of wanted to make him actually ask. But on the other hand, he appreciated the boldness of the move.

"Hop in," he said, unlocking the door.

El continued to be an enigma. "Do you mind if we make a quick stop?" he asked as Cody pulled away from the park.

"Is it at a costume store?" Cody asked. "Gonna get me a little chauffeur outfit?" He laughed, but when he glanced over at El, he was looking Cody up and down as if that wasn't such a bad idea. Which just made Cody hot under the collar.

"No," El eventually said. "I just need to stop by the market for a minute."

"For what?" Cody at least knew where the store was around here, so he didn't have to rely on El's distracted driving directions.

"Milk."

"Milk?" Cody scoffed. If that wasn't a lamer excuse to hang out than bringing over misplaced mail, he didn't know what was.

"What?" El asked, looking genuinely innocent and confused. "I ran out this morning and didn't have time before the game."

"Uh huh, sure," Cody said. He shot El a quick smirk. "I believe you."

El pouted, actually *pouted*, and looked out the window until they arrived. There wasn't any open space close to the store, so Cody parked about a block away and they started walking.

"You don't have to come in with me," El said as they approached the store.

"Why not?" Cody asked. He shoved his hands in his pockets and smiled at El. Finally, he was getting the upper hand here. "Afraid I'll find out you were just making stuff up?"

El gave him a prim look and then walked rather purposefully into the shop. Cody laughed and trailed after him. They wound their way through the shelves, got El's milk, stood through check out, and emerged to a rumbling sky.

"*Now*, it looks like rain," Cody said.

They hurried back to the car but only got about halfway before the shearing sound of rain spelled imminent danger. El grabbed Cody's arm and pulled him under a nearby awning, just as a torrential downpour cascaded upon them.

Cody huffed and looked down the street at his car. "We could make a run for it," he said. "It's not that far. We wouldn't get too wet. Nature's shower, and all that, eh?"

"Perhaps," El said. "Or..."

"Or?" Cody looked back at El. He was looking up at Cody with a suggestive expression, lips recently licked to a nice shine. "Oh, yes. Or."

Cody nodded and stepped closer, placing a hand on El's cheek. He leaned down and pressed their lips together. El's kiss was as soft as anything, and his lips had such a delicious slide to them. But before Cody could really get into it, the rain came to a sudden stop, about as sudden as it had started.

Fate giveth – fate taketh away.

Cody looked up at the sky with a glare dark enough to match the clouds.

"Well, should have no trouble getting to the car now," El announced. He stepped out of their hiding place and started heading down the sidewalk.

"What about the or?" Cody asked, wishing desperately that the rain had lasted longer. An hour at least.

El turned around, now walking backwards. "It's not raining," he called out. "So, we don't need an or."

Cody deflated with a sigh. He shook his head clear of those delightful kissing fantasies and followed after El.

Chapter Four
Practice Date

Cody had allowed himself to get fully roped into the games because of El. But they weren't the only two teams in the league. And Cody was back to regretting his decision to join when he showed up for the next game against the Brainy Bunch. But as he trudged his way from the parking lot to the dugout, his outlook brightened a little.

"Hey," Cody said, walking up to El on the bleachers. Their games usually didn't have too many spectators, just a few friends and family of the players and a couple locals who had nothing better to do with their time than watch people fail at playing baseball.

"Mm, hello," El mumbled around a mouthful of popcorn. He hurriedly finished chewing and gulped, smiling up at Cody. "Good day for a game, right?"

"Yeah, sure." Cody thought that any day playing the game wasn't good, but it was a little better with El here. And since they hadn't seen each other in about a week, Cody was pretty excited. "You always come to the games you don't play?" He gently nudged his bat against El's leg. "Like hassling players even off the field?"

El chuckled and scooted over. Cody took the offer and sat down. Briney would yell at him for being late, but he didn't care. "I just like to watch sometimes," El said. "Have to study the opposition, you know. Stay up to date on techniques and all that. Plus, the park is just a walk away."

"Makes sense," Cody said. "You gonna want a ride home after this match? Or is that only when you play?"

El smiled, a small blush forming. "Well, if you're offering..."

Cody laughed. "I guess I am."

"Then I would love a ride, thank you."

"Hey, quit making nice with the opposition already," Rich said, walking up from the dugout. "We have a game to play."

"I won't occupy any more of your time," El said. But then he patted Cody's knee, which he figured was going to occupy all of his time.

"What are you even doing here?" Rich asked El. He scoffed a little and crossed his arms. "Never seen you at an outside game before."

At that, Cody raised his eyebrow and stared at El as he blushed even more.

"Just because you've never seen me, doesn't mean I wasn't here."

Rich looked at the sparse gatherings of people on the bleachers. "Hard to miss you."

"Well, maybe you're just blind," Cody said. He thought it was kind of sweet that El came out here just to see Cody play. So, if he could help him cover up the truth, he would.

Rich just sighed. "C'mon, get a move on."

"I'll see ya after," Cody said. He winked at El and couldn't wait to get the game over with.

El hummed happily and continued eating his popcorn as the game started. He kept noticing Cody looking at him while waiting in the dugout. But every time El caught his eye, he was quick to look away. Which made El chuckle. Cody really was cute.

Then Cody was up to bat. He made an excellent hit and ran to first with no trouble. El figured he was just about the best player in the league right now. He briefly wondered if maybe Shades of Infernal had 'hired' a professional just to get ahead, what with him showing up late in the games. But El knew from Cody's grumblings and mumblings that he disliked the game too much to do it professionally.

Which had originally begged the question as to why Cody kept playing in the first place. But then El thought about him bringing that letter over. And he felt both a little guilty that he was the reason Cody was suffering through the games and a little more excited that Cody liked him so much. Because he liked Cody so much back.

And he really liked messing with him.

That kiss the other day had been perfect and deliciously yummy. But more delicious was the confused look on Cody's face when El walked away from him. El was looking forward to another kiss, however. So, even if the to-read pile was stacking up at home, he decided to take himself to the game and enjoy the show.

And what a show it was. Not the game of course, that was fairly boring. But Cody was a wonderful player, despite his protests to playing. He rarely struck out, and when he made a hit, he ran like his life depended on it. At one point, Cody even slid his way into third, a delightful display that brought a soft gasp to El's lips.

By the time the game had ended, Cody's team leading 3-2, El had managed to work himself up a bit too much. The problem with not playing the game: El didn't have anything else to really focus his energy on, other than thinking about Cody. He was thankful as the team took to cheering and celebrating for a few minutes so he could calm himself down before going to meet Cody at his car.

"Enjoy the show?" Cody asked as he walked up, a strange little bounce in his step.

"Very much. You play well."

Cody smirked, unlocking the door and tossing his bag in the back. El settled in the passenger seat, thinking of whatever he could to keep the day going that was much better than buying milk.

"Need any errands run today?" Cody asked, a bit of a goading smile on his face.

El couldn't think of anything that wouldn't give in to that satisfaction. "Mm, nothing I can think of." And he frowned a bit, upset that the day would have to end soon anyway. And it was such a lovely day.

"Mind if I run a few?"

El's heart swelled. He tried not to smile too much. "Don't mind at all."

"Perfect."

Cody drove them through the town a few blocks and pulled up in front of a little cafe. It was newer to the area. El had always seen it on his way home, but had yet to go in. El looked around but couldn't see anything that looked like a store or any other place you'd go to run errands.

"What errands do you have to run here?" he asked.

Cody smirked. "Oh, I don't actually have any errands." Then he got out and walked around, opening the door for El.

El continued to fight his smile as he got out and followed Cody into the cafe. They got a few looks with Cody still in his dirty uniform, but no one really paid them much mind. And El thought the little bit of dirt made Cody look charming.

They went up to the register and El looked over their menu. They had quite a selection of teas and coffees. And in the display cases around the counter there was a lovely mixture of pastries. He would have to start making an effort to come in here more often. Cody ordered himself a coffee and some kind of croissant. El got some tea and one of the strawberry-flavored desserts.

"And an extra-large water, please," El added.

"Thirsty much?" Cody chuckled.

"It's not for me," El said, handing the water bottle over to Cody. "It's for you." Cody looked at it, refusing to touch it. "I saw you hardly drinking anything during the game. You need to stay hydrated."

Cody grumbled a bit and rolled his eyes. But he took the bottle from El with a small smile playing at the edge of his lips. El followed Cody to a table by the window, determined to make sure he drank at least half of the water while they were there.

"You played expertly today," El said before taking a sip of his tea. "It was very impressive."

"Thanks. You were the best spectator one could hope for."

El chuckled softly and bit into his desert. He couldn't help but let a little moan of delight slip past his lips as he savored the delicate flavors and textures. He always did have a sweet tooth.

"That good, huh?" Cody asked.

El blushed and wiped his lips on his napkin. "Mhm. Don't forget your water," he added, nodding at the neglected bottle by the edge of the table. He didn't want to be too pushy, of course, but *someone* had to make sure Cody was drinking well after a game. And Cody certainly didn't seem interested in that job.

Cody shook his head and made a show of picking the bottle up, strong arming the top open, and taking a big swig. Only, he moved a little too fast, and about half of that big swig splashed out over his face and neck. El hid his mouth behind his hand and tried very hard not to laugh.

"Yep," Cody said, carefully putting the cap back on and setting the bottle down. "That happened."

"Here." El grabbed some spare napkins from the holder to the side and handed them over.

"Thanks." Cody started patting himself dry, laughing a bit himself, which gave El the permission to let a little giggle through. "How'm I doin'?" Cody asked. "Best first date ever or what?"

"Or what," El answered. Although this was just about the best date he could think of so far. "But, you know, it doesn't have to be our first date."

"No?"

El shook his head. "It could be a warm-up, if you'd like. A practice game before the real one."

Cody nodded along. "Yeah, I could get behind that. But then, uh, when *is* the real one?"

El got a marvelously brilliant idea and smiled. "How about next week? After our match." He gave Cody a challenging, yet playful, stare. "Loser buys dinner."

"Oh, now that is interesting." Cody leaned back in his seat, looking El over as he thought about it. "I'm in."

After they had finished eating and chatting, Cody drove El home, but he didn't get out of the car right away. No, he was still looking forward to that next kiss. And he couldn't wait a week for it.

"Everything alright?" Cody asked.

"Oh yes," El said. "I was just thinking. Since this was a practice date, perhaps we'd better make sure we practice everything."

"Everything?" Cody asked. El gave him a knowing look. Really, for how confident he acted, Cody could take a while to get the hint. "Oh! Oh, everything. Yes, yes, we should definitely practice everything."

El smiled and leaned over, meeting Cody halfway. It was a longer kiss this time, and one that sent El's nerves all buzzy. Cody certainly knew how to kiss, and he had some quite interesting things he could do with his tongue. Things that sent a shiver of delight right down El's spine and into his pants.

No matter how much he wanted to keep kissing, he figured it was still a bit too soon for that. So, he pulled away with a slight cough and smiled bashfully at Cody.

"How's my form?" Cody asked.

El laughed at him. "Perfect."

"Well, you know, there's always room for improvement." He tilted his head down a bit, looking up at El in a suggestive fashion. "If you want to keep practicing."

Oh, he was going to be trouble, of that El was sure. But a little trouble could be just what he needed. "Oh, I don't think you need the extra help. But feel free to practice on your own if you want."

Chapter Five
The World's Best Catcher (But Worst Hitter)

El hummed as he flipped through his files. He was getting ready to go on an expedition to one of the nurseries today. It was both the best and worst parts of his job. On the one hand, he got to be away from the office and do some traveling. On the other hand, however, he had to deal with managers that thought they knew better on how to run their nurseries.

The worst part about that was that they usually did. And El could only do so much to help them.

El's phone rang just as he found the folder he was looking for. He dropped it on his desk and picked up the phone, greeting Valerie's bright and cheery voice.

"Hello," she greeted. "Mr. Lawrence and Ms. Michelle would like to see you up on the 20th."

El stifled a groan. He hated the 20th floor. Lawrence and the others only met on the 20th when they were getting ready to change things up. Which usually meant more work for El.

"Tell them I'll be right up," El said. He took a deep breath and made his way. When the elevator doors opened, he groaned so loud he worried he sprained something.

Lawrence and Michelle were standing before a whiteboard, a schematic of the ballpark drawn up. Spreadsheets and binders were laid out on the meeting table. The two stood close to each other, talking in excited and hushed tones. They always obsessed over this game a bit much, El thought, but this was taking it to a whole new level.

"You wanted to see me?" El said, getting their attention.

"El!" Lawrence greeted. "Good timing. We were just talking about you."

"Fantastic," El said under his breath. But then he gave them a professional smile. "What is it you need?"

"I know you're supposed to go to the Conoway Property today," Michelle said. "But we need you to stay here."

El looked at all the baseball notes and wondered, well, hoped, that he had read the situation wrong. "Is there some kind of crisis?"

"I'll say." Lawrence grabbed a file and flipped it open, sliding it down the table to El. He saw Cody's picture and knew his hopes were squashed. "The Infernals are becoming a real threat." He wondered exactly what they were a threat to. It's not like there was any money on these games. Not even a trophy. It was literally just bragging rights.

Unfortunately, Lawrence and Michelle loved to brag.

El stifled another groan and sat down, waiting for the nonsense to be over. At least he was technically getting paid for this particular bout of nonsense.

"And this has what to do with me going to the Conoway Property?" El asked. He was all for a little healthy competition, but this was perhaps going a bit too far. Especially for something as low stakes as a company league.

"It's supposed to storm this afternoon," Michelle explained. "What if the roads flood and you're stuck there? We need you here for tomorrow's game."

"I hardly think the storm's supposed to be that bad."

"That's not a risk we can take," Lawrence said. He tapped on Cody's folder. "We need you to stay put and stay safe. We don't know what this guy is going to throw at us, and our best catcher needs to be ready."

El sighed. "Mr. Conoway asked to see me personally," he explained. "He wants to get permission for a new store layout."

"And Jonathon is perfectly capable of handling that," Michelle said.

"But we're supposed to be building relationships with our franchisers," El said, most certainly not arguing, of course. "How can I do that if I don't go meet with them?"

"It's one meeting, El," Lawrence reminded him. "And this is important." He pointed back at the whiteboard.

El thought their jobs and actual work were more important than a silly baseball game, but he wasn't going to argue. There would be no point.

"Very well," El said. "I'll make sure Jonathon is properly briefed on the work that needs to be done, and I'll stay here."

"Excellent." Michelle smiled at him and El got up to leave.

"Oh, and El, one more thing." Lawrence leaned over the table. "You are, without a doubt, the best catcher we could hope for."

"Mhm," El said, not liking the but that was sure to follow.

"But your hitting, it could use some work," Lawrence continued. And Michelle nodded in agreement. "So maybe get some extra practice in between games, hm?"

"Sure."

"Good man."

El turned around and rolled his eyes. He would not be doing any practicing; of that he was certain. Because the very last thing he wanted to do with his time off was play more baseball

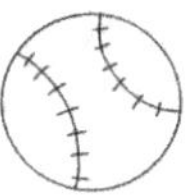

Cody was in the zone. It was the first time he was actually looking forward to one of these stupid games. The bet made things infinitely more interesting. And even if he lost, he still got a date with El, which he considered a win.

The Gardeners were up first, and as the designated hitter, Cody got to watch comfortably from the dugout. The other team had some good hitters, sure, but anything hit to the outfield was just a waste. The triplets were shit at the plate, but they were nothing if not a well-oiled machine out in the field.

But El's team still managed to score two runs before they were out. So, Cody had some making up to do.

"Not a word," he warned El as he stepped up to bat.

He heard El chuckle, but that wasn't a word, so he let it slide.

Cody readied himself and managed a double on the first hit, earning a "good job," from El as he left.

Rich made a nice hit himself, after two strikes, and Cody tucked his head and made a run for it. He knew the play was good when Rafael didn't do his annoying shout. He rounded third and made a beeline towards El.

The dilemma: Cody looked up just in time to see El catch the ball, thrown back in from the outfield. He *could* turn and run back, but that would make him look like a coward, and he'd probably just end up stuck in a game of monkey in the middle.

So, he had two options. He could either keep running like usual and let El get the tag. Or...

Yeah no, letting El win here wasn't an option.

Cody sped up a bit and then went for the slide, angling his body just right so he'd knock into El, aiming to hit him in the shin guards, of course, so he didn't actually hurt him. He felt El topple over him, landing half-on him as Cody stretched his leg out, cleat securely on the base.

He looked over at El's hands as the dust settled.

"Oh, that's an out!" Rafael declared as El smiled, holding up his hand with a firm grip on the ball.

"Impressive," Cody said, looking at El's eyes through his face guard.

"Thank you," El said, smiling as always.

"You okay?" Cody checked.

"Yes. You?"

"Yeah."

And then they just stayed there, laying tangled up on the field, too lost in each other's eyes to move.

"Ahem." Rafael knelt down, looking between the two of them. "I said you're out," he told them. "As in, get up and get off the field?"

Cody glared at him, but El just laughed as he worked his way to his feet. He offered a hand and Cody took it, dusting himself off a little.

"Good effort," Briney said, giving Cody a shoulder pat as he passed.

"Don't look too dejected," Lily agreed. "Not the first one of us to think he'd be an easy one to take down. He's something else."

Cody smiled out at El as he got back in position. "Yeah, he sure is."

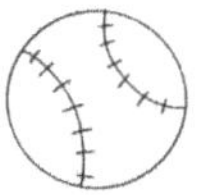

The game was a bit of back and forth, which made El worry. He was used to games that had a bit more of a grip, one way or the other. But their teams kept swapping the lead, run by run, until they ended up at the last inning, with the Infernals leading 9-8. El wrung his hands together and watched as Michelle made a nice hit that was immediately caught by one of the outfield players.

"I thought we talked about no outfield," Lawrence said as Michelle stormed their way back.

Michelle didn't even respond, and El gulped.

Derek was up next. He managed a double and that loosened the knot in El's stomach. This was good. Valerie was up now, and she could hold her own. She made a nice bunt that got Derek to third but got her out at first.

El looked at the scoreboard and his mouth went dry.

"One sec," Lawrence told him, before calling time and jogging out.

"He won't let you switch hitters," El called after him, but Lawrence just turned around and gave him a thumbs up with a confident smile.

Everyone waited, tense, in the dugout as Lawrence talked to Rafael. They seemed to argue for a bit, then Lawrence bounded back over, looking a little disgruntled, as expected.

"I told you he wouldn't let you," El said. Even though he did wish someone else could bat instead. He knew himself well enough to know that he was not going to do well.

"It doesn't matter," Lawrence said. He shook his head and then smiled. He grabbed El by the shoulders and looked into his eyes with a scary determination. "You can do this, okay?"

El nodded.

"Derek's already on third. All you got to do is get him home and we tie."

El nodded again, but the knot in his stomach was back.

"Get him home and not get out," Amy called from the bench.

"Yes, thank you," Lawrence said, shooting her a bit of a glare. He went back to smiling and looking at El. "You'll do great."

El gulped and Lawrence sent him on his way, a little reassuring pat on the back for support. Not that El felt very supported. He knew he wasn't going to do well.

El caught Cody's gaze from the opposite dugout. Cody gave him an encouraging nod, but all that did was enhance his anxieties. Not only was he about to let his whole team down and cost them the game, but he was about to fail spectacularly in front of his date.

"Deep breath, buddy," Rafael told him.

"Hey, stop taking sides," the opposing catcher said.

El did take a deep breath. And then he proceeded to strike out in what he assumed was the quickest strike out in the history of the league. He deflated with a sigh as the other team started to celebrate. With his head hung a little low, El walked back to the dugout.

"That's alright," Lawrence said, patting him on the back again. "We'll get 'em next time. Just...practice, yeah?"

El nodded slowly and slumped to his seat.

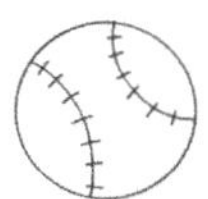

Cody knew that El wasn't the best hitter, but that had been borderline spectacular in how terrible it was. First, he swung at what was clearly a ground ball, then he hesitated on what would have been the perfect throw, and to top it all off, his third swing missed the ball by so much you could have fit an entire mitt between the bat and the ball.

But Cody figured there had to be a bit of give and take in athletic ability. Sure, El couldn't hit, but he was built strong and stout. Cody's hip had actually started to get a little sore from their earlier contact. As far as he saw it, El had nothing to be ashamed of.

But shame was the clear expression in his slumped body language as El waited by Cody's car.

"You okay?" Cody asked as he walked up to meet him.

"Yes," El said. He was doing a good job of hiding it on his face, but he looked absolutely crestfallen. Cody leaned against the car and gave him a look that said he wasn't buying it. "Well…a little disappointed perhaps," El admitted. "It's not that I mind losing, and I certainly don't mind paying for dinner, I just…"

"Are really bad at batting?" Cody offered, with a small smile to soften the blow.

El sighed, deflating a little. "Yes, that. I don't mind it usually, just not when it actually has to matter. Like today."

"Well, you know, I am pretty good myself," Cody said, only partially as a boast.

El rolled his eyes, but his smile was starting to come back. "Yes, yes, we all know you're good."

"So, maybe I could give you some pointers one day," Cody finished. And then El's smile and bright eyes were back in full force. "If you'd want," he added for a little extra fun.

"Well, that certainly would help," El agreed. "As long as you won't get in trouble for helping the opposition, of course."

"Ah, screw 'em," Cody said. Sure, he'd probably get a talking-to. But it's not like helping someone in a dumb company league was grounds for firing or anything. "If they get mad, they get mad. It's not like they can actually *do* anything about it."

"True." El's smile widened just a bit further, and Cody considered his job well-done. "In that case, I would love to take you up on your offer."

Chapter Six
The Real First Date

Cody dropped El off and then went back to his place to shower and change (and ignore the dishes in the sink again). El had originally tried to convince Cody to pick where they would go for dinner, as he was the winner. But Cody managed to successfully get El to pick as a sort of 'consolation prize'. Not that El needed much convincing.

Cody was still trying to figure El out, but the one thing he had come to learn was that El was very good at pretending he didn't want something, but then caving as soon as it was offered in earnest.

El had hummed and hawed over the decision, and decided on a nice little bistro that wasn't too far from where he lived. He claimed it was supposed to be a pleasant evening and they could walk together.

El was already waiting for him outside, and Cody smiled upon seeing him, especially seeing how El smiled back. Heaven help him that smile would do him in one of these days.

"Isn't it just the perfect night for a walk?" El asked.

"Oh, yes," Cody agreed. "Perfect indeed."

El gave Cody a bit of a suggestive look, holding his hands behind his back. Cody shook his head a little, unaware what he was waiting for. He had always been a little slow to pick up on cues. But El had never made him feel weird about it. Which was weird itself. It's not like El did anything different than anyone else. Code just hadn't been lying when he said that El seemed naturally trustworthy.

El's eyes glanced briefly at Cody's arm. With a nod, Cody held it out to him. "Shall we?"

"We shall." El's smile grew and he linked his own arm with Cody's, leading them down the sidewalk.

"So, er, what sort of first date topics would you like to start with?" Cody asked.

El chuckled. "Hm, well, how about work? We are in a company league, after all. And yet I'm not really sure what you *do*."

Cody didn't like thinking or talking about work outside of work, but he was awfully interested in learning what El did. Or what the Gardeners of Eden did in general. Plants, right? Had to be plants.

"Well, we're in fashion design, you know," Cody said. El nodded and they turned the corner. Cody could spot the bistro just at the end of the road. Not far from El's place at all. "And I technically run the brand 'Fork and Tail'."

"You *technically* run it?"

There was a small line outside, but El pulled them past. He gave his name at the front, and they were led inside to a reserved table. Cody was impressed that El was able to get a reservation when they only just decided a few hours ago to eat here.

"Yeah, I'm the 'brand ambassador'," he said. "Whatever that is."

Their waiter brought over some menus and water. El ordered them a bottle of wine as well. Cody briefly considered offering to pay at least for part of the dinner, but El had lost fair and square. And if he decided to buy a bottle of wine, more power to him.

"You don't actually know what your job is?" El asked.

"Eh." Cody shrugged as he looked over his menu. "I mean, you know, they pay me to show up at things. Tell people to do the jobs they're already doing. I dunno, be around if something happens. But nothing ever happens, so…" Maybe Cyrus would have been able to do the job well enough, come to think of it. Cody still didn't know why he had been put up for it in the first place. He did his best to not try at his job. Maybe he needed to actively work on being bad at his job?

"That must get pretty boring," El said.

Cody looked up at him surprised. Most people, upon hearing Cody's take on his job, thought it was the dream. Getting paid to show up and basically do nothing. But El understood. Of course he would. Cody smiled.

"Alright, then." Cody tapped his fingers on the table. "Your turn. What is it *you* do?"

"I am a regional manager."

Cody laughed. "Yeah, if that isn't more of a made-up job than brand ambassador."

El chuckled and nodded, taking a sip of his wine. The waiter returned to take their order before he could continue. El got a roasted duck platter and Cody ordered the garden salad.

"Just a salad?" El asked. "You know you don't have to pick something cheap on my account. I'm perfectly comfortable with paying."

Cody smiled at him with a soft chuckle. "I don't doubt it. Just not much else as an option here."

El's face fell. "Oh, dear. You have an allergy? I'm so sorry, I should have asked."

Cody waved away the panic and worry that was quickly forming on El's face as he fidgeted in his seat. "Nope. Just a preference," Cody told him. "Don't eat meat."

"Well, why didn't you tell me? I would have picked someplace more…option friendly."

"It's fine, El, really. I like salad." He also didn't want anyone to make a fuss over him. Especially when his diet was a choice. He wanted El to eat where he wanted to eat.

"Are you sure?" El asked. He looked like he was ready to get up. And do what? Cody wondered. Go somewhere else? Make a big deal about it?

"I'm positive," Cody assured him. El seemed to settle down, but he looked at Cody with a slightly hesitant look. Like he wasn't sure. Like Cody was lying. Like Cody's comfort was worth El's own. They needed to change subjects. Fast. "Anyway, enough about my food habits. Get back to this regional manager nonsense."

El finally smiled again. "Well, I'm afraid it's not much more exciting than your job. Mostly micromanaging people that really should be left to their own devices, but what can you do? At least I get to do some traveling, which is always nice."

"Yeah, nice. So, the people you manage, they work for the Gardeners?"

"Er, sort of?"

"Sort of?"

"See, it's a franchise. The owners, they work for themselves. But they're under our, erm, guidance? And so, they follow our rules. But they don't, you know, directly 'work' for us."

"So, you get a bunch of money to show up and tell people to do the job they're already doing," Cody said, a smile playing at his lips. "You have an entire company that does my job."

"It's not just that," El argued, looking a bit angered and the insinuation, but also like he kind of agreed with it. This Cody was much more comfortable with.

"Oh, no? What else is it?"

"Well, we...we brand them!" El said, a bit of gusto in his voice. "They become Gardens of Eden, and we help them, you know, promote themselves and improve their shops and nurseries and all that."

"You do know that's a terrible name, right?" Cody asked.

El nodded. "Yes, well, I don't know who exactly came up with it, but it is a bit...much."

Cody chuckled. "Do you like it?" he asked. "Your job."

El thought about it for a moment. "You know what? I do. I may have a lot to say about how it's run, or some of the specifics of things. But overall, yes. I like my job. You?"

"Eh." Cody shrugged. "It's alright."

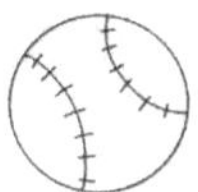

They spent a wonderful evening chatting and laughing and getting to know one another. By the time they were done, El truly felt like he had known Cody his whole life. And Cody was learning, quick to offer his arm again as soon as they stepped out into the lovely night air.

"Well, thanks for dinner," Cody said, walking El up to his door.

"Thank you for the lovely company."

Cody smiled and leaned against the doorframe. "You know, I, uh, I did take your advice."

"And what advice would that be?"

"Practiced a bit on my own."

El felt the tingles starting up inside him already. "Well, we'll just have to see if it paid off any."

He stepped closer and leaned in for a kiss. And *oh* did it pay off. El hadn't been entirely convinced that Cody did 'practice', especially since he didn't need to, as the last kiss had been marvelous on its own. But clearly, he did something, because whatever this was, it was about ten times better.

El leaned in even more, hands instinctively coming to rest on Cody's waist. And Cody's hands wrapped around him, one holding his back as the other messed itself up in his hair. Cody's tongue started doing those *things* again, and El let out an airy breath into their kiss.

Before long, El was out of breath and hot all over. He pulled back and the devil was smirking at him. Which only set off more of his tingling.

"You know," El said as he tried to catch his breath. "I do have some delicious decaf tea inside. If you'd like to extend the evening a bit."

Cody smiled and placed his hand back on El's cheeks, looking deeply into his eyes. "Sounds perfect."

"Okay, good." El smiled at him and turned to open the door. He got halfway through before he startled and turned back, smacking into Cody, hand reflexively coming to a rest on his chest. He briefly forgot what he was going to say as he looked at where they touched.

"Everything okay?" Cody asked.

El shook his head clear. "Yes, sorry, perfectly. I just, ah, wanted to make sure we were on the same page about tonight."

"Why don't you tell me what page you're on," Cody said. "And then I'll tell you where I'm at."

El nodded and looked back up into Cody's eyes. He was a little nervous. He knew he had just used the most obvious line for sex in the book, but he hadn't really been thinking about it when he said it. He tended to do that a lot.

"I don't think we're ready for sex *quite* yet," he said. It was their first date, after all. He noticed no change in Cody's expression. "But I would very much like to make out with you for a decent portion of the evening."

Cody smiled, and that settled all the butterflies in El's stomach. "Funny, I was thinking the exact same thing."

El had a suspicion that wasn't true, but Cody didn't at all look disappointed in him for changing up the mood a little. "Then I guess we are on the same page."

"Looks like it."

"Good."

El opened the door again and led Cody inside. They never even drank the tea.

Chapter Seven
The Morning After

El sighed peacefully as he stretched and opened his eyes. He hadn't slept that good in ages. Which was strange, given the odd weight laying on him. He wondered, in his still waking mind, if maybe something had fallen off a shelf in his room and landed on him while he slept.

But he wasn't even in his room.

El's eyebrows rose in surprise as he looked around him. He was lying on the couch in the living room, his head resting on the arm. And the comfortable weight on top of him was Cody, spread out over El, head on his shoulder.

"Oh, dear," El said. He gently nudged Cody awake.

"Hmm?" Cody took a deep breath and slightly opened his eyes, still swollen with sleep. "What?"

"I'm afraid we fell asleep," El informed him.

Cody lifted his head and looked around. "Huh. Looks like it." Then his eyes couldn't stay open anymore and he dropped his head back down on El's shoulder. He was asleep again in an instant.

El sighed but smiled. Cody looked awfully cute when he slept. His face was very soft and peaceful, and despite not actually resting on a pillow or anything, his hair had an adorable tousle to it. Of course, that could have been from all the making out last night. El hated to disturb him.

"I'm sorry, but I do have to get up now," El said, nudging Cody awake again. "Pretty urgent, actually."

Cody grumbled but rolled to the side. El tried to catch him, but he was still suffering the momentary lack of muscle awareness that came with just waking up, and Cody tumbled over, landing on the floor.

Which at least woke him up. He sat up straight, eyes wide. "El?" he asked.

"That's me." El got up and smiled at him. "And I'll be right back." He rushed off to the bathroom and returned to find Cody exactly where he left him, sitting on the floor, still looking around in confusion.

"Did we fall asleep?" Cody asked. "On the couch?"

"It seems like it."

"Did we do anything fun?"

El's mood fell a little. "You don't…you don't remember?"

"I remember kissing a lot," Cody said. He staggered to his feet and smiled. "Definitely remember the kissing."

"And I'm afraid that's all there was," El announced. "So, no, nothing fun." He tried not to let his disappointment show. It wasn't that he felt they should have slept together last night. But he did wish he wasn't always the one taking things slow. Too slow, in some cases. Hopefully not in this case. "Coffee?"

El turned to head into the kitchen, but Cody cut him off, racing around to block his path.

"The kissing was fun!" Cody said. "The most fun I've had all decade probably."

El gave him a less than earnest smile, then stepped around him. He knew Cody liked him. He knew was probably just overreacting. But he couldn't help that the rejection stung a bit. Cody groaned and followed him into the kitchen.

"I didn't mean that the kissing wasn't fun," he reiterated. Only the more he said it, the less El believed that to be true. "Sometimes I just, I dunno, I say things without thinking and I don't really mean what they seem to mean. I'm sorry."

El glanced up from the coffee machine. Cody did look honest. And El also often said things without thinking about what they would really mean. As had happened last night. "You really enjoyed the kissing?"

Cody smiled and stepped closer. He gently grabbed El's chin in his hand. "I really, *really* enjoyed the kissing." And then he leaned over and placed a very sweet kiss to El's lips that somehow had the same tingly effect as some of their more intense make outs last night.

"Alright then." El gave Cody a real smile. There was no use worrying over something that Cody would go to such lengths to lie about.

"Still can't believe we just fell asleep like that," Cody said. "Does your neck hurt?" He reached over his shoulder and rubbed his neck a bit. "Cause my neck hurts."

"You did fall asleep with your head at a weird angle," El said.

"Yeah," Cody chuckled softly. "I can see that."

El raised an eyebrow at him. "What can you see?"

Cody tilted his head and looked at El's neck. El reached up and felt around, fingers roaming over various bumps. He gasped and rushed back to the bathroom. He had still been half asleep earlier, he hadn't even looked in the mirror properly. And there were about a dozen hickeys spread about his neck.

"*Cody*," he hissed.

Cody popped his head in. "What?"

"I told you to be gentle!"

"I was gentle! You can give gentle hickeys."

El huffed at him. "I have a very important meeting tomorrow, Cody. What if they don't heal by then?"

"Well, then you should have said 'don't make any hickeys,' not 'be gentle'."

El sighed. "You're impossible." The coffee machine beeped and El slid past Cody to make them some mugs.

"I'm sorry," Cody said, trailing after him. "Won't happen again, promise."

"Just, ask next time."

Cody shoved his hands in his pockets and smirked. "And, uh, when is next time, hm?"

El tried to fight his own smile. Cody could be too cute for his own good when he needed to be. "When are you free?"

"Thursday?"

"Oh, I'm afraid I can't. I promised some of the others I'd go to the silly batting cages with them for practice." He shook his head, telling himself not to get started. "It's just easier to go along with it sometimes."

"Well, why don't you tell them you're getting some more *private* lessons. Date on the diamond doesn't sound all that bad, does it?"

El smiled, because that didn't sound too bad at all. "It's a date!"

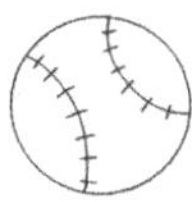

"My, my." Cody jumped at the voice that assaulted him as soon as he got back to his place. He turned and spied Trish sitting in the chair in his living room, one leg crossed over the other, smiling at him. "Coming in early in the morning, hair all a mess, clothes from the night before…someone had fun last night."

Cody looked at the door, the dishes in the kitchen, then back at Trish. "How did you get in here?"

"Childhood habits die hard, huh?" Trish reached behind her and pulled out Cody's spare key, shaking it a little. "Found this under your mat. That's really unsafe, you know."

"Okay, let's go for *why* you're here." Cody tossed his jacket over the back of the couch and flopped down.

"Well, I was just in for business," Trish said, adjusting her seat to a more relaxed position. "And I heard some very interesting news."

"Oh, yeah? What's that?"

"This," she reached into her bag and pulled out an old photograph, "little boy, who complained so much about having to go to games, is back to playing baseball." She tossed the photo over and it landed perfectly on the coffee table.

Cody scoffed at the photo their parents had taken on the first day of little league. He was the only one in the group not smiling. "It's not really anything important. Just some dumb company league I got roped into."

"And I thought the only thing you hated more than baseball was your job." Trish smiled coyly. "So, who's the guy?"

"Shuddup," Cody said. He yawned, feeling the effects of his long night that wasn't quite as long as he wanted. Which was a good thing, probably. Going too fast was always his problem. Trish just kept staring at him with that little smile. "Not that it's any of your business, but his name's El."

"Mhm." Trish looked entirely too pleased with herself.

"I'm sorry, what exactly were you doing here again? Work, was it?"

"Yes, just some business to attend to."

Cody wasn't buying it for a single second. "Oh, yeah? What, uh, what business would that be?"

Trish's smile faltered. "Business business," she offered. She was entirely too confident in herself for someone who was so shit at lying.

"They sent you, didn't they?" Cody accused.

Trish dropped the act with a sigh. "They just asked me to check in. You never call!"

"I call," Cody said. He sat up. "Why, I just spoke to them last, uh…" He snapped his fingers in memory and pointed to her. "Dad's birthday!"

"Cody, that was three years ago."

"*No.*" Trish nodded her head. "Really?" Another nod. "Huh. I guess time flies when you're having fun." Of course, moving to the city and getting away from home hadn't been as fun as he initially thought. Although it was picking up.

"They just want to make sure you're okay," Trish said. "And now I can tell them that you are." She smiled that devious smile of hers again. "And that you have a boyfriend."

"Oh, well don't *tell* them."

"Whyever not?"

Cody groaned and rolled his head back. "Because then they're gonna want to meet him! And it's really too soon for that. It's always too soon for that. I mean, we only just went on our first date."

Trish looked at Cody's disheveled state with a raised eyebrow.

"Nothing happened," he told her. "We stayed up late talking and accidentally fell asleep."

"Wow. Did that line ever work on anyone? Ever?"

"Oh just, shut it and go make your little family spy report, hm?"

"Alright, I will." Trish stood up and smoothed down her skirt. "I'll just see you at the next game."

"Oh no you will not!" Cody said, pointing at her as she left the room. "You better not show up there, Trish. Trish!" He heard the door slam and groaned, laying back down on the couch.

Chapter Eight
A Lesson in Hitting

El was both excited and nervous as he walked his way to the park on Thursday night. He was excited to see Cody, of course, but he was nervous because he had a very clear idea of how he wanted the evening to go. He just wasn't sure if Cody was on the same page. After having denied sex a few nights ago, El worried if he would be able to set the mood properly again. The last thing he wanted was for Cody to always feel unaware of what the expectations were. Or, worse, disappointed with the expectation.

El rounded the corner to the park and spotted some candles on the field. Cody had set up a little picnic, and El chuckled softly. Seemed he wouldn't need to worry about setting the mood at all.

"I thought we were playing baseball," El said.

"We will." Cody smiled at him over his shoulder, knelt on the ground as he laid out a spread of fruits and cheeses. "Wine?"

"One glass couldn't hurt." El knelt down next to him and took the glass offered. The whole spread looked truly delicious. "Wouldn't want to throw my balance off any."

"Sometimes a thrown balance can be good for hitting," Cody said. "Cheese?" He held up a little platter with a lovely spread. El had already had dinner, but he hated for such efforts to go to waste.

"Thank you." He picked up a few slices and grabbed some grapes from a nearby plate. "You eat some, too." He nodded with a smile. "You'll need your strength."

"Well, we'll both need our strength," Cody said.

El just nodded and sipped at his wine. Cody gave him a cryptic look, and El wondered just what he was thinking. He probably wasn't jumping to the immediate conclusion that El was suggesting, but he clearly was making some kind of insinuation.

"This really is very romantic, dear," El said. "Thank you." He leaned over and kissed Cody on the cheek.

"Yeah, well, you know, I try." Cody smiled and then gave El a real kiss. "I'm just glad I have such a lovely companion to share it with." Then he went in for another kiss. If El wasn't careful, he could let Cody derail the whole evening earlier than planned.

"Baseball," El mumbled against Cody's lips. Then he forced himself to pull away and get up. Cody frowned after him in that adorable fashion of his but did eventually follow him over to home plate.

"Alright, let's start with your stance. Show me what you got."

El nodded and picked up the bat. He gripped it tight and held it up, looking like he figured a batter should look.

"Okay, I think I see the problem." Cody walked up behind El and wrapped his arms around him, hands resting atop his on the bat. Which was exactly what El had been looking forward to all day. "See, your grip is too tight."

"I've never had any complaints before," El muttered, a soft smile playing on his lips.

Cody stalled for a moment, giving El a knowing look. Then he shook his head and refocused on the lesson. "You don't want to strangle it." He rubbed his fingers gently over El's hands and he loosened his grip. "You have to be soft. Tender. Gotta treat your bat like a lover, you know?"

El nodded, his mouth going a bit dry as he thought about treating Cody to something soft and tender. "Just promise you won't get jealous," he said.

Cody chuckled and backed away. El tried not to pout too much.

"No promises. But now that you've got your stance straightened out, that'll do wonders for your swing." He stepped a few paces away and picked up a mitt, grabbing a ball from a nearby basket. "Ready?" El licked his lips and nodded. Cody gave him an easy and gentle toss. El managed to make a hit, which was good in his book, but it would have been a foul in a real game.

"Better," Cody said. "But, hmm, you're moving your body all at the same time." He shook his head and dropped his glove, jogging back over. He was quick to slide against El's back again. El smiled as he leaned into him a bit.

"How would you like me to move my body?" he asked. And he smiled as Cody's lesson stalled for a second time.

Cody cleared his throat and then shifted his stance a bit. "You want to move fluidly, kind of like a wave, right? Gotta start in your toes and then work your way up." Cody placed one hand gently on El's right arm, and then slid his other hand down to rest on El's left hip. "Crest with your hips," he said in a whisper. El's body shook as Cody's hand placed a firm pressure on El's hip, urging him to move it back as he pivoted into Cody's body further. "Then crash it down with the hands." Cody's other hand pushed on El's arm, leading him through in a swing. Then he reset them and ran him through it again, the grip of his fingers on El's hips sending a wave of delight right up his spine. "See?"

"Oh yes," El said. "Hips *before* hands." He chuckled an airy laugh. Oh, he was having too much fun with this. "I think I just get it mixed up."

"Why's that?"

El turned his head, giving Cody a suggestive look. "Usually, I work with my hands first."

An absolutely beautiful flush covered Cody's face. But El wasn't done with the lesson. So, when Cody leaned in for a kiss, El turned his head and let Cody's lips fall on his jaw. Not that that deterred him from kissing away.

"I'm not sure what this has to do with baseball," El said, even though he did tilt his head a little to give Cody better access.

Cody hummed against his skin. "Yeah, me neither."

Cody kept kissing, dipping lower and lower until El was sure he would be in danger of getting another hickey. And just after the others had started to heal.

"I'll make you a deal," El whispered.

"Mm, love deals."

"You help me get a real hit, and I'll take you back to my place for something...*fun*."

Cody's head popped back up, looking into El's eyes with a heavy gaze. And El could *feel* his interest in that statement.

"Right. Okay, so." Cody backed up a bit. "Wave from your hips to your hands. Grip not too tight, and most importantly, don't think about it too much." He walked back over to the mitt and picked up a new ball. "Let everything else fade away until it's just you and the ball."

"Me and the ball," El said with a little nod.

"No work, no company league nonsense, no family stuff." Cody got the pitch ready. "Just you and the ball. And maybe the adorable catcher behind you making weird jokes about your butt."

El chuckled softly, and was too busy thinking about that exact moment, that his swing missed the ball completely. Cody tsked and shook his head at him.

"You were thinking too much," he said.

"It's your fault," El argued. "You said something funny, and I lost my focus."

"Yeah." Cody smirked as he picked up another ball. "See how annoying that can be?"

El scrunched his face in fake anger as Cody laughed. Oh, he'll show him. Nothing but himself, the ball, and Cody's entirely too smug face.

Cody wound up another pitch and El swung at it with all his might. He felt a strange vibration in his arms as the bat made contact, and then he dropped the bat with a gasp, watching Cody dive to the ground to avoid getting beamed in the head.

"I'm so sorry!" El raced over, dropping to his knees next to Cody. Cody's head popped up, looking at El with a wide, astonished stare. "I didn't mean to aim for you, I promise!"

"That was a nice hit!" Cody said.

El wasn't sure if Cody was being serious or not. Maybe the ball had clipped him just a little on the way. "Are you alright?"

Cody smiled and laughed a bit. "Yeah, I'm good. How do you feel?"

"Well, I hit it," El said, letting himself feel a little proud of that.

"Yeah, you did!" Cody agreed.

"And it wasn't a foul."

"Not even close."

But then the guilt set in. "And I almost killed you!"

"Let's just focus on the good things, yeah?" Cody laughed again and sat up next to El. "And next time, I'll make sure I wear a helmet."

El let himself relax a little, seeing as Cody wasn't bleeding or concussed or anything. "I really am sorry. Maybe aiming should be the next lesson."

Cody's smile grew. He tilted his head to the side and looked up at El with the cutest expression on his face. "I can't wait."

El smiled back. "I think perhaps it's best we don't continue tonight." Cody nodded. "So, why don't we head back to my place, and I can make it up to you." He reached out and placed a hand on the side of Cody's head, loving the feel of Cody's hair between his fingers.

"Oh, ow, you know what?" Cody reached up and felt around his head. "I think you might have nicked me a little," he said. El rolled his eyes. "Yeah, yep, there's a bump. Oh, that's gonna take a lot of making up for."

"Well, the night is young," El said. And he pulled Cody in for a kiss, the promise of a long and thoroughly enjoyable evening on the horizon.

Chapter Nine
A Night of Debt

Cody probably drove a bit too fast on the way to El's, but it wasn't his fault. He had known El to be a flirt, sure, but what he did on the field that night was just plain evil. Cody was surprised he had managed to hold it together as long as he did. Heck, as soon as El had sat on the picnic blanket, all Cody wanted to do was pounce on him and get those hickeys to come back out.

But something told him that what was coming up next would be much better.

As soon as they were in the door, El grabbed Cody's shirt and pulled him close for a hungry kiss. Cody managed to get the door kicked shut as El tugged him along down the hall, still kissing like his life depended on it. And his needy and desirous kisses were so much different from the soft and gentle kisses of their last make out session that even if this was again all they did, Cody wouldn't mind one bit.

The steps got a little tricky, however, as they couldn't both fit up sideways and El did not seem interested in stopping their kissing even for the few seconds it would take to get up there. El just pushed Cody against the wall at the base of the steps and pressed their bodies together, moaning into their kiss.

"So pushy," Cody whispered with a smile in the few milliseconds of breaks between each kiss.

And then El proved how pushy he could really be, sliding a leg in between Cody's and pressing ever so gently against his groin. Cody's body stiffened at the pleasurable pressure, and he cupped El's face in his hands, giving him one last long and languid kiss before he forced them apart.

"Unless you wanna do this on the couch, we really should get upstairs," he said.

El pouted, looking positively divine with his lips all kiss-bitten and his face a full flush. He looked between Cody and the stairs. Then he glanced over his shoulder into the living room. "Well, the couch is closer..."

Cody laughed and pushed himself away from the wall, taking El's hand and leading him up the steps. "You know, I've been told patience is a virtue," he said.

"Is that so?" El asked. They reached the top landing and he once again pressed Cody to the wall, getting right back into that tortuously delightful position. "I suppose I ought to be in some kind of trouble for not having any, then, hm?"

Cody cocked an eyebrow. "Well, I guess we could let this one slide," he said. "Given the right price, of course."

"Oh, of course." El kept Cody pinned with his body, his hands drifting down to undo his pants. "I wouldn't possibly think of not paying my dues."

"You are racking up quite the debt, there," Cody said. "What with first beaming me in the head when I was only trying to help and all."

El gave Cody a bit of a smug look, and then dropped to his knees, pulling Cody's pants down in one quick motion that was so smooth Cody would have guessed El did it for a profession. Maybe plant nurseries was just the dumbest coverup for brothel ever invented.

El looked up at Cody as he grabbed the base of him in one hand, the other gently toying with the tip. And that look in his eyes was enough to send a shiver through Cody's nerves. El had quite the devilish streak, Cody knew, and so he figured El would find a way to pay him back while still somehow coming out with the better end of the deal.

But not like that.

"One sec." Cody grabbed El's arms and pulled him back up. "Where's the bedroom?"

"Why?"

"Because knee pain is a terrible way to pay off your debts," Cody explained. "And I'm just not that kind of debtor."

El's expression melted away as he looked at Cody with a soft smile and gentle eyes. "Just through here."

He gestured to the left and disappeared into one of the rooms. Cody hopped out of his pants and followed. The bedroom looked much the same as the rest of El's home; cozy, brown, with lots of books tucked away everywhere. But there was little time to appreciate it before El's hands were back on Cody's body, pushing him to the bed.

Cody settled himself up against the headboard as El climbed up, laying between his legs. Hardly a second had passed before El grabbed Cody's dick in one hand, lips gently wrapping around the tip.

Cody let out a moan as El started to slide up and down, keeping his motions shallow as his hand did most of the work. His lips felt so delicate and soft, a smooth sensation that felt like it wrapped itself around Cody's entire body. And as El's saliva started to work its way down Cody's cock, his hand began a lovely slide that worked opposite his lips.

"Fuck," Cody breathed out, his head falling back against the headboard. But he couldn't tear his eyes away from the wonderful work El was doing. His head and hand worked in perfect unison, creating a conflict of sensations that kept Cody both confused and needy. And with every down pass El made, his lips slid further and further, as if testing the waters on just how far he could go.

And he got pretty damn far.

Cody reached down instinctively, placing his hand on the back of El's head. "This okay?" he asked, once he realized what he was doing.

El nodded, adding some extra pleasurable pressure as he hummed a soft yes. Cody busied himself with running his fingers through El's hair. It was soft, just like the rest of him. And Cody hadn't had too much soft in his life. He was liking it so far.

After a minute or two of pure bliss, El pushed up, Cody instantly dropping his hand.

"Sorry," El said, taking some deep breaths. He kept his hand working, which made it a little difficult to focus on what he was saying. "It's been a while. And the last one was considerably shorter."

Cody let out a laugh and sat forward, scooting down a bit so he could place his hand on El's cheek. "Hey, nothing to apologize for. I'll take whatever you give me."

El got that devilish look in his eyes again. "As will I." And that certainly got Cody half an inch away from coming right on the spot.

El smiled and then tried to worm his way back down. But Cody held him up. "No, no," he said. "It's your turn."

"My turn?" El asked. And he looked so genuinely confused that Cody was just about ready to go rampaging on anyone who had ever made him feel like sex was one-sided. "But I'm paying off a debt."

"It's been paid," Cody told him. He leaned even closer and pressed some kisses to El's jaw. "In fact, I think you paid too much. So now we gotta even it out, you see."

"I promise you," El continued, "that I'm really perfectly comfortable continuing on."

Cody hummed and shifted back so he could look El in the eye. He had been with his fair share of partners before, and he had an idea of what was going on. He had just been so taken with El's confidence in their flirtations, that he hadn't figured him to be insecure in bed.

"You know," Cody dropped his voice to a whisper and let his eyes wander over El's body. "I find you incredibly attractive. A very sexy package." At this, El turned his head and squirmed a bit. "And taking off your clothes is not going to change that. I can tell you right now, all it's gonna do is spike up the sexy-o-meter."

El chuckled softly and looked back at Cody with just a hint of trepidation in his eyes. But Cody knew El would find nothing but the truth as he looked at him. Because Cody wouldn't be able to stop staring at El like he was the damn most gorgeous thing on this planet even if he wanted to.

"Well, alright."

El shuffled off the bed and started undressing. Cody pulled his shirt off and tossed it to the side before settling in and watching the show. El was slow with his movements, but not because he seemed worried about getting naked anymore. He was just particular about making sure everything was done carefully and got folded up after he was done.

"There we are," El said, walking back up to the bed. But he was still wearing his underpants. And Cody sat at the edge, putting a hand out on El's waist to stop him. "What?"

"All of it," Cody said.

"Why?" El asked.

Cody smiled. "Are you asking why your penis is necessary in sex?" He laughed when El rolled his eyes. "Because that's really a more complex kind of discussion."

"You really want to see it?" El asked.

"Oh, I really want to see it," Cody said. And touch it. And lick it. And suck it.

El huffed. "Fine." Cody pulled his hand back and El pushed his underpants down, kicking them to the side and crossing his arms over his chest.

"Oh, it's quite girthy, ain't it?" Cody smiled and reached out to grab El's cock. It wasn't by any means long, but it quite made up for it in thickness.

"I suppose," El mumbled.

"I love it," Cody told him. And then he bent forward, taking El in his mouth and showing off just how true that statement was.

"Ah!" El let out a surprised gasp and stumbled forward a bit. Cody placed his hands back on El's hips, able to keep El in his mouth with no problems. Well, a small problem; just a little bit of a stretch in his jaw as his lips fit around the width of it. Do this long enough and he'd end up with an ache.

"C-Cody," El huffed. And if his name didn't just sound heavenly coming from El's lips. El placed a hand on Cody's hair, his fingers reflexively grabbing a fistful. But the tug only accentuated Cody's pleasure.

Cody could feel El starting to waver as he worked, so he took a brief pause to pull El down to the bed. He rolled El over and quickly got back to work. His hands grabbed El's thighs, feeling with a hum of delight how muscular and thick they were. Squatting all day for games was certainly doing nice things for him.

"Cody," El moaned again. But it was a very specific kind of moan. The type that's followed very quickly by the best pleasure on the plant.

So, with a smile, Cody pulled away and took over with his hand, watching with bright eyes as El came, dropping some deliciously thick looking globs of cum on his hips. Cody rubbed El through it and then brought his hand up to clean himself off. Delicious indeed.

El breathed heavily for a few moments, laying back with one arm flung over his face. And his neck was just sitting there, perfectly presented. Cody figured one little hickey certainly couldn't hurt. Afterall, a neck like that was just made for them.

"That was…" El started as Cody laid next to him and got to work on his kissing. "I mean, I never…"

And that got Cody's attention. He popped his head up and looked over at El.

"Never what?"

El moved his arm away, looking up at Cody with lust-laden eyes and hair all a mess. "Sorry?"

"You just said you never," Cody said. "So, never what?"

"Oh, well, uhm, that." El shrugged.

Cody squinted at him. No. No, he couldn't be suggesting that.

"You've never been on the receiving end of a blowjob?" Cody asked. And it sounded so ridiculous, he was just waiting for El to laugh and say it was something else. It had to be something else.

But El just shook his head, looking a bit *ashamed*.

"Well, that just won't do." Cody shifted to the side until he was laying over El, raised up on his elbows. "I hope you didn't plan on getting any sleep tonight," he warned. "Because your past sexual encounters have clearly built up quite the large debt, in your favor. And as your current lover, it is my duty to pay that off."

El looked a bit like he was going to argue, but the fight quickly died down. "Well, if that's what you'd like," he said in his usual way of pretending he didn't want what he really did.

"Can't think of any other way I'd want to spend my time," Cody said. "Except for maybe covering every inch of your neck in hickeys."

"That," El told him, "is not happening."

Cody gave a big, dramatically fake sigh. "Fine. A hundred blowjobs it is."

Chapter Ten
Playing Hookie

"Cody, get up!"

Cody grumbled and did no such thing. He was perfectly enjoying his morning, curled up next to El, buried under the blankets. It was just about the best sleep he'd ever had, and certainly much better than the couch. But then El had to go and get out of bed, which made his morning take a sour turn.

Cody tried to reach out and keep him in, but he was still too sleepy, and El escaped his grasp easily. Cody peeled his eyes open and frowned as El opened his closet and started pulling out clothes.

"What's the hurry?" Cody asked.

"We must have slept through my alarm," El told him. Cody glanced over at the bedside table. He briefly remembered a moment of convincing El that five more minutes wouldn't hurt. But more than five had passed.

"Okay, but why are you in a rush?"

"Because I'll be late for work!" El stepped into a pair of pants and huffed at Cody. "As I also suspect you will!"

"Well, let's just not go then." Cody pushed himself up to a sitting position and smiled at El, thinking that his morning could make a quick turnaround back to perfect.

"Not go to work?"

Cody nodded. "Yeah. We can just call in sick."

"I...I don't think I've ever had to call in sick to work before." El stood before the bed, still half dressed, thinking. And Cody really, really, just wanted him to get back in the bed, naked if he could swing it. "It seems a little dishonest."

"Oh, it's a lot dishonest. But that's part of what makes it so fun. The morning sex is the main fun, of course."

El glanced around the room, eyes finding their way to Cody before glancing away again. And he was trying awfully hard not to smile as he bounced a bit in place. "I don't think I can."

"Well, then let me help." Cody got to his knees and crawled to the edge of the bed. He grabbed El's waist and pulled him close, pressing open kisses to his neck.

El's body shivered. "Yes, alright, I'll call in."

Cody chuckled and smiled to himself as El sat on the side of the bed, pulling out his phone. Cody was quick to settle behind him, getting back to his kissing.

"Don't you have to call, too?" El asked, trying to shrug Cody off.

Cody sighed and fell away. "Yeah, alright." He looked around, trying to remember where he had left his phone. Probably in his pockets. "Where are my pants?"

El furrowed his eyebrows for a second as he held the phone to his ear. "I think they're in the hall?"

Cody rolled off the bed and peeked his head out the door. Yep, sure enough, there they were bunched up at the top of the steps. He smiled to himself as he remembered El's pushy attitude and how much he could not wait to get back to having more fun this morning.

Cody fished his phone out of his pocket and sent Briney a quick text that he wasn't coming in today. Then he dropped both phone and pants by the side of the bed and sat down next to El as he finished up his own dirty deed.

El giggled a bit as he set his phone down on the bedside table. "I feel so excited," he said.

Cody smiled at the pure ray of sunshine that was now in his life. He had never fallen so fast or so hard for a guy before. But El sure was something special. He reached over and cupped El's face in his hands, pulling him close for a kiss. He was quite looking forward to a lazy morning spent in bed.

But then El's phone rang, and he broke away from the kiss, looking at it with wide eyes. "They knew I was lying," he whispered.

"I doubt it," Cody said. "Just don't answer it. They can't make you go in if you don't want to."

El bit his lip and then grabbed his phone, much to Cody's demise. "Oh!" he said. "I actually really do need to take this. One moment."

El got up and walked out into the hall as he answered. Cody sighed and laid back on the bed, looking around at El's room. Then a sneaking thought wrapped into his mind. One that tried to convince him that whoever had called was someone he needed to worry about. But he didn't like that thought, so he distracted himself by reading the titles of books on the shelf next to the window.

"Sorry," El said when he returned. "I'm afraid I'm going to have to cut the morning short."

Cody tried not to think anything too much of it. "Everything alright?"

"Oh, yes. Just a little kerfuffle with my sister. Nothing to worry about."

"Do people still say kerfuffle?" Cody asked. "Did people ever say kerfuffle?"

El chuckled and sat on the edge of the bed. He placed a hand on Cody's arm. "I really am sorry."

"Nothing to worry about," Cody assured him. And he tried to assure himself. "Is it anything I can help with?"

"Not unless you want to spend your day off moving furniture and boxes around."

Cody shrugged. "Got nothing better to do," he said. Plus, if it meant hanging out with El more, he wouldn't mind it one bit.

"Are you serious?" El asked.

"Yeah."

El seemed to think it over for a few seconds. "Alright then! Your help would be greatly appreciated. Now, let's get dressed."

"Oh, well, you didn't say anything about getting dressed." Cody fake moaned. "I've changed my mind, it's not worth it."

El just got up and laughed, tossing Cody's pants at him. "I promise we can get naked again once we're done."

Cody eagerly rolled off the bed. "I'mma hold you to that."

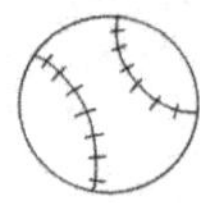

El was very thankful that Cody had agreed to come that day. Even though it was probably still too soon in their relationship to meet family, he knew having him there would be helpful both for carrying things and for dealing with Clara. His sister was a sweetheart but wasn't always 100% there. And given enough time, even El could lose his patience.

But Cody seemed to have the exact calming and carefree attitude that would help make the whole thing go over smoothly. Hopefully.

"So, your sister just *forgot* that she was moving today?" Cody asked as he drove them over to Clara's new place.

"Not so much that she forgot it was today, just that she forgot she needed to hire movers to help," El explained.

"Well, what else are big brothers for, right?"

El chuckled. "I'm just glad I'm able to help. If I had gone into work this morning, I could have ended up too wrapped up in something."

"So, is it a good thing or bad thing we played hooky?" Cody asked with a laugh.

"Good," El assured him. Especially since they were still spending the day together, even if it wasn't in bed as planned.

They pulled up to Clara's new building, spotting the moving truck outside. At least she had managed to get her stuff to the building. It was just a matter of getting everything inside. And up all those steps.

"Thank you for coming to help," Clara said, greeting them as they stepped out of the car. She rushed over and pulled El into a big hug. "Oh! And you've brought a friend!"

"Ah, yes." El smiled and introduced the two of them.

"Come on up!" Clara headed for the door, but El held her back.

"Wouldn't it make more sense to carry something up with us?" he suggested. The less trips up and down he had to make, the better.

"Oh, duh!" Clara chuckled. "You're absolutely right."

She led them to the truck and they each took a few boxes with them as they ascended. Clara didn't live on the top floor, thankfully, but four flights of steps was still a bit much for carrying heavy objects.

"Something smells like gas," Cody commented as he entered after Clara. And El noticed it as well. Very pungent.

"I know, right?" Clara said. She set her box down and looked around. "Been like that all morning. I opened the windows though!" She pointed to the other side of the room at the open windows.

"Erm, your stove is on." Cody leaned over, studying the stove and the little light that was on it. He reached over and turned it off.

"Oh, is that what that light means?"

Cody gave El a worried look. A sentiment that was perfectly shared. Cody wandered over and whispered in El's ear. "She doesn't know how to work a stove?"

"We had very sheltered childhoods," El explained. "I was a similar way when I lived on my own for the first time."

"Is it such a good idea *for* her to live on her own?"

"It's the only way she'll learn."

But El wasn't entirely confident in that statement himself. Forgetting movers was one thing, but somehow accidentally turning on the stove and not knowing how it worked was another. He had been worried about Clara moving out on her own for a while now. She had stayed at home while in college, and a little bit after while she was finding her footing. But now she was truly on her own.

And El couldn't take the stress.

"You know, Clara, there's actually an apartment for rent in the building next to mine," he offered. At least if she was right next door, he could keep a better eye on her.

"That's cool," Clara said.

"It's much nicer than this one," El continued. Cody gave him a strange look.

"Oh, I couldn't afford that part of town," Clara said.

"I'd be happy to help," El said.

Clara stood in the center of the room, a soft frown on her face. El gave her a gentle smile. She'd still be living on her own. He'd just be nearby if something happened. And he'd be able to sleep at night knowing she wasn't going to set her place on fire or anything.

"Didn't you already sign a lease?" Cody asked. And he stepped up next to El and put an arm around his shoulders as if he didn't just ruin his perfect plan.

"Yeah," Clara said. "Twelve months."

Cody gave El that look again. "Makes no sense to move, yet."

"Hey, good point!" Clara smiled again and then headed back downstairs for more boxes.

El frowned at Cody. "I appreciate your help with moving," he said, choosing his words carefully. "But I was handling that."

"Yeah, I know." Cody made a little face and then turned around, running a hand through his hair. "Sorry."

El's frown deepened. He wanted to tell Cody off for getting involved where he shouldn't. But he didn't want to ruin their day. Or lose out on a helper.

"It's alright," El said. He sighed. "I'll just have to visit her more often."

Cody turned back with a half-smile. "Nothing worse than hanging out with family, huh?"

Chapter Eleven
Lessons Pay Off

For as much as El didn't want to rush into anything of sorts with Cody, he couldn't seem to say no to his presence. Despite Thursday night having only been their second official date, they had already spent the last twenty-four hours together.

After helping Clara finish her move (and sticking around a bit to make sure she didn't accidentally break everything they just moved in), Cody had driven El home and successfully talked his way into a shared shower. It did save water, after all.

And then El had offered to make Cody something for dinner as a way of thanking him for his help with the move. And now they were curled up next to each other on the couch, working through the last of El's cookies as they watched a movie.

"I think this officially counts as the best unplanned day off ever," Cody said. He pulled his legs up, leaning more on El. It felt comfortable.

"Certainly a good first impression," El agreed. "I may just have to do it again sometime. Well, maybe."

Cody chuckled. "Well, I'll be happy to help you out with that at any ol' time."

El smiled and reached his hand over, wrapping his fingers with Cody's. He liked the way their hands fit together. And then El caught the time on Cody's watch and sighed.

"Everything, alright?" Cody asked. He leaned his head back from its perch on El's shoulder, looking up at him.

"Yes, just thinking I should get to bed. I have that morning game tomorrow."

"Ya know," Cody said, sitting up a bit. "You could just skip it. You were sick today, after all. I don't think anyone would think twice about it if you called out tomorrow."

El laughed. "I don't think I could. Wouldn't want to let anyone down."

"Yeah, alright." Cody looked down at their held hands. "I guess I should...go home?"

It would probably be for the best, El thought. After all, they were still early in their relationship. They weren't even officially in a relationship, as it were. Spending another night was perhaps moving a bit too fast. But, then again, El had slept rather comfortably last night with Cody wrapped up around him. And waking up with him had been an enjoyable treat.

"I really do need to get my rest," he said. And Cody nodded, already pulling away. But El increased his grip on Cody's hand, holding him back. "So, no funny business."

Cody smiled and leaned back in for a kiss. "Oh, there's nothing funny about what I have planned."

El hummed happily to himself as Cody drove them over to the park. He had successfully managed to stick to his guns, despite the many attempts at funny business Cody had done last night. El had allowed a very yummy make out session, of course, but that was it. And he was feeling very proud of himself.

"Oh, you're staying?" El asked as Cody followed him out of the car.

"Of course," Cody said. He took El's hand and walked with him towards the ball field. There was some kind of child's birthday party going on in the main park, lots of little kids running around and screaming. El hoped it wouldn't be too distracting. "Gotta study the opposition and all, right?" He winked, and El blushed a bit.

"Just as well," El said. "Now you can observe the effects of your teachings."

"Oh, yes. Cannot wait to see you beam someone in the head."

El swatted Cody gently on the arm and shook his head.

"What?" Cody asked with a laugh. "It's a very effective maneuver."

El looked ahead and smiled when he saw Clara already in the stands. She had been all too eager to come see El play when he had mentioned the game yesterday. He started to lead Cody over to her. At least someone could keep an eye on her so he wasn't distracted while trying to play.

"How long do you think it'll be before she falls off the stands or gets hit by a foul?" Cody asked.

"Well, with you there to keep her company, I'm sure she'll be just fine."

"Good morning!" Clara said, getting up to greet them. She tripped on the corner of the stand as she went, almost tumbling over, if not for El catching her by the arm.

"Careful now," Cody said, growing a wide smile. He grabbed Clara's other arm and helped her straighten up.

"Thank you," she said with a small laugh. "I guess El got all the athletics."

"Oh, hardly," El said. He felt a tingle on the back of his neck and looked to the dugout. Lawrence was standing by the entrance, arms crossed, giving El an icy stare.

"Yeesh," Cody said. He took a seat next to Clara and grimaced. "What's his problem?"

"I'm not sure," El said. "We're not late, are we?"

"Annoyingly on time," Cody announced, checking his watch. "As requested."

"Well, I'd better go and see what that's all about. Enjoy the game, you two."

"Oh, we will," Cody said.

"Go get 'em!" Clara added.

El smiled at the both of them and then took a deep breath before heading over to Lawrence.

"Good morning," he said with a cheerful smile. Lawrence just frowned at him. "Something the matter?"

"What is going on with that?" Lawrence pointed to the stands.

"Oh, well, my sister wanted to come and watch," El said. "I hope that's not a problem."

"Not your sister," Michelle said, standing up and joining Lawrence in a cross-armed stare. "*Him.*" Michelle pointed at Cody with a sneer. When he noticed, Cody just smiled at them and waved.

"Cody?" El asked, pretending to be ignorant of their insinuations. Maybe they'd just drop the subject. "He gave me a ride this morning. Decided to stay and watch."

"More like stay and spy," Derek said from the bench.

"Why did he give you a ride?" Amy asked. El hadn't even seen her show up.

"Because we were coming from the same place, and he was being friendly," El said. Not that they needed to know anything about his personal life. But he figured telling the truth was a lot quicker than trying to make up lies.

"El," Lawrence said with a deep breath. "You cannot just go around socializing with the enemy!"

"First of all," El said, "Cody is not the enemy. None of them are 'the enemy'." Lawrence's eye roll seemed to disagree. "And secondly, we are not 'socializing'." El smiled at the thought of the other night. "We're dating."

"Ew," Michelle said.

"That's worse," Amy agreed.

Lawrence pointed a finger at him. "You most certainly cannot sleep with the enemy either."

"Oh, for goodness sakes." El rolled his eyes and shook his head at them. "Stop taking things so seriously. It's just a fun little game. And Cody and I like each other. There's nothing wrong with that."

"I think it's sweet," Valerie said. "And I fully support you."

El smiled at her. "Thank you."

"You're on my list, too," Lawrence told her.

"What list?" El asked. He was thoroughly fed up with his teammates now; they were taking all of this way too far.

"We don't have time for this," Lawrence said, checking his watch. Rafael was already on his way over to get the game started. "Just, stay focused out there, hm?"

"Yeah," Michelle agreed. "We don't want a repeat of last game."

"Of course not." El took his seat and shook his head. He didn't want to take the game as seriously as they all did, but he did want to do his best. Especially in front of both Cody and Clara. All he had to do was hope that his short lesson did pay off.

-

The game itself was pretty lack-luster, as most games were. But Cody was having a hell of a time watching it with Clara. She got overly excited at the smallest thing but didn't actually seem to understand the rules of the game. She just went along with what the few others in the stands did, sometimes even rooting against El's team, not that she would know it.

And in between innings Cody got her talking about El and was banking up quite the list of fun stories he could play with.

"And he was on the chess team," Clara told Cody. "He wasn't the best, but he was still amazing! And he would take me to his matches sometimes and let me move the pieces!"

Cody chuckled at the thought. It must have been strange, having such an age gap between siblings. If Trish had been ten years older than him instead of two, they might have actually gotten along better, too.

"Must have been hard when he moved out, huh?" Cody asked.

Clara's face fell a little. "Yeah..." Her bubbly disposition disappeared in an instant.

Cody knew he probably shouldn't push it, but ignoring his curiosity was never really his strong point. "Everything alright?"

Clara made little motions with her mouth as she thought. "He just kind of disappeared, is all. For a couple of years. And when he came back, he seemed so much more like an adult, you know?"

"Yeah." Cody was still waiting for his 'seems like an adult' bit to kick in.

"I think being alone made him better," Clara continued. She looked up at Cody almost as if she was afraid of the answer to, "Do you think it would work for me to?"

Cody popped his lips. "Well, that's a tough one." He's been alone for almost five years, and he wasn't really sure he was better for it. "Are you sure he was actually alone all that time?"

"You mean like a second family?"

Cody chuckled. El had only introduced him as a friend. And he hadn't been very affectionate during the move. There was a good chance his family didn't know he was gay. "Maybe he was seeing someone."

Clara made a face. "El doesn't *see* people."

Cody laughed. "Well, I guess you'll just have to ask him what he was up to that helped make him better."

"I guess...Oh, look!" Clara pointed over to the dugout. El was standing off to the side, practicing his swings. "That means he's gonna be next, right?"

"Yup. One sec."

Cody hopped up and made his way over to El. "Perfect form," he said with a smile.

"Are you attempting to distract me as revenge for the previous games?" El asked.

"Maybe. Is it working?"

"Afraid not."

Cody smiled, watching El swing at nothing. He did look much better at it already. "Just remember to keep your grip loose," Cody said.

El nodded, his stance relaxing a little.

"El!" Lawrence called over, instantly scowling when he saw Cody there. "You're up."

"Right." El took a deep breath.

"Hey, don't forget your hips, yeah?" Cody winked at him and the little blush on his face as he walked away. Alright, that *had* to be a good distraction.

Cody rejoined Clara on the stands, laughing at how energetic she was. She was practically shaking with it.

El got a strike on the first throw. And Cody made a mental note to practice some curveballs with him later. He had only thrown straight pitches before. El hesitated on the next pitch, which ended up bringing a second strike to his score. Visibly upset, he shook his head and looked up at Cody.

Cody gave him an encouraging smile and a thumbs up while Clara stood and started clapping.

El nodded and took his stance. The next pitch was a fastball, but El was able to keep up, making a nice hit that had the ball driving down between second and third. He froze for a second, probably surprised by the hit, and then startled and raced off towards first. Cody thought the call was a little close, but he certainly wasn't going to argue with Rafael about giving El a safe. Cody stood up and clapped with Clara, earning him a big, bright smile from El.

Unfortunately, El's team was out before he could make a run, but he had gotten a good hit in and that, Cody figured, was something to be proud of.

Of course, El's real skill shined as a catcher. And Cody could watch him work all day at that and never be bored of it. And not just because watching him squat reminded Cody of how lovely and wonderful his thighs were. El moved with ease and fluidity, never missing or dropping the ball no matter what came his way. He was the last line of defense between a runner and a score, and he wasn't going to let anyone slide. Not even Cody, he remembered with a fond smile.

In the end, El's team won by one run, and El walked up to them with the best of smiles on his face.

"You were fantastic!" Clara said. And this time when she got up to hug him, she didn't trip.

"Well, I have Cody to thank for that," El said. He turned his smile to him. "Your lesson was very helpful."

"Well, it's easy with such a great student," Cody said. "Celebratory drinks?"

"Actually," El looked over his shoulder at his team. "Lawrence is taking everyone out to lunch to celebrate. Why don't you join us?"

"Yeah," Cody looked at the guy who would not stop glaring at him. "Don't think so." He laughed a little, just to show El everything was fine.

"Can I come?" Clara asked.

"Of course," El said. He gave Cody another look. "Are you sure you don't want to come? I promise you they'll be civil."

"Nah, that's alright. I should probably get home anyway. Check the mail, water the plants, you know. That kind of stuff." Do the dishes, finally.

El smiled softly at him. "Of course." He stepped forward and leaned up to kiss Cody on the cheek. "Thank you for everything these last few days." Well alright, maybe his family did know.

"You're welcome," Cody said. He smirked and gave El a proper, long kiss, smiling into it a bit as he heard the groans coming from the dugout.

Chapter Twelve
The Lace Bet

Cody would have loved nothing more than to just hang around with El for the rest of the weekend, maybe convince him into a Monday off of work, too. But even he had to admit a break from all the fun was necessary. Except all he did the rest of the day was spend his time thinking about all the fun. He very nearly called El to see if he was done with his celebration until he remembered that in all their revelry, they had never actually exchanged phone numbers.

But he did know where El worked. So, on Monday afternoon he paid another lunchtime visit, only this time without any sort of flimsy excuse. The receptionist smiled at him and sent him on his way up with his little visitor's badge.

El greeted him with his patented bright smile. "Hello, dear," he said. "More mail today?"

Cody chuckled, shoving his hands in his pockets. "Afraid not." He rocked on his feet a bit. El was looking particularly nice and dressy today, and Cody spied a packed briefcase sitting on the edge of his desk. "Goin' somewhere?"

El followed Cody's gaze to the case and nodded. "Yes, I have a meeting at one of the properties today. Playing catchup with a little mishap from the other week, I'm afraid."

"Sounds like fun," Cody said. But also put a damper on his plans to get El out to lunch. "Erm, well, anyway. I did come by to give you something." He pulled his fancy little business card out of his pocket and handed it over.

El took it with a small smile. "Ya know, just in case you wanted to stay in touch or anything."

El chuckled softly. "I most certainly do." He pulled out his phone and a few seconds later Cody's own buzzed. "There, now you can stay in touch, too."

Cody chuckled. "Great. I'll, uh, I guess I'll see ya around, then."

"Yes, most definitely."

Cody smiled a bit awkwardly and left. He may not have gotten the full afternoon of fun he had been banking on, but he had El's number now, so that was a good thing. And he was going to just focus on the good things.

The next day, as Cody pretended to work while thinking about El, he got a text from the very person in question. It read: *How about another bet?*

Cody smiled and did a quick check of the league schedule. The two were slotted to play against each other again on Saturday. *I'm game.*

He waited anxiously, watching the little typing dots for what felt like an eternity. *Loser has to do more than just pay for dinner.*

Cody smirked. *I don't intend to lose, so hit me with your worst.*

The minutes dragged on, and Cody got a kick out of watching the dots appear and disappear. He could just imagine El looking all adorable and nervous as he thought and backtracked over whatever he was working on.

"Don't you ever do any work around here?" Jean asked, slipping behind Cody's cubicle with a fresh cup of coffee in hand.

"Not really," Cody told him. "But don't let on, yeah?"

His phone buzzed and Cody was quick to check it. *Loser has to wear something ~fancy~ on the next date.*

Cody chuckled. *How fancy we talking?*

I was thinking something with lace...

Oh, you'll look mighty pretty in lace.

So would you.

It's on.

Cody chuckled to himself and slipped his phone back in his pocket. Oh, but the idea of El in a cute li'l lace outfit was driving him insane. Needless to say, he really didn't get any work done that day.

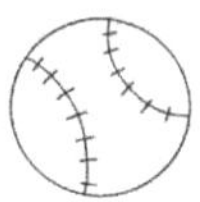

"No," Cody said, upon immediately spotting Trish in the stand.

"Yes," Trish replied with a small smile. "I told you I was going to come watch. Just be glad I didn't bring mom and dad, hm?"

Cody rolled his eyes. Yes, it would be unbearable if his parents were here, but just having his sister here was horrifying enough.

"What's wrong?" Trish asked. "Afraid you aren't as good as you think you are?"

"I'm fantastic, thank you very much," Cody informed her. "I just don't need you here heckling me." He would get enough of that from El.

"I shall keep my heckling to a minimum," Trish promised. Not that Cody believed her for a second.

"Hello, dear," El said, approaching from behind.

Cody startled and turned to face him. El's sister had also made an appearance, trailing behind her brother.

"Er, hi," Cody said. There was no way he could let this get out of control.

Trish's foot nudged the back of Cody's leg. "Aren't you going to introduce us?"

"Nope." Cody grabbed El's arm, dragging him off to the other side of the field. He looked back over his shoulder, in horror, as Clara sat down next to Trish, chatting away excitedly. Trish cut Cody a smug glance, and he knew it was all over.

"Everything alright?" El asked, hurrying along beside him. "Who was that?"

Cody sighed and slowed his pace, since the cat was already out of the bag. "That would be *my* sister," he explained.

"You don't sound too happy about that," El said with a soft chuckle.

"Yeah, well, you know how you and Clara get along great and everything?" Cody asked. El nodded. "Trish and I have a more of a classic sibling rivalry thing going on. Love her but hate her, you know?" And it didn't help that every time he saw her it just reminded him of how stupid he was as a kid.

And how stupid he probably was still being.

"Ah, I see." El smiled and pulled his arm free so he could grab Cody's hand instead. "Well, I certainly hope she won't prove too distracting." Then he leaned over and gave Cody a kiss before dropping his hand and heading to his team.

Cody flushed and looked back at Trish. She was looking entirely too pleased again. Cody sighed and dropped his shoulders, slumping his way over to his own team. This was going to be one hell of a game.

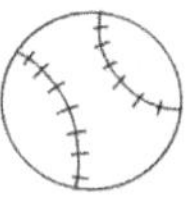

Cody stood on the field, staring down the scoreboard. It was Trish's fault really. Her very presence threw Cody's game off so much that now they were at risk of losing. Top of the ninth, down by two runs. If they didn't pull something out of the bag now, it'd be over. And Cody's dream of El in his pretty little lace would slip away.

"Anytime you're ready, dear," El said.

Cody cut him a glare and then finally stepped up to the plate. He was usually one to let his emotions lead the way, so he kept up his hopeful thoughts of El in lingerie and hit himself a homerun on the first pitch.

"Lovely hit, dear," El said, standing up to watch as the ball sailed away. Cody leaned against his bat and smirked. "But you are still down by one run, and I do believe one of the Mackinson's is up next."

Cody's smile dropped. Great. Two outs and one of the worst batters up. He looked over El's body and frowned. He was really getting attached to the idea of lace on that lovely skin.

"Don't look so glum," El said. He pointed to first base and gave Cody a little pat on the butt. "You've got basses to run."

Cody tossed his bat aside and did his little required jog around the diamond. Unsurprisingly, Anwar struck out and the game was over. Just like all of Cody's hopes and dreams.

"Well, now I'm really glad I didn't bring mom and dad," Trish said, walking up to torment Cody even more. "Would have hated for them to see you lose so spectacularly."

"It was a close game," Cody growled.

"If you say so." Trish gave him a little smile and then flitted away, entirely too happy with how things turned out.

And then El was there to rub it in.

"Good game," he said, holding out a diplomatic hand. Cody just glared at it. "Oh, don't be a sore loser." El smiled and placed his hand down on Cody's waist. "Just think of how lovely you'll look in your new outfit, hm?"

Cody huffed a laugh at him. "You may have won this time, but I want a rematch."

"Well, I think we play again in two weeks' time," El said.

"I meant specifically about this," Cody said. "I'm getting you in lace one way or another, understand?"

El's smile widened, hiding a bit of a mischievous glint in his eyes. "Well, if you say so."

Chapter Thirteen
Gotta Love Lace

It was a little itchier than Cody figured, but that kind of made the night exciting. The cris cross of lace across his back tickled his skin and left goosebumps every time he moved. And the lace of his underpants rubbing against his cock made things even more tantalizing. And thinking about El enjoying all of this lace on his body certainly helped.

"You're squirming again," El commented, popping a roll of sushi into his mouth.

"It's itchy," Cody said. He reached over his back with his chopsticks and scratched his shoulder.

"Oh, well, here." El scooted closer and started scratching Cody's back for him. Which certainly felt wonderful. But then El's fingers stopped scratching and started mapping out the straps.

"Ah, ah, ah," Cody said, shrugging him off with a smile. "No cheating. You'll just have to wait until later tonight to see."

"I can't help it," El said, his fingers tracing over one of the loops in Cody's back. "Thinking about what you're wearing is driving me crazy." And then he started squirming in his seat as well.

"Well, consider this a lesson in patience," Cody smirked and kissed El's cheek. "You could do with some of that."

El's hand dropped and he pouted at him. Then his face brightened considerably. "Oh! Dear, grab me that gunkan, would you?" El pointed to one of the plates that passed by, and Cody snatched it up for him.

"What is that?" Cody asked as El's eyes lit up at the goopy mess on top of the roll.

"It's roe," El said. And he smiled happily as he popped it in his mouth.

"Roe...isn't that like fish eggs or something?"

"That's exactly what it is." El hummed and rocked a little in his seat as he chewed. Cody smiled at him. Strange food likes aside, El was the most charming, beautiful person Cody had ever met. "Would you like to try some?" El held a roll up and Cody leaned back.

"No thanks." He picked up a roll from his own plate. "I'll stick with the California boys."

El laughed. "Next time you can pick where we eat."

"And you'll be the one in the pretty lace outfit," Cody whispered.

El gave him a cryptic look. "We'll see."

El was a little excited to see Cody's place. It only seemed fair, after all, since he had seen El's. Cody drove them back after dinner, with El's overnight bag in the back of his car. After what had happened on their last date, El had been sure to add extra clothes and supplies in case a night turned into another weekend. Not that he would have minded. Not one bit.

"Alright, welcome to casa Cody," Cody announced, throwing open the door. He swept his hand in in a grand gesture and El smiled as he walked in.

It wasn't quite what El had expected. He figured Cody's sense of style would be more on the modern side, sure, but it was a bit minimalistic. El took Cody to be the type to have many unique and wild decorations hanging about. But El felt like he just walked into a catalog for home design. It was lovely, of course, just not what El had thought.

"So, what do ya think?" Cody asked, slipping in behind El.

"It's very nice," El told him. Then he figured he should change the subject before his lie was caught. "Where's the bedroom?"

Cody laughed and led the way, carrying El's bag for him. "So much for those lessons in patience."

"Well, it was only my first one."

El smiled brightly, thinking about the fun of the evening as Cody showed him into the bedroom. This room, at least, felt a little more like Cody. The bed was large and plush and had what looked like silk sheets in a dark gray color. A red rug covered most of the floor, an intricate and unique design woven in gold.

"Very cozy," El said. "Lots of pillows."

"Yeah, I'm a burrower," Cody said. Which explained why he loved to curl up so close to El while they slept. "Have a seat."

El tested the mattress, finding it was a bit firmer than it looked. But it was comfortable all the same. Cody left El's bag by the door and then wandered to his dresser, messing about with his phone.

"Aren't you going to join me?" El asked. Because oh, how he wanted to see what Cody had under those infuriating clothes of his.

"All in good time," Cody said. A soft, almost jazzy song played from his phone at a gentle volume. He turned around and gave El a smirk. "But first...a little show."

El felt his heartbeat quicken as Cody moved closer, staying out of arm's reach. He moved his hips along with the music, giving El a sultry look as he slowly started undoing the buttons on his shirt.

El smiled and squirmed in his seat, his own little surprise becoming awfully tight as his arousal grew.

Cody did put on quite a show. He got his shirt unbuttoned but left it on, running his hands over his chest. All El could see was two thin straps that ran along the side of this chest and stomach, little hooks connecting to fabric on the side and *something* underneath.

And the idea of that something excited El even more.

"You're a very skilled dancer," El said, a little mesmerized by the turning of Cody's hips. He seemed quite flexible. And El was looking forward to seeing just how flexible he could be.

"You don't know the half of it," Cody said with a smile. Then he turned around, and El almost missed what Cody was doing with because he was too busy staring at his ass.

But he looked up in time to see Cody shrugging the edge of his shirt off one shoulder. It revealed a large strap of fishnet material. But before El could fully appreciate it, Cody was covering it back up again.

"Tease," El said with a pout.

Cody spun back around and stepped closer. He placed his hands on the bed next to El and leaned down over him. "Consider this your second lesson." Then he placed a quick kiss to El's lips and was back out of reach before El could do anything about that.

"I don't think I'll be able to retain any information in this state," El said, once more distracted by Cody's moving body.

"Oh, I'm sure you can," Cody said. He turned back around and El crossed his legs at the anticipation.

Cody slipped both of his shoulders out of his shirt, holding the fabric tight across his back. He slid it down inch by inch, dreadfully slow, revealing more fishnet straps that matched what El had felt in the restaurant. The straps made two loops in Cody's back, accentuating the lean muscles there.

And there were two more hooks that connected to whatever was underneath Cody's pants. And it was driving El crazy not knowing.

"How you doing back there?" Cody asked, looking over his shoulder. Every movement drifted the straps across his skin, showing off different parts of his back.

"Suffering," El said with a huff.

Cody laughed and turned back around. Which was slightly worse because there was no fabric obscuring El's view of his chest and abdomen. "Well, we can't have that."

Cody walked up to the bed again and placed his hands on El's shoulders, bracing himself as he straddled El's lap. He kept their groins pressed deliciously together as he kissed El deeply, then he sat up on his knees, until his stomach was perfectly in line with El's face.

And he wasn't going to let the opportunity pass him up. El grabbed Cody's waist and pressed open-mouthed kisses to his stomach. He loved how the muscles tickled and twitched under El's touch. El's hands itched, fingers curling to play with the hem of Cody's pants.

"Someone's antsy," Cody crooned. He moved one hand up to run through El's hair, letting off a soft sigh.

"Mhm," El hummed. He kept kissing his way down Cody's stomach, sliding down on the bed a bit so he could position himself in front of Cody's crotch. He bit on the material of Cody's belt, pulling it out through the loop.

"Holy *fuck*, El," Cody breathed through a moan. "That's hot."

El chuckled and smirked at Cody. "You don't know the half of it."

"I don't think I'd survive it," Cody said with a laugh of his own.

El decided to take mercy on him and finish undoing Cody's pants with his hands.

"Slowly now," Cody said as El started to slide his pants down. El thought about being particular anyway and just tearing them off, but Cody had gone through all the trouble of making it a process.

So, El inched Cody's pants down, licking his lips in anticipation. The strap hooks connected to a pair of red, lacey briefs. Thick, dark straps surrounded the lace, and the material wove together in a delicate pattern of interconnecting leaves and vines.

"Oh my," El said with a deep breath. A pocket sat at the front, bulging out under Cody's effort. A simple movement of fabric to the side would reveal the opening, letting Cody's dick out. But El wanted to enjoy the lace a little bit more.

El moved his head forward and mapped out Cody's cock with his mouth. He slid his hands around to Cody's ass, humming with delight to find that the lace of his outfit curved around the top, leaving his cheeks out for El to fondle. And fondle he did.

Cody gave a breathy laugh, his body wavering slightly as his hand tightened in El's hair. El smiled and shifted the thin material out of the way, taking Cody into his mouth and making him make that lovely little moan of his.

"You're seriously too good at that," Cody said, his voice heavy.

El smiled, working his lips up and down. He hadn't even gotten his tongue involved yet, and already Cody was singing his praises. Well, he could sing praises all night long if he wanted. That would suit El just fine.

Cody's hand on El's shoulder tightened its grip a little, and the one on his head started moving about, ruffling El's hair before smoothing it down again. It felt very calming, and El closed his eyes as he worked, humming softly. Which only made Cody moan even more.

"I ought to wear lace more often," Cody said with a laugh. And El just nodded. "Alright," he said after a few more minutes. "Your turn."

Cody's hand gently pulled El's head back, much to his disappointment. Not that he didn't want it to be his turn again and again and again. "But you haven't finished yet," El explained with a pout. He just didn't like to leave a job unfinished was all.

"Plenty of time," Cody said. He lowered himself back down, rubbing their groins together. El's pants would get all kinds of messy, but that's why he had packed extras.

Cody pressed forward and kissed El, his hands running up and down El's arms. Then they slid forward, moving up El's stomach and tickling the fabric that rested across his chest.

Cody raised an eyebrow and pulled back. He studied El's shirt as his fingers felt around, causing a shiver to run through El's body.

"What's that?" Cody asked.

"Well, uhm, see, the thing is," El started. Cody nodded but kept his focus on El's chest as he slowly undid the buttons of his shirt, starting at the bottom. "I, er, well, I didn't really anticipate winning, you see?"

"Uh-huh."

"And, so, I had sort of already bought myself something for the bet." Cody made an animalistic noise and licked his lips, his eyes widening. "And, well, I figured I shouldn't let it go to waste…"

Cody popped the last button on El's shirt and took a deep breath in as he pulled it off him. He let it out in a deep growl. El had gone for something a little simpler with his design. The top was nothing fancy, just a soft white lace in a floral pattern that rested in a thick band around his chest.

"*Fuck*," Cody hissed. He licked his lips again and then finally snapped his attention up, looking El in the eyes. "Please, *please* tell me there's a matching bottom?"

El smiled coyly. "Perhaps you should go find out."

Cody scrambled off the bed and El laughed. He let out a surprised gasp as Cody grabbed his hips, flipping him onto his back as he wiggled El's pants off.

"What happened to lessons in patience?" El asked.

"That's only for you."

"Oh, I see."

Cody got El's pants off and then joined him on the bed, laying on his side as he stared at El's crotch. Which was a sentiment El was not used to having, making him squirm a little under all the attention.

"Fucking adorable," Cody said, reaching out to play with El's own lace design. The bottoms had a little pouch for his cock that was tucked away beneath a short flowy skirt in the same floral pattern as the top.

"The ruffles make it look bigger," El informed him, blushing a bit.

Cody chuckled and toyed with the little bow at the front. "And what's the bow do for ya?"

"Oh, well, that just looks cute."

Cody laughed again and dropped his head. "I love you," he said. And then his whole body stiffened.

"I'm sorry?"

"It!" Cody said. "I love it! The bow!"

El nodded. "Right. Of course."

Neither of them said anything. El wasn't even sure if he *should* say anything. Cody certainly seemed eager to not admit to what he had just admitted to. But El didn't want Cody to think his feelings weren't returned. Even if they weren't so far as *love* on El's side.

"Fuck, I'm sorry." Cody flopped onto his back and covered his face with his hands.

"There's nothing to be sorry for," El said. He turned on his side and grabbed one of Cody's arms, pulling it away. He just spread the fingers on his other hand, covering the full shade of red. "Darling, please." El leaned over and kissed Cody's hand, willing it away.

Cody huffed and dropped his hand to the side, staring up at the ceiling. "I understand if you want to leave."

"Well, that's the last thing I would want to do," El said. He snuggled closer and wrapped an arm around Cody's waist, fighting the urge to get too handsy right now.

"Really?" Cody looked at him with a look of disbelief.

"I enjoy being with you," El said, pressing gentle kisses to the hand he still held. "And I would very much like to stay and continue our evening."

Cody took a deep breath. "Yeah, alright. I didn't mean it, ya know?"

El smiled. "It's okay if you did."

Cody pursed his lips slightly. "Might have, just a little." He held up his free hand with his thumb and pointer finger close to touching.

El smiled and leaned in for a kiss. "Now then, I do believe it was my turn?"

Cody smirked, his attention wandering down El's body. "Can't believe I almost ruined this perfect moment," he said, fingers going back to playing with the textured lace of EL's lingerie. El's body jerked a little with each tickling touch. It was exhilarating.

"Didn't even come close," El assured him.

Cody took another deep breath, that animal look returning to his eyes. "Right. To work!"

Chapter Fourteen
The Saturday Off

Cody took a deep breath and snuggled up closer to El, feeling him shift slightly in his arms. Lazy mornings in bed were the best kind of mornings, especially if you had someone like El around to cuddle with. He had really thought he ruined everything last night. It wasn't the first time he brought up the L word so early in a relationship. Most people either got scared off or thought he was just lying because who could fall in love so quickly?

But fate must have known what it was doing when it brought that piece of mail to Cody's work. And he wasn't going to question that if he could help it. Cody pressed his nose up against El's neck and then started getting to work on making it all pretty and purple.

"You'd better not be trying to give me hickeys," El said, his voice all cute and sleep-mumbly.

"Just one?" Cody asked, because how could he not? A neck like that just didn't look right without a show of love all over it.

"Not even one," El insisted. His hand reached around Cody and gently grabbed his hair, pulling his biting away. "I have to stay presentable for work."

"I can show you how to cover them up," Cody offered.

"No, thank you."

With a sigh, Cody dropped his head on El's shoulder. He looked down and smirked. "What if, I give you a hickey that's not on your neck?"

El hummed for a bit, his lips pursed in thought. "I suppose that could be acceptable. As long as it's in a place I can easily cover with clothing."

"Oh, it is." Cody squirmed his way down under the blankets, chuckling at his own brilliance. "Not that I think you *should* be covering them up. Ever."

He wrapped himself around one of El's legs and pressed a gentle kiss to the inside of his thigh. El's thighs were certainly more muscular than meets the eye, but there was still plenty of lovely fat there for Cody to enjoy. And enjoy he did.

He enjoyed the way El's skin molded under his touch, giving way at the very suggestion from Cody's lips. He loved how, at the first true bite, El's hand was back in his hair, tugging with a gentle pressure that made goosebumps run down Cody's neck. And he simply adored the soft noises El made as his body shivered with delight.

Cody wanted nothing more than to spend the day between El's legs, covering him all over in love bites. But he had said just the one, so, with a bit of a grumble, Cody wormed his way back up after a satisfactory job.

El giggled a bit and held Cody close. "Thank you, dear. It feels like a little secret down there."

Cody smiled and kissed him. "Yeah. Something to help distract you during work." El laughed and Cody laid his head back on his shoulder. "So, what would you like to do today?"

"I'm not sure." El's hand went back to playing with Cody's hair, fingers gently scratching his scalp. It was the most relaxing sensation ever. "What is it you normally do on Saturdays? Suppose I wasn't here. What would you do?"

Cody shrugged. "Sit around and think about you?"

Cody instantly worried he had come on too strong, too fast again. But El just chuckled. "Suppose we never met." A thought which made Cody shudder and hold El closer. "What would you do?"

"Honestly? Can't even remember what I used to do with my time before this damn league." Cody laughed and rolled onto his back, staring up at his ceiling. Usually, he'd spend the weekend catching up on cleaning and stuff. But he had gone into a cleaning frenzy that week when El suggested spending the night here. "It's like the last two months have been nothing but baseball this, and baseball that. I don't remember who I was before."

"I know exactly how you feel," El said. He patted Cody's hand. "It's nice to actually have a weekend where neither of our teams are playing."

"Yeah." Cody looked over at El with a smile. "Ya know, we could go and watch the other teams play today." El's look was thoroughly unamused, and Cody laughed at it. "Alright, what is it you would do alone with your time, hm?"

"Oh, I'm afraid I'm pretty boring," El said. "I mostly just sit around and read. Occasionally I'll go to a movie or show, but most of the time I just get myself lost in a book."

Cody turned back on his side and raised himself up on his elbow. "I've got a few books laying around here somewhere," he said. "You're more than welcome to them."

"I wouldn't do that to you, dear," El said. He reached up and placed a hand on Cody's cheek, rubbing his thumb over his skin. "I'm here to spend the day with you, not a book."

"Who said you can't do both?" Cody smirked at him. "You can read your book, and I can spend that time covering every inch of coverable skin on your body with little bites." His eyes roamed down El's body, a hunger growing within him. "Nothing I'd love more, honestly, than to keep you in bed all day." He looked back into El's eyes with a bit of worry. "Unless that's too much?"

Cody did believe what El had said last night, but he also knew El, for as much as he could be a bastard, was genuinely a nice and accommodating guy. Mr. Never-Had-a-Blowjob before couldn't be the most upfront with what he wanted when it came to sex or relationships, Cody figured. And he wanted to make sure he wasn't unintentionally taking advantage of that and putting El in a position he was uncomfortable with.

"Oh, my darling." El turned and raised himself up to match Cody's height. "I think that sounds wonderful."

"Really?" Cody raised an eyebrow at him. He saw nothing but honesty in El's eyes, but how could he be sure that the guy wasn't just a really good liar?

"Of course. I love how expressive you are, dear. And how intensely you feel your emotions."

"Ya do?" Because no one's ever been of that opinion before.

"I do. See, most people I know tend to be more...repressed, by nature. I find you entirely refreshing and very charming."

Cody smiled at him. There was no way El could possibly be lying with the way he was looking at Cody. Cody leaned forward and kissed him. "Alright then, here's the game plan." El nodded, his eyes opening a bit wider in eager anticipation. "You peruse the wares, while I make us some French toast for breakfast."

"Sounds good already," El said.

"After we're done eating, we get back in bed, and you read while I get to work."

El chuckled and leaned in for another kiss. "I love it."

"And," Cody said, not letting El lean back until at least three more kisses were had, "you have to read out loud to me. Because you have a very sexy voice."

El laughed again and nodded. "I think that sounds agreeable."

"Good. We can take breaks whenever you need."

"The same goes for you."

"Oh, I don't think I'll be needing any," Cody said, his free hand reaching over and mapping out the curves of El's body. He stopped on El's waist. "And uh…maybe you wear the lace thing again?"

El's smile grew and he placed his hand back on Cody's cheek. "Whatever you desire, my dear."

Chapter Fifteen
A Love Returned

El's day was full of busy work. Which was why he wasn't so disgruntled as usual to be called back up to the 20th floor. The last week or so had been full of these meetings, which consisted of Lawrence (and often Michelle) running through various strategies for the games with El and the others. They had even come up with the insane theory that the other teams had figured out their code, and so El had to learn a whole new set of hand signals.

"We need to have a serious conversation about Cody," Lawrence said, as soon as El arrived.

"Oh boy." El sighed and took his seat across from Lawrence. Valerie was sitting next to Lawrence, taking notes and avoiding eye contact. "What exactly about Cody do we need to discuss?"

"We need intel," Lawrence said.

"I'm sorry?" Surely talking so detailed about their relationship broke some kind of H.R. rule somewhere.

Lawrence leaned back in his chair and put his hands together before him. "I've decided to turn your betrayal into an advantage." El had to bite his tongue to keep himself from saying anything too rude in response. Lawrence was still his boss, after all. "With your help, we can win."

"Mhm," El said, trying to choose his words carefully. "Well, my batting skills have been improving. So, I'm sure our skill as a team will really shine." He nodded a bit too eagerly.

Lawrence frowned. "That's not what I was talking about." As El figured. "We need you to get some information for us."

"Information?"

"About the Shades of Infernal team," Lawrence explained. "With your *connection* to Cody, you have an in."

"Why did you say connection like that?" El asked. "We're in a relationship. There's nothing air-quotey about that."

"However you want to phrase it, you can get us details."

El took a deep breath and then stood up. "I'm not going to spy on Cody's team for you. And this conversation is over. I have actually important work to do."

Not that El wanted to do any of that work. But it was better than sitting around here talking such nonsense. Lawrence started to protest, but El just left, not giving him any time to argue. If they wanted to talk genuine strategy, that was fine. But El would not entertain the idea of cheating. Especially if it put his new relationship in jeopardy.

El got back to his office and sat down, already dreading getting back to his pile of paperwork. But then his phone buzzed in his pocket and he pulled it out with a smile. Cody had texted him: *Got lunch plans tomorrow?*

Not yet.

Wanna meet up at 1? Doing a photo shoot all day and would welcome the distraction

Sounds perfect. What should I bring?

Just your beautiful self. We have an excellent caterer for events

El's smile grew and he wiggled a bit at the prospect of both spending time with Cody and seeing what kind of spread they had. *Can't wait.*

Me either

"E-excuse me, Mr. El?"

El looked up, a little more than surprised to see Valerie standing by the elevator. More surprising was how nervous she looked. He gave her a smile and waved her in.

"Do come in," he said, gesturing to one of the chairs opposite his desk. "Is everything alright?" He wouldn't be surprised if the poor dear had gotten the earful from Lawrence after El just walked out like that.

"I just wanted to ask you something," Valerie started. El gave her an encouraging nod.

"Well…how did you get the courage to date Cody?"

"Ah, well, I suppose I had suspicions that he liked me," El explained. "So, in this case there wasn't much fear of getting rejected."

"No, I mean, you know, with him being the opposition and all."

"Oh." El gave Valerie a slightly pitied smile. "Valerie, see, he isn't really the *opposition*. I know that Lawrence and Michelle and some of the others can make it seem like that, but it really is just a game." El laughed a bit. "I don't even think there's a real trophy this year. Just bragging rights."

"But they love bragging rights," Valerie said.

"That they do. Which is why they take things so seriously. But I assure you, there is absolutely nothing wrong with getting along with or liking anyone on any of the other teams."

Valerie seemed to relax a little.

"So, who is it?" El asked.

Valerie scrunched down a bit, holding back a smile as she looked away. Then she sighed and looked back at El, a longing in her eyes. "His name's Altan," she said. And El smiled with a nod. "He's cute, and sweet, and *so* funny, even when he's not trying to be!"

"He sounds like the perfect match," El said. "And if you like him, I promise you have nothing to fear. And if anyone gives you any trouble for it, you just let me know."

Valerie nodded and stood up. She hesitated and then looked nervous again. "I do believe what you said," she added. "But, uhm, could we maybe just keep this between us? For just right now."

"Your secret is safe with me." Lord knows El would never wish this kind of nonsensical stress on anyone else.

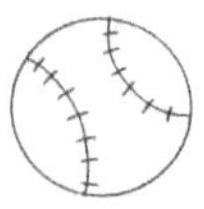

Out of all the events Cody had to go to and 'supervise,' photo shoots were generally some of the more interesting. But this one was turning out to be particularly boring. There had been no wardrobe malfunctions, no diva drama between the models, and the designer had even been mellow about the few suggestions to the set made. All of the things that made a shoot entertaining were missing.

But Cody managed to make it through the morning by thinking about El. El and his lovely personality, smokin' body, and genuine presence. Fuck him, Cody was in deep. If he had one less brain cell, he'd go out and propose already. But even if El had been accepting of his incredibly early love confession, Cody knew anything else was guaranteed to scare the guy off.

"Those are some interesting shoulders," El said.

Cody smiled and turned to look at him. "Hey, you." He leaned over and gave him a kiss, feeling better already.

"Yeah, believe it or not, they actually used to be bigger but rounder. Then someone decided sharpness was the way to go."

"I can't tell if that was a smart decision or not," El said. He held Cody's hand as the two of them watched the shoot unfold.

"Me either. I guess I should really pay more attention to fashion trends, huh?"

El chuckled. "Well, you do work in the industry."

"Eh." Cody shrugged and turned his focus back to the vision of beauty next to him. "Hungry?"

El's face brightened and he nodded. Cody led him over to the craft services table. It was filled with a make-your-own-sandwich spread. Not quite as sophisticated as usual, but El seemed to have no qualms, already getting to work on making himself a delicious looking bun.

"You ever thought about being a model?" Cody asked.

El turned to him with a cocked eyebrow, midway through a bite. "Me?" he mumbled around his sandwich.

Cody chuckled. "Yeah, you." He leaned against the table and just had the time of his life imagining all the lovely little outfits he would put El in.

El finished his bite and gave Cody a sympathetic smile. "I don't really think I'm cut out for that kind of work."

"It's not that hard," Cody said. "You just stand around and let people poke and prod you all day." He shrugged. "You could be photo exclusive, then you don't have to deal with catwalks or anything."

"I meant more that I'm not built for it," El clarified. "Physically."

Cody made a face. "What are you talking about? You're gorgeous!"

El smiled. "Well, I'm glad you think so, dear. But I'm afraid this beauty is only in the eyes of that beholder."

"Nonsense." Cody picked up a bagel and bit into it bitterly. "Look, the modeling world is really opening up these days. And all the guys like me, who love a body like yours, are gonna drool all over themselves the second they see you."

El laughed and turned back to the set. "Yes, quite the spectrum of body types."

"Well, not this stuff." Cody walked around and blocked El's view. He didn't need to be competing with those guys for El's attention. "But, ya know, good stuff."

El patted Cody's arm and gave him one of those bright, dazzling smiles. "Thank you, dear. But I'm quite comfortable where I am."

"Fair enough." Cody shrugged. "Alright, let's say you could have any job in the world. What would it be?"

El hummed and thought about it as he continued eating his sandwich. "I think I'd like to own a used bookshop," he said. "But only so I could get the best ones for myself."

Cody laughed. "That does sound like the perfect job for you. Maybe I could be your assistant? I have lots of experience in standing around and doing nothing. Perfect for that kind of work, right?"

"Well, if we're in a universe where dream jobs are available, what would yours be?"

Cody tilted his head and tried to come up with a good lie. Because the truth was certainly not one he could speak aloud. Especially after his love trip-up. "Erm, well, I dunno. Professionally retired?"

El chuckled and reached his foot out, nudging Cody's gently. "C'mon. I told you mine."

"Yeah, but yours wasn't embarrassing."

El shook his head, looking down with a soft smile. "It can't possibly be that bad."

"Alright, alright, if you really want to know the truth…" El gave him an encouraging nod and Cody rubbed the back of his neck. "I kind of always thought about being one of those…ya know, stay-at-home husband/dad types? I dunno." He shrugged and looked down at his feet, hating how awkward he was being. How was he going to get El to reciprocate his love if he was such a dork?

"A little busier than being retired," El said. He reached out and grabbed Cody's arm. "But I think it would suit you perfectly."

Cody allowed himself a little smile. "I just wanna take care of the people I love." And, boy, would a therapist have a field day with that one.

El stepped closer, pulling on Cody's arm until he looked up. El leaned up a little and kissed him. "I love you, too."

Every inch of Cody's skin set on fire. "You do?"

El nodded and kissed him again. Cody smiled into the kiss and tossed his bagel away so he could wrap El up and kiss him deeply and properly. It was the most perfect moment in all of existence, until something crashed behind him.

Cody growled and rolled his eyes as he pulled his head away, looking over his shoulder. One of the light riggings had fallen. Thankfully it didn't look like it had hit anyone, but the set was a complete disaster.

"Of course, something interesting happens as soon as I need it to stay calm."

El giggled and placed his hands on Cody's chest, smoothing his shirt down. "I suppose I should let you go deal with that, hm?"

"I mean…yeah, probably." Cody sighed. He really hated his job.

"How about we pick this up tomorrow?" El asked. "It is a three-day weekend."

"Don't we have a game Saturday?"

"Well, if you're over, then you can give me a ride."

Cody liked the sound of being over. "I'll bring my uniform. Want to do dinner?"

El looked at his hands, continuing to play with the fabric of Cody's shirt. "I was actually thinking we could meet earlier. Maybe eat...after?" He looked up at Cody through his eyelashes.

"After?" Cody asked, his mind short-circuiting a little. El's eyes just sparkled when he did that. "Why?"

"Well, *you know.*" El stepped closer, pressing suggestively against Cody. Which did not help his concentration.

"Uhhh, do I?"

"Don't you?"

"Don't think so."

El cleared his throat and looked around, dropping his voice to a whisper. "If we eat before, it could get...messy."

"...Messy?"

"Oh, good lord, Cody! I want you to fuck me."

"Ohhhhhhh!" Cody smiled wide, already dreading the wait until tomorrow. "Yeah, that would be good."

"Then it's settled." El stepped away, finally giving Cody the atmosphere needed to breathe. "I'll see you at, say, four?"

"Why not three?"

El smiled back. "Good. And text me which condoms you prefer. I'd like to have some extra on hand for whenever."

"Will do."

Chapter Sixteen
Toe-Curlin'

Cody had a skip in his step as he walked his way up to El's door. He knocked and bounced on his feet as he waited. After a few seconds, he checked his watch to make sure he wasn't arriving at the wrong time. El had been texting with him just before he left, too, so it's not like he didn't know Cody was coming over.

"Sorry for the wait," El said, finally opening the door. He looked a little flushed in the face and held the door open. "Just finishing up getting everything ready." He took Cody's bag from him and immediately led him upstairs.

Cody trailed after him with a chuckle. "Boy, do you know how to treat a guy."

El's bedroom had been completely transformed. With the dark shades drawn, even the bright afternoon sun couldn't find its way in. And only the romantic flicker of candlelight gave illumination to the space around them. Scents of vanilla filled the air and gentle, classical music played softly in the background. El had even gone so far as to lay out a towel on the bed.

"Just thought it would be nice," El said. He set Cody's bag down near the closet and then moved in for a kiss. "Don't you agree?"

"It's perfectly nice," Cody said, taking his time to properly nip at El's plump lips. "Much too nice for li'l ol' me."

El laughed and placed a hand on the back of Cody's head, pulling him in for a deep, proper kiss. Cody wrapped his arms around El's waist and pressed flush against him.

He had been getting himself excited on the drive over, sure, but El was already hard as a rock.

"Well, hello there," Cody said, looking down between them.

"Couldn't help myself," El explained. "Thinking about you, about this…" He moaned softly and pulled Cody's head back up for a kiss.

Cody laughed into the kiss and walked El back until they were next to the bed. He started carefully undoing the buttons of El's shirt, taking time to make sure his fingers brushed against the skin of his stomach and chest with each motion. El's body shivered a few times, and his own hands went to Cody's waist, squeezing him close as they kissed.

Cody pushed the shirt off El's body and tossed it to the side. Then he moved his kisses lower, trailing over El's jaw, his neck, his chest, lowering to his knees as he kissed across El's stomach.

"Oh, Cody," El said with a haggard breath.

Cody glanced up with a smirk and a raised eyebrow. "Yeah?" Then he pushed forward and pressed his open mouth against El's clothed erection.

El moaned again and his knees buckled. He sat heavy on the bed, supporting himself with his hands as Cody did his work. He felt out the shape of El through his pants, tongue tracing the outline before he peppered it with hard kisses. El placed a hand on Cody's head, pushing gently, trying to get more.

And who was Cody not to give it to him? Cody kept his kisses up on El's pants as his hands reached up and made quick work of his belt and zipper. He pulled El's pants down, grinning in delight as he revealed his lover, inch by inch. El lifted his hips to help, and then eagerly kicked his pants off and to the side.

Cody kissed his way up one thigh, placed a lavish lick to the underside of El's cock, and then nipped his way down the other thigh. He figured he could live nestled between these thighs and be perfectly happy.

"My dear," El said, hand brushing through Cody's hair. "While I do appreciate it, I don't think I'll last for you for very long like that."

Cody smiled, crossing his arms over El's knees and resting his chin on them so he could look up at El. His eyes were half-closed, lids heavy with lust. And his cheeks had such a lovely flush on them.

"You're gorgeous," Cody said.

El smiled. "Still not modeling."

Cody laughed and pressed a kiss to El's thigh before he stood up. "Where's the goods?"

"Over on the dresser there," El said, pointing to the side. "Everything you should need."

Cody wandered over and his smile grew. El had gotten a box of the condoms Cody had texted him, as well as a few other brands and types. And a small collection of various lube bottles and packets were spread out as well. The guy really did go all out.

"How would you like me?" El asked as Cody looked over the options of lube.

"However you'd like," Cody responded.

El huffed. "Don't be like that." Cody glanced over his shoulder. El was pouting in the most adorable way possible.

"Don't be like what?" Cody decided he couldn't be far away from that face for too much longer, so he just grabbed a random bottle and made his way back over.

"Indecisive," El said. His pout had lightened a little, and by the time Cody started shedding clothes, it was practically gone.

"I'm not being indecisive," Cody said. He smiled and sat down next to El, kissing him. "I'm being considerate."

"Well, I *am* indecisive," El said, pout starting to come back. "So, really, the considerate thing to do would be to just make a decision."

Cody hummed as he studied El. Truth be told, Cody didn't really have a preference when it came to positions. Sure, he had some that he liked better than others, but overall, sex was good no matter how you swung it. And he figured sex with El would be fantastic in any position. But if El was the same way, then one of them would have to make some kind of decision. But Cody was still trying to figure out if El really was indecisive, or if he had just never been given the chance to find out what he really liked.

"What is the best position you've ever had it in?" Cody asked.

"The best?"

"Yeah. Like, what's the last position that really got your toes curlin'?"

"Hmm, I'm not really sure." El adjusted his seat and placed his chin in one hand as he thought about it. Cody figured El wasn't the kind of guy that went and slept around much, but it was still a little sad to know he couldn't even remember that last good time off the top of his head. Cody just had to dedicate this time to being perfect, then.

"How about," Cody leaned over and pressed soft kisses along El's jaw, "you on your side? With me spooning ya?"

El made a happy little noise and melted against Cody's touches. "That sounds lovely."

Cody reached over and placed a hand on El's cheek, turning his head for a proper kiss. Then he pulled back and looked into El's eyes with all the sincerity he felt. "I need you to promise me something."

El gulped, a little tinge of worry spreading in his gaze. "What's that?"

"You'll let me know if anything starts to hurt or get uncomfortable?"

Relief returned, and El smiled with a nod. "I promise."

"No matter how small," Cody urged. "Even if it's just a sore muscle from being in one place for too long."

El pressed his own hand over Cody's, leaning his head against Cody's palm. "I promise. But you have to promise the same."

"Deal." Cody leaned forward and sealed it with a kiss. "Now," he gestured his head to the rest of the bed. "On your stomach."

El started to move but stopped halfway. "I thought we were spooning?"

"Oh, we will." Cody popped the bottle of lube open and spread some on his fingers. "But I gotta get you ready, first."

"Ah, no need for that," El said with a bright smile. "Already taken care of."

Cody raised an eyebrow at him. "Already taken care of?"

El sat back down slowly, looking a little worried again. "I just thought you'd want to get right to it," he said. He picked at his fingernails, looking down at his lap.

Cody reached over, rubbing the lube on his fingers over El's cock, worried that this shift in mood might shift some other things. "Hey." He pressed a kiss to El's cheek.

"I love you," he reminded him. "No harm, no foul." That, at least, got a little chuckle out of El.

"I promise that next time I'll be more patient," El said. He finally looked back up at Cody, breathing a little heavy as his hips pressed up against Cody's touches.

"Or I'll just be earlier," Cody whispered back. He pressed a gentle kiss to El's lips. "Of course, I will have to inspect your handiwork."

El smiled and kissed him back. "Of course."

Cody placed his free hand on the back of El's head and laid them both down. El's legs spread open, and Cody's hand made its way down, slick fingers seeking out his entrance.

El lifted his hips a bit and moaned into their kiss as Cody's fingers pressed against him. Cody hummed his approval as one finger easily slipped inside. He kept note of how El's body reacted as he moved that finger inside, feeling an easy stretch. El seemed perfectly content and relaxed, even as Cody pressed a second finger in to join the first.

El pulled away from their kiss, giving Cody a brief pause before he huffed out, "air."

Cody laughed and went back to scissoring his fingers, finding no physical signs of pain or discomfort. He tested the waters with a third finger, finding it a little bit of a tight fit, but not enough to make it difficult or to pull any reaction other than a deep moan from El.

"You really do prepare, don't you?" Cody asked with a soft chuckle. He curled his fingers a bit, searching until he found that spot that made El's body jerk with a sharp breath.

"Good?" Cody asked, gently pressing against that spot, eyes glued to El's face for any grimaces or wavering.

"Perfect," El breathed out. He laid there with his eyes closed, head tilted back, hands grabbing at the towel around them. El's dick started to leak a bit of pre-cum, and Cody figured they'd better get the show on the road.

"Alright, *now* on your side," he said. He pulled his fingers out and wiped them on the corner of the towel before he went to put on the condom.

"L-let me know if you n-need anything," El said, words interrupted by haggard breath. Cody watched him move, slowly at first, as he rolled to his side, then with surprising agility as he positioned himself more near the center of the bed.

One of El's hands reached up, grabbing at the air as he tried to reach the pillows above. Cody smiled and laid down behind him, grabbing two pillows and placing one under El's head.

"Thank you, dear," he said.

Cody placed the other down next to it and got himself nice and cozy, all curled up to El's back. He reached behind him for the lube and rubbed it on himself as he snaked his other arm under El's body, holding him close.

El's hand gently brushed against Cody's arm as his head leaned back against Cody's. Cody got one leg between El's, opening them slightly just so he could guide himself in.

El's ass was tight and hot, and felt oh so divine. As soon as Cody had gotten the head of his cock in, El was pushing back, arching his back a bit to help rush Cody all the way inside.

Cody laughed as he grabbed El's leg and held it up for him. "Pushy, pushy," he chided.

"Oh, hush," El whispered back.

Cody kissed the back of El's head and then made a shallow thrust, trying to see which way he needed to angle his hips to hit the right spot. When he had suggested this position, he figured it would be close, intimate, and romantic. Which it was. But it was also a little difficult to get the right traction as he slid in and out of El. And that just wouldn't do, not when it needed to be the best time of El's life.

"Okay, this isn't working," Cody mumbled.

"Feels fine to me," El said.

"Yeah, well, fine isn't good enough." Cody eased his way out and then sat up, trying to recalculate.

"Is everything alright?" El asked, sitting up next to him.

"I just want to make it good for you," Cody said.

"Because you like taking care of the people you love?" El asked.

"Well, yeah!" Cody looked him in the eyes. How could he not want to give El only the best of everything?

"Darling, it doesn't need to be perfect." El placed a hand on Cody's cheek and rubbed his thumb over his skin. "As long as I'm with you, I'm happy as a clam." He kissed him softly.

Cody knew that was true. And the sentiment was certainly returned. But he'd be damned if that truth got in the way of his mission.

"Here, you lay down." El moved his hand to Cody's chest and gently pushed him onto his back. "And we'll try this."

El swung a leg over, straddling Cody backwards, hands bracing him against Cody's thighs.

"You won't get tired?" Cody asked, although he was already twitching at the lovely sight before him.

"Hardly," El said, almost as if offended by the insinuation. "My legs have quite the stamina for this, if you recall."

And, oh, did Cody recall. He licked his lips and placed one hand on El's hip, using the other to guide himself back in. El once more pushed his way down, taking Cody deep inside him. It was an intoxicating sight.

But it was nothing compared to El moving in that position, his leg muscles clenching and relaxing as he bounced himself on Cody, taking his pleasure with a fast pace that knocked the wind out of Cody's lungs.

"Oh, this was a bad idea," Cody said with a huffed laugh.

El slowed a bit. "Why's that?"

Cody ran his hands over El's thighs, hips spasming upwards to seek more of that delicious friction. "Because now I'll literally never be able to concentrate during a game."

"Hm, sounds like a good idea to me, still."

Cody chuckled and gave El's ass a playful, light swat. El looked over his shoulder at him with a raised eyebrow and Cody's entire body froze.

"Surely you can do better than that," El said, a hint of goading in his voice. Which got both of Cody's eyebrows to rise.

"Yeah?" He smacked El's ass with a bit more gumption, still not wanting to get too hard, too fast.

El shrugged. "Better." Then he turned his head back and picked up the pace.

So, he liked it a little rough, huh? Cody smirked. He could do rough.

Cody grabbed El's waist with both hands and held him still, thrusting up into him more than letting El ride him. He slid up just a bit, angling his hips down and earning a series of sharp gasps as his reward.

"C-Cody," El moaned out. And never had Cody's name sounded so sweet.

Dangerously close, Cody growled a bit and pushed up, needing to get some better traction. He slipped out as he rearranged them, getting El on his hands and knees as he knelt behind, but he was quick to get back in. He leaned over El's back as he continued thrusting, reaching one arm around his waist to pump him off in time with his thrusts.

"Cody," El moaned again. "Oh, y-yes!"

Cody dropped his head, focusing on the sounds and vibrations of El's body as he came so beautifully for him. And with El's ass squeezing all around him, Cody wasn't too far behind in perfect bliss.

Cody enjoyed the moment, still curled up against El's back, ignoring the sticky feeling in the condom as he breathed in El's scent, which mixed perfectly with the vanilla. But then he felt El's body start to shake a little, and knew it was time to move.

Cody gently pulled out, carefully holding the bottom of the condom until he was clear. Then he was quick to get out and tie it off. He helped El to lay down and then hopped off the bed to dispose of the condom. El hadn't moved an inch by the time he got back.

With a chuckle, Cody grabbed the pillows and moved them to the foot of the bed. He slid one under El's head and then settled down next to him.

"You okay?" Cody asked. El had his eyes closed, but he was smiling.

"Oh, yes," El said. He peeled his eyes open a bit. "Darling, that was lovely. Thank you."

Cody smiled and leaned over for a kiss. "I should be the one thanking you," he said. Because that was certainly up there in the list of best times ever.

"But you made my toes curl," El said, wiggling his feet for emphasis.

"And I always will," Cody promised.

Chapter Seventeen
What are the Odds?

"We didn't make a bet of any kind," Cody commented as they stood off to the side, waiting for the game to get going. Thankfully Trish hadn't shown up to this one. But the two had stopped by Clara's to pick her up that morning. El still worried about her safety while living alone, but she hadn't burned down the place yet. Sure, she was a little ditzy, but Cody thought El might be overreacting a little bit.

"I don't think we need a bet each game," El said. "Do you?"

Cody shrugged. They didn't *need* one, sure. But it was fun all the same. "Makes things more interesting."

El nodded and hummed. "We could do something simple," he said. "Winner gets to pick the next date spot."

"We could," Cody said. "Or," he smiled just thinking about it, "we could do the lace thing again." He turned his smile to El. He really wanted to do the lace thing again.

El chuckled. "You can just ask to do the lace," he said. "It doesn't need to be won."

Cody leaned his head down, lowering his voice to a whisper. "Will ya wear the lace thing tonight?"

El smiled, a hint of pink on his cheeks. "Yes." Cody did a little celebratory dance. "But that still leaves us without a bet."

Cody crossed his arms and pursed his lips, thinking about what would work best. Something as simple as choosing dinner or a movie was too lame to work that hard for. It had to be something with some drive behind it.

"Oh! I got it!" He smiled back at El. "If I win, you let me give you a hickey!"

El's face looked repulsed by the suggestion, but his eyes wandered a little bit, as if actually considering it. Cody bounced excitedly in place. "Just one?"

"Just one."

"Alright. And if I win?"

Cody shrugged. "Well, what do you want?" And as long as the answer wasn't 'never give me a hickey again,' Cody could go along with it.

El mulled it over for a few minutes. Either he had a lot of things he wanted and couldn't decide on which to bet for, or he had a minimal pool of things he knew he wanted. Cody really hoped it was the former.

"If I win, you have to come with me to the bookfair that's in town next week and help me carry all my books," El finally said. "Without complaining."

Cody smiled. He'd have done that anyway if El had asked. But he was just glad El had been able to think of anything at all.

Cody held out a hand. "Deal."

El shook it. "Deal."

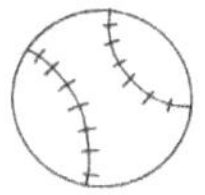

Thankfully, Cody didn't need to concentrate much during the game unless he was up to bat. Which was very good because he couldn't stop staring at El even if he wanted to. Which probably wasn't good for his health, but who could blame him? The guy was hot, especially since Cody could now imagine that body all naked and hot and panting.

"Cody!" Briney called out. "You're up."

Fuck. Cody shook the images from his head, but he hadn't regained full composure by the time he walked up to the plate.

"You know," El said, making Cody chuckle and shake his head. Of course he would start the mind games right away. "It's really a shame that the batters are in front of the catchers. Should be the other way around."

"Wouldn't make much sense to the game," Cody said. He readied for the pitch and made the mistake of swinging at an obvious ball, earning himself a strike. Seeing El in that position last night really was a bad idea.

"I suppose this does work out better for me," El whispered.

"Why's that?" Cody asked. He readied up again and this time restrained from hitting the curve that went wide to the right. El caught it expertly, of course.

"Because this way I get to stare at *your* butt during the games instead," El said, very matter-of-factly.

Cody huffed and made a second strike. He shook his body loose. "You can stare at my butt anytime you want, El."

"True," El said with a slow, musing voice. "But you'll get to see mine much more often, I'm sure."

And the image of El's ass riding him was enough to stall Cody's entire body for a full two seconds, letting the third strike whiz right into El's mitt.

"Alright," Cody said, grumbling as he turned to face El and Rafael. El was smiling all proud behind his mask and laughing softly. "That's gotta be illegal, man, c'mon."

130

Rafael shrugged and tilted his head back and forth a bit. "Eh, it amuses me," he said. Literally the worst person to ump a game ever. He pointed a finger at El. "But if this gets more graphic, there will be red flags."

El chuckled again. "And if we were playing soccer, I'd be very worried."

Cody gestured to El with a wild stare at Rafael. "Seriously? You're going to let that slide."

Rafael just shrugged again. "Yeah."

Cody rolled his eyes and groaned his way back to the dugout. He'd need to come up with some kind of anti-El's comments system while up there.

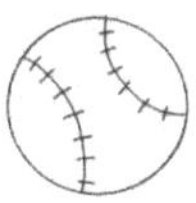

"What are you doing?" El asked, laughing as Cody walked up to the plate, a wad of napkins stuffed in each ear.

"Sorry, what?" Cody asked, shouting a little for emphasis. He pointed to his ear. "Can't hear you!"

El just laughed again and gave Cody a look that told him he was being silly. And he was awfully cute when he was silly. It was one of the things El loved the most about him. There wasn't enough silliness in life these days. But Cody was certainly working on fixing that up.

El crouched down, ready to make the catch as needed. Cody needn't go through such dramatics, however. El wasn't going to mess with him *every* time he came up to bat, of course. That wouldn't be very sporting. Besides, picking and choosing his times carefully would add more suspense and flavor to the games.

Michelle steadied, ready for the pitch, and out of the corner of his eye, El saw the runner on first take a few cautious steps. As soon as Michelle threw the ball, the runner was off. El kept his eyes trained on the runner, trusting that he would catch the ball as Michelle was pretty regular with her fastballs, meaning it would land right in his mitt if Cody didn't hit it.

The harsh thud of the ball in his glove told El that Cody had gotten a strike. But before he could even really process that information, his body was already moving and reacting as if by second nature. He was quick to stand and grab the ball from his mitt. With one long stride forward, he lobbed it over Michelle's (quickly ducked) head. The runner made a dive for it, but he wouldn't be quick enough, El knew. It was a well-earned out. One that ended the inning.

"Holy shit," Cody whispered.

El slipped his helmet off. Cody was staring at him with wide eyes. Which worried him a little. They had always had fun with the game, and Cody had gotten a little upset at a few plays or comments. But there was an entirely different look in his eyes now, and El had no idea what to make of it.

"Nice one, El," Michelle said, jogging past him as the teams switched out. "I didn't even see him make a run for it."

El gave her a polite smile and then turned back to Cody. "What?" he asked. Better to just get it over with, he figured.

"That was hot," Cody said.

Oh. It wasn't a bad look at all, was it? El smiled, feeling relief wash through his system.

"I'm sorry you didn't get to finish batting," El offered. Because he really did like to see Cody's talents himself.

"Don't be," Cody said with a short laugh. His eyes grazed over El's body, making him hot under all his gear. "That was worth it."

"Alright, let's keep it PG here, folks." Rafael stepped between them and ushered them back to their respective dugouts. Cody kept looking back at El with that same look in his eyes. And El decided he wanted to see more of that look.

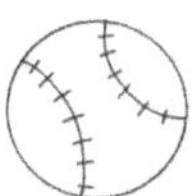

Games never seemed to get as close when they weren't playing against each other. But there they were, tied at the bottom on the ninth. Two outs. Cody on third. El shivered as the next batter stepped up. Cody was already crouched, smirking as he stared El down.

Cody should know by now that a dive wasn't likely to knock El out. But he had a challenging look in his eyes that said he was going to try all the same. El was more than ready for a challenge.

Michelle readied the pitch, and El turned his attention back to her. A fast ball should be enough to strike this batter out. El wouldn't have to worry about hiding a hickey, and he'd get some help carting books around. No more having to narrow down his choices based on carrying capacity, not this year!

Michelle nodded and threw the pitch. The ball made contact with the bat, of that El was sure. But as soon as he saw and heard the hit, the world went dark with a force of pressure against all sides of his head.

El stood up, his brain taking a second to process that. He wasn't unconscious, but he could hardly see out of his mask. Like someone had draped a cloth down the center. No, not a cloth. A ball. The ball had bounced off the bat and lodged itself firmly in El's helmet.

Cody was over to him in an instant. "El!" His hands grabbed at El's body, but it was hard to see him much with the ball still obstructing his view. "Shit, are you okay?"

"I'm perfectly fine," El said. But the adrenaline put a shake in his voice all the same. "It's why we wear these things, after all."

"Yeah, but still."

"El!" That was Michelles' voice, and El turned to face the direction she had come from. He was getting all closed in and disoriented now. "You alright?"

"Yes, yes, I'm fine." El held his hands out, raising his voice a bit to quell anyone else's concern. He could already hear Lawrence running up as well.

"Hell of a play," Rafael said. His presence grew closer, no doubt bending over to study the way the ball was lodged in the helmet. "That takes some precision."

"Erm, yes, something like that." El shrugged Cody's tight hold off his shoulders and slipped his mask off. Everyone, the batter included, gathered around to stare at it.

"Here." Rafael took the mask and started trying to dislodge the ball. "Wow, that's really in there."

"You aren't hurt, are you?" Cody asked, his hands quickly back on El's shoulders. He twisted and turned El's body, looking him over from every angle.

"I'm okay," El assured him. "A little shaken-up, but fine."

"That could have killed you," Michelle said in a soft whisper.

"Which is why it's a good thing we wear protective coverings," El told her.

"I'm glad you're okay," Lawrence said, smiling at him. Then he dropped his smile and turned to Rafael. "So, Cody's out, right?"

"Huh?" Rafael and Cody said at the same time, though in much different tones. Rafael's was distracted, still trying to get the ball out of the mask, whereas Cody's was enraged.

"He left the base," Lawrence said. "That's illegal or something, right?"

"It wasn't a fair ball," the batter argued. "We'll just reset."

Oh good. El didn't want to miss their big showdown, after all.

"Er, technically-" Rafael popped the ball out and gave a celebratory shout. "Sorry, technically Cody gets a free run."

"What?" everyone asked, also in varying tones.

"Official rules," Rafael said, shrugging. "Look it up. If the ball gets stuck in the catcher's gear, the runners get to advance one base."

"That's ridiculous!" Michelle argued.

"It's true," Lawrence said, phone already in hand.

"Alright!" The batter patted Cody on the back and ran off to tell the rest of the team the good news.

"This is bullshit," Michelle said, stomping off to their dugout to relay the bad news.

Lawrence pulled Rafael, who was still studying the ball and mask with interest, off to the side and started his pointless arguing. El turned to Cody with a soft pout.

"Winning on a technicality shouldn't count," he said.

Cody laughed and wrapped his arms loosely around El's neck. "Oh, I think it definitely does." And he was eyeing El's neck rather hungrily. It sent a shiver of delight down his spine. "But I'll tell ya what." Cody took a step forward and tilted his head. "Since you are clearly incredibly lucky, I'll still go with you to the book fair to tote your haul around."

And that perked El right back up. "Really?"

Cody nodded. "But! I do get to complain a little."

El chuckled. "That sounds fair." He closed the gap between them and gave Cody a kiss. Technicality or not, Cody had performed most spectacularly during the game. And El figured he really did earn that hickey.

Chapter Eighteen
A Well-Earned Reward

El hummed happily to himself as he looked through another box of rare finds. The book fair this year had been exceedingly fruitious, and he was happy to have Cody's assistance. And despite his insistence to complain, Cody seemed to enjoy himself as well. Although El couldn't see what could capture Cody's attention, as he didn't even buy anything for himself.

"Are you going to have room for all of this?" Cody asked, lugging the third box up to sit on the desk in El's study. "Your shelves are looking full to burst already."

El smiled at him and pulled the box closer. "Mm, yes. I plan on taking some time this weekend to rearrange everything, bring a few books into the office. That should make plenty of room for these new acquisitions."

"My shelves are pretty empty, as you know." Cody slid up behind El, wrapping his arms around his waist and looking over his shoulder into the box. "Could always store some there, if you want."

"A very kind offer." El turned his head and kissed Cody on the cheek. "And I just might take you up on that."

"But you should only bring over the ones you read all the time," Cody said. He buried his face in El's neck, kissing along various spots. Ever since winning the bet, he's spent the week trying to determine the 'perfect spot' for his hard-earned hickey.

"But then I wouldn't have them here to read," El said. He tilted his head to the side slightly, giving Cody more room to work. The longer he spent ruminating over where to place the hickey, the longer El could avoid it altogether.

"Oh *no*," Cody said, moving his kisses to the other side of El's neck. "Then you'd have to come over *all* the time. What a *shame*."

El giggled under Cody's touches and words. The idea of spending more time with Cody filled him with warmth. But he much preferred the homier touch of his own place compared to the minimalist approach in Cody's. "Perhaps we could find something of yours to put here for the same purposes," he suggested.

"Yeah?" Cody pulled his head up and leaned forward, looking over at El. "All the reason I need for visiting is right here." He placed a kiss to El's cheek.

El chuckled and left his books unattended as he leaned back into Cody's embrace. "If I may ask, darling, how is it that someone as sweet and attentive as you hadn't already been snatched up by now?"

"I was just thinking the same thing about you," Cody said. His arms tightened their hold on El, bringing their bodies flushed together.

"Well, I don't get out much," El whispered. Not that the opportunities to get out didn't appear. He just liked ignoring them. He rested his head back against Cody's shoulder, closing his eyes and enjoying the warmth of his touch. He might have paid more attention to them if he knew someone like Cody was out there waiting. "Not many chances to meet someone, you know."

"You're awfully skilled for someone who doesn't get out much," Cody said. "I don't buy it."

"I've done some self-practice," El informed him. "One needn't be in a relationship to *explore*."

Cody hummed and nuzzled his way back to El's neck. His breath tickled hot against El's skin. "I'm sure you've done plenty of exploring." He chuckled deeply before getting back to kissing all over El's skin.

"And you have been avoiding my question," El noted. Cody sighed, ceasing his kisses and resting his chin on El's shoulder instead. El gulped. "You don't have to talk about it," he whispered. "If you don't want." He would want to know eventually, of course. But he wouldn't push Cody to talk when he wasn't ready. They had grown together so quickly; it was hard sometimes to remember that they were still early in their relationship.

And there were certainly some topics El wasn't ready to talk about either.

"Nah, it's alright. I've been told I'm 'too intense'. Figure that's why no one stuck around."

"I'd hardly call you intense," El said. Excitable surely. But that was endearing.

"I told you I love you on, what, our *third* date or something?"

"I didn't mind." El's own love hadn't been all that slow to follow, after all.

Crowle let out a soft laugh. "Yeah. Most people I've been with think I'm either crazy or lying." The thought that Cody had been lying never even crossed El's mind. Anyone who knew him even a tiny bit could tell he was more open and free with his emotions. "Just makes me grateful to have you." He placed a kiss on El's shoulder and then straightened up, releasing his hold. "Guess that whole 'never met the right one' deal was true after all, huh?"

El spun around and gently grabbed Cody's arms, looking into his slightly downcast eyes. He didn't mean to bring up what was clearly a sore topic. But 'the right one' did seem to fit. "I feel the same way about you, I hope you know."

Cody smiled and leaned his forehead against El's. Then he groaned.

"What's wrong?" El asked.

"Nothing. Just..." he groaned again and shook his head, rocking it gently against El's. "We owe our relationship to *baseball*." He shuddered, and El laughed at him.

"I'm sure our paths would have crossed at some point," he said. He slid his arms down and grabbed Cody's hands, lacing their fingers together. "Something as wonderful as this was bound to happen, wasn't it?" El hadn't been the biggest believer in 'fate,' but he couldn't deny that this right here was meant to happen.

"Mm, couldn't have said it better myself." Cody tilted his head back and kissed El with a deep breath. "And, I think I've found the perfect spot for my love-bite." Cody moved his head, positioning his lips just a bit below El's right ear. "Right here." He placed a gentle nip to the skin, humming in delight.

"Are you sure you don't want to give it any more thought?" El asked with a little waver in his voice and nerves. Cody's hands found their way to El's hips, pulling him closer and creating goosebumps up and down his arms.

"Oh, I've been thinking of nothing else since the game," Cody mumbled. He pushed closer, until El's legs were pressed against his desk. His kisses against El's neck became hungrier too, a small growl building in the back of his throat as he nipped.

"Wha-now?" El asked. He moaned gently under Cody's bites. The way his teeth skimmed over his skin, pinching and pulling so delicately yet with just enough of a sting to keep things interesting, was enough to send shivers up and down El's spine.

"Problem with that?" Cody asked. His strong hands tightened on El's waist, a quick squeeze the only warning before he was lifting El up, sitting him down on the desk with an excited gasp.

El's hands were quick to wrap around Cody, fingers of one hand tangling up in Cody's hair as the other bunched the back of his shirt in a passionate grab. El had never been desired so desperately before. And feeling how much Cody wanted him was an elation he didn't know he had been longing for. "I-I suppose not."

El closed his eyes and leaned his head to the side as he enjoyed Cody's work. He often found himself growing rather bored with most activity like this, part of why he avoided it. But he would never want to avoid such things with Cody. He always kept everything just interesting enough to not be boring. Like right now, for example, his hands were pulsating on El's hips, fingers making deep impressions at odd intervals that El could never predict. And he felt himself getting excited.

El opened his legs, shifting forward a bit so he was sitting just on the edge of the desk. Cody took the hint and angled slightly. His thigh pressed against El's groin in a way that pulled a deep moan of pleasure from El's lips.

"You sound so beautiful, El," Cody mumbled as he took a softer-kiss break on El's neck. "Heavenly, even. Angelic."

El breathed out a laugh. "Oh, I don't know about all that."

Cody growled again and moved his leg, rubbing against El's erection as his bites grew more intense. El's hands flexed in response, another deep moan escaping as his nerves set afire. If only hickeys weren't so hard to get rid of or hide, El might just be more open to them in the future.

"Like I said," Cody said, giving one last, gentle, kiss to the spot he had been working over. He pulled back, his face flushed red, his eyes wide and dilated. "Angelic."

He cupped El's face, looking deep into his eyes. "My angel," he said in a gentle whisper.

El felt a shiver rock through his entire body, zeroing in on where Cody's thigh pressed so delightfully against him. He tried to close his legs and prevent the inevitable, but all that accomplished was pinning Cody between his knees as he came.

Cody chuckled and looked down, his hands still holding El's face, which was now as hot and red as El figured it's ever been.

"S-sorry," El said.

Cody just smiled and pressed their foreheads together. "I love you," he said, his voice sounding distant yet close at the same time.

"I love you, too," El said. It was a little difficult to find the energy to talk, so he simply closed his eyes and enjoyed the moment.

"Are you *sure* you only want one?" Cody asked, a bit of goading in his voice.

El mustered up a chuckle. "Positive."

"Well, only one *visible* one, right?" Cody moved his hands down to El's thighs, grabbing them tightly.

"Yes, alright," El conceded with no hesitation. "Let me just grab a book for the evening, hm?"

Chapter Nineteen
Walkin' Home

Cody frowned as he walked El and Clara over to the stands. "What are you still doing here?"

Trish turned to him with a small smile. "What? A sister can't come to watch her brother play? Clara does it."

"Clara lives here," Cody mumbled.

"I think it's nice," Clara piped up. "She's being supportive!"

"No, she's not." Cody crossed his arms and glared at Trish. "She's being sneaky and up to something."

"Honestly." Trish rolled her eyes. "You're so distrusting."

"Of *you*, yeah."

El had been standing a bit away, watching in silence. And Cody could imagine how El felt when moving Clara in, trying to deal with family stuff on his own only to get interrupted. But if El got involved, who knew what might come out.

"C'mere." Cody gestured to the side and stepped away from the stands. Trish followed, the smile dropping from her face. "Seriously, Trish. What are you doing?"

Trish sighed. "I'm seriously just here to watch you play." Cody squinted at her. "And maybe talk to El a bit, what's wrong with that?"

"A-ha!" Cody pointed a finger at her. "You're doing more spying for them!"

"I wouldn't have to spy if you would just talk to them once in a while." Trish sighed again, and she got that look on her face that meant she was about to get all 'big sister' on him. "Look, Cody, you gotta realize that they aren't going to stop caring about you. No matter what. They didn't stop caring when you almost went to Juvie. They didn't stop caring when you turned eighteen. And they won't stop caring just because you moved two hours away to the city." She crossed her arms at him. "It's been *twenty* years. When are you going to realize that they love you?"

Cody frowned and turned away. Only he was now looking at El, who watched him with a concerned eye. Cody stifled a groan and forced a smile before turning back to Trish. "Look, I get that I have issues, okay? That's pretty fucking obvious. But *telling them about my day* isn't going to fix that. So, drop it."

Trish shook her head. "You're an idiot."

"Shocking, I know."

"Fine. Go avoid your problems. I'll be over there," she pointed back at El and Clara, "with the other well-adjusted members of society."

Cody scoffed at her as she left. Then he gave El another smile and a thumbs up before heading to the dugout. He didn't have time for Trish's mind games right now.

Trish was doing a whole lot of talking. Cody tapped his foot and imagined all the different ways he could torture her, depending on exactly what she was talking about. El burst into a fit of laughter and Cody groaned. This game needed to be quick and fast so he could shut that down.

It's not like the game was even that important. Cody's team had already secured their spot in the league finals with their last win, technicality and all. This was just part of the pecking order for the rest of the teams. It was El's game tomorrow that would determine whether or not their teams would be playing each other in the finals. Cody really hoped they would.

"You're up, go show 'em we mean business," Briney said, patting Cody on the shoulder. Cody did not mean business, but he did need to put on his 'impress-my-boyfriend' pants, since Trish was clearly undermining all his cool-guy efforts. And he did enough of that on his own without her help.

Cody made the mistake of glancing over at El as he was getting ready to bat. El sat on the edge of his seat, hands grasping over his thighs, staring at Cody with such bright and glittering eyes. It was more than enough for Cody to miss the first pitch entirely.

Clearly the 'don't pay attention to El' rule had to apply while he was just in the stands as well. Cody shook his head and focused his attention solely on the pitcher. When they threw the next pitch, Cody was ready. He felt pretty good about it as he started running. The ball continued right between two of the outfielders. It was a safe and easy double. But Cody needed to show off. And in a game that didn't really matter for the main score, he could afford a few risks.

Cody saw El stand up as he rounded second and made a beeline for third. He knew El would be tracking the ball, making calculations in his head, thinking Cody was a fool to try. But if Cody could make it, he'd certainly win some cool-guy points for sure.

Yeah, he was never gonna make it. Cody was hardly half-way around when he heard the thud of the ball in the short-stop's mitt. Thankfully, Cody was both quick at thinking on his feet and quick on his feet. He skidded to a stop and raced right back to second. It was a pretty close call, but his foot was securely back on base by the time the second baseman tagged him.

Cody caught his breath as the next batter readied up. He looked up to see El shaking his head but smiling softly. Cody just gave him a shrug. Couldn't blame a guy for trying, right?

"He's really talented, isn't he?" El said as he settled back in his seat. It was, of course, foolish for Cody to try and get the triple with that hit, but he was able to realize his mistake and adjust his run to match. Which took a certain amount of skill itself. El turned his attention back to Trish. "Was he this good as a child?"

Trish scoffed. "Oh, he was good, if he could be bothered. First half of the season he wouldn't even try to hit the ball. It wasn't until the other kids made fun of him for being bad that he actually showed up and showed off." She smiled a bit coyly. "Kind of like he's doing now."

El blushed, knowing he was one Cody was trying to show off for.

"You really think someone's been bullying him?" Clara asked, leaning over El to stare wide-eyed at Trish.

"Hardly," Trish assured her. "If someone was antagonizing him, believe me, you'd be able to tell."

"Oh?" El perked up a bit, eager to learn more about his boyfriend. Of course, he knew to always take anything a sibling says with a grain of salt.

"He wounds easily," Trish said. "And he doesn't hide it well."

"He is expressive," El agreed. Then he smiled, because that was what he loved so much about Cody. "It's very refreshing."

"You absolutely cannot tell him I said this." Trish leaned closer and lowered her voice. "But I'm glad he found you. And if he does anything stupid, you have to promise to tell me all about it so I can yell at him."

El laughed. He wasn't sure, originally, what kind of relationship the two of them had. But he could see now that they did care about each other. They just had more of a friendly sibling rivalry whereas El and Clara were both closer and farther apart in different ways due to their age gap.

"What is that on your neck?" Clara asked. She reached over, poking at the spot where Cody had left his mark.

"Oh, er, nothing," El said, swatting her hand away with a nervous chuckle.

"Is that makeup?" Clara examined the substance that had smeared a bit on her finger. It was this cursed heat, making El sweat off his careful coverup.

"My, my," Trish crooned. "Makeup on the neck? Aren't you two a little adventurous?"

El chuckled again, a nervous reaction he's always had. "It's nothing like that." But he knew the blush on his face was not doing him any favors.

"Let's just have a little look," Trish said. She reached a hand out to grab El's chin. But he was quick to stand up.

"Oh, look," he said, pointing to the field. "Cody's about to make a run."

And what a perfectly timed run it was. As Trish laughed softly behind him, El just smiled at his love and clapped as he ran across the home plate. Cody smirked at him and jogged back to the dugout.

El knew that if he sat back down between Clara and Trish, he'd just get questioned endlessly about things that really were none of their business. And as much as he wanted to get to hear more stories about Cody, he wanted to avoid accidentally telling any himself.

"I think some water might be in order," he said, already scooting past Clara towards the small concessions stand. "Anything for the two of you?"

Despite not actually mattering, the game seemed pretty intense. The other team was trying, which had thrown their team for a loop in the first few innings. Now they were at a risk of losing. Which, again, didn't matter. No that anyone else seemed to care about that.

"Damn it!" Briney shouted as Anwar struck out again. "You're useless."

"I know," Anwar said, slinking back to her seat.

"Lay off her, eh?" Cody said. He grabbed his bat and stretched his arm a bit as Jean went up to bat. "She's doing alright."

"She hasn't gotten a single hit all game!" Briney said.

"All season," Lily corrected from the bench.

Briney looked at her slightly bewildered. "Is that true?" Lily nodded. Briney turned their murderous gaze back to Anwar, who tried to quickly hide behind her siblings.

"Relax," Cody said. "We're still in the finals no matter what happens today." He was seriously beginning to think the others forgot about that. It was one thing to get crazy about games that mattered, but to go yelling at people for something with no risk at all was a bit much.

"And we'll be taking the world's worst hitter with us," Briney said. They sneered at her again and Anwar winced.

"But we'll have the best trio of outfielders as well," Cody reminded them. "Nothing like a hivemind for organized sports, eh?"

He patted the sated Briney on the shoulder and went to wait for Jean to finish hitting. He made a decent hit and ended up safe at first. If Cody could land a homerun, they'd be tied, and maybe Briney would just lay off the triplets for a while.

Cody briefly glanced at El as he made his way to bat. El gave him a smile and an encouraging nod. Which was all the extra motivation he needed. He'd get that homerun alright.

Cody stepped up to the plate and readied his bat. He stared the pitcher down, consciously not looking into the stands, but turned back once he heard shifting. The other team's catcher was standing up, arm stretched to the side, mitt ready to catch the obvious ball.

"You gotta be kiddin' me," Cody grumbled. But they were not kidding him. The pitcher tossed the ball right into the catcher's glove. Even Rafael sounded disappointed as he called it out.

Cody leaned against his bat and placed his free hand on his hip. The pitcher gave him a small apologetic shrug, and then pitched another obvious ball.

"This is ridiculous," Cody muttered under his breath.

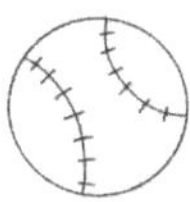

"This is ridiculous!" El nearly shouted.

"What's going on?" Clara asked.

"They're intentionally walking him," Trish said.

"What's that mean?"

El gripped his hands in tight fists to stop himself from walking over there and giving the other team a piece of his mind. "It means he doesn't actually get to bat. He'll get to first, but that's that."

"He could still score a run, though, right?" Clara asked. "Isn't that a good thing."

"It's poor sportsmanship," El said. He huffed and crossed his arms. "Not letting a player get a proper shot."

"You're just upset because you want Cody to show off more for you," Trish said, that coy smile on her face again.

El blushed and refused to dignify that with an answer. Even if it was partially true. El did appreciate it when Cody put on a good show. And he wasn't being allowed that opportunity.

El frowned as Cody walked to first. And then the next hitter struck out and the inning was over.

"Well, maybe he can find other ways to show off, hm?" Trish laughed, nudging El's arm with her elbow. He sighed and shook his head at her.

Chapter Twenty
Growing Up

"You would have won if they let you actually hit," El said as Cody drove them towards Clara's place. She sat happily in the back, looking out the window and smiling.

"Yeah, well, can't win 'em all. No big deal." Cody shrugged at the wheel, but El could tell he was just as steamed.

"But you were performing so spectacularly," El said. "It's disappointing that you weren't allowed to showcase your true talents." Very disappointing indeed.

"Don't look so glum." Cody smiled over at him. "You'll get to see all my talent in the finals. With a front row seat." He winked.

El chuckled. He did like the idea of that. "That's only if we win our game tomorrow." He gulped. "A feat I'm not so confident in. The opposing team has a very strong pitcher, you know. And I'm still so behind on my batting skills."

"Maybe another practice session is in order," Cody suggested.

"I certainly would appreciate it," El said. "But I fear there's no time. It's only tomorrow afternoon, after all. And I really should get some rest before the game."

"Ya know, relaxing really can help you prepare," Cody said. "Maybe I can help. I've been told sex is a great stress reliever."

"*Cody*," El hissed.

"What?"

El gave him an exasperated look and gestured towards the back seat.

"Oh, fuck. Sorry." Cody grimaced a bit and focused very hard on the road before him.

"It's alright," Clara piped up. "I already know you two are sleeping together." And she said it with such a bright and innocent face that it threw El for a loop.

"It's still not something we should discuss," he said. "You're my kid sister for goodness sake."

Clara frowned softly and looked back out the window. She mumbled something under her breath.

"What?" El asked. It wasn't like her to not say what was on her mind.

Clara didn't respond, but after a moment of awkward silence, Cody did. "She said she's not a kid."

El glanced at Cody, who looked about as uncomfortable as a person could be while driving, and then back at Clara, who was staring very hard out the window. El huffed softly and settled back in his seat. Of course she wasn't a kid. He knew that. But she was still young. And impressionable. And maybe if someone had been looking out for him like he looked out for her, he wouldn't have made so many mistakes.

Two turns later they arrived at Clara's place. But when she tried to open the door, Cody was quick to lock it. "You should talk to him," Cody said. Then he got out of the car.

El turned around in his seat. "What's going on?"

Clara curled up a bit, her shoulders hunching over, looking exactly like a kid who had just got caught doing something they shouldn't. "I don't know," she said, her voice small.

El looked at her features, the way she was physically making herself small, the way she was desperately avoiding eye contact while also keeping an eye on him. He saw himself. Everything he had been trying to protect her from was right there, front and center. And it felt like everything inside him broke all at once.

"Clara," he said, trying to keep his voice steady. "You can tell me anything. I promise I won't get upset."

Clara pursed her lips and glanced away for a second. "I'm twenty-six," she said.

El sighed. "I know."

"I...I can take care of myself," she added, a bit more fire returning to her voice.

El didn't entirely agree with that, but she had managed to stay out of trouble so far. "Yes, you can."

"So, maybe you could..." Clara squirmed in her seat a bit, her face contorting as she tried to find the words, "not treat me like a kid?"

El gulped. "I suppose I have been a little overprotective," he admitted. Clara nodded. "I'm sorry." He took a deep breath. He wanted to explain everything to her, but he didn't want to make this all about him. "I love you," he said. "And as your big brother, I feel it's my responsibility to make sure you're safe and protected." He looked down. "But I suppose I take that a little too far sometimes."

"Yeah."

"I'm sorry, Clara," El said. "I promise, I'll try to be better."

Clara looked up at him with a hesitant smile on her lips. "Are you mad at me?"

"Of course not!" El reached back and grabbed one of her hands. "You've done nothing wrong. This is on me. Not you." Clara finally smiled. "And I hope you know that, in the future, if I get too big-brothery, you can tell me. And I won't be upset."

"Really?"

He gave her hand a squeeze. "Really."

They both got out of the car and Clara pulled him into a tight hug. "I love you, too," Clara said. "And I'm glad you're my brother."

El smiled and hugged her back. Then she waved over at Cody before heading up to her place. Cody nodded at her and stood beside the car with his hands shoved deep in his pockets.

"Sorry," Cody said, to which El furrowed his eyebrows. "I know I shouldn't get involved." He sighed and closed his eyes.

El shook his head and quickly walked around to the other side of the car. "I'm glad you did." He pulled his hands together and picked gently at his fingernails. "I might never have realized she was so upset with me." And he hated that he had acted in such a way that made her so uncomfortable.

Cody nodded. "The more you care about someone the harder it can be to talk about stuff like that, I guess."

El knew that all too well. "Cody?"

"Yeah?"

"Promise you'll never care so much about me that you wouldn't tell me if I was hurting you." A vice gripped at his stomach, and El clenched his hands together so tightly he worried he would break a finger. He would never forgive himself if he had unknowingly hurt him.

But then Cody gave him a crooked smile, and it was like every muscle released in a big wave. "I can't promise to care less about you," he said. He closed the distance between them and gently untangled El's fingers. "But I can promise to be honest with you as long as you're honest with me. Deal?"

El nodded but didn't trust his voice to confirm it. Cody leaned back and gave him a bit of a knowing look.

El gulped. "I'm sorry," he whispered. "I'm fine. I promise. Just a little wound up after all that." Maybe one day he would tell Cody everything. But that would be an exhausting conversation. And he was already too tired.

Cody kissed his forehead, and El closed his eyes. "You want I should help unwind you?"

El smiled and leaned forward, resting his head on Cody's shoulder. Cody slid his arms around him, hands rubbing softly up and down his back. El figured it would be best to be alone, to process what had happened and feel the true weight of his guilt so it wouldn't happen again. But Cody was soft, loving, and gentle. So he nodded.

"Nothing too strenuous," El said as they pulled apart. "I do still have a game to get ready for tomorrow."

Cody smiled and chuckled softly as he walked El to the other side and opened his door for him. "Who said anything about strenuous? I'm thinking we get back to your place, I'll give you a very nice full-body massage, and you can just lay there and relax while I take care of ya."

El felt his entire body flush. "I think that sounds perfect." He's never had someone want to take care of him in such a way. El was so used to taking care of himself, and then taking care of others, sometimes too much, as it turned out. It felt nice to have someone like Cody who wanted to cherish him so.

If only El didn't feel so deeply guilty about taking advantage of that, things would be perfect.

Chapter Twenty-One
A Half-Body Fully Experienced

Cody hummed and placed his chin in his hand as he looked over the assortment El had pulled out for him. If it was possible, the guy had more oils than he did lube, and he had had a lot of lube. And then there were the candles to consider. With the right combination, Cody could make the perfect relaxing environment to help El prepare for tomorrow's game.

"Everything alright over there?" El called from the bed. He had already set up gentle music to play and had been tasked with making himself comfortable while Cody picked out the goods.

"Yeah, just trying to pick the best ones," Cody said. He picked up a lavender candle and gave it a tentative sniff. "Why do you have so many things?"

"I had an aromatherapy phase," El said.

Cody scoffed and looked at the collection that spanned the entire length of El's dresser. "Big phase."

"Long phase," El corrected.

Cody nodded and grabbed the bottle of frankincense oil. Those two should go together nicely. He placed the candle on the bedside table and lit it before dimming the lamp. El let out a happy sigh as the scent started to reach him.

"How ya doing?" Cody asked, opening the bottle of oil. "Comfy? Not too cold?"

"Perfect," El said. He snuggled deeper into the mattress, pressing his body against the fluffy towel laid down. Cody wished they had a proper massage table for this, but he would make it work.

"Just let me know if you need anything adjusted." Cody crawled onto the bed and knelt before El's head, warming up some oil on his hands as he planned out his massage path.

"I wouldn't mind if your pants were off," El mumbled. But he made no effort to move, keeping his arms wrapped around the plush pillow that supported his head and neck.

Cody laughed and leaned forward. "All in good time." He started at El's shoulders, pushing the oil around in circles, small at first, then getting wider in diameter.

El took a deep breath in and then released it in a happy sigh. "That feels wonderful."

Cody smiled and focused on his work, not the gorgeous sounds El was making. The guy had rocks for shoulders. Which made sense given his tendency to pour over books all hunched up all day. Cody wouldn't be able to loosen him up like he needed, but some relief could be expected.

After spending enough time getting the shoulders worked over, Cody moved his hands closer together and then gently dug the palms into El's muscles as he pushed his way down along the sides of El's spine. El let out a shuddering moan as Cody worked, morphing into a satisfied gasp when Cody's hands spread out over his butt cheeks.

"You're very tense in the gluttonal area," Cody informed him. But, oh, he just really wanted to spend as much time as possible grabbing and squeezing that lovely ass.

El chuckled. "Well, I trust you to loosen that up for me."

"Of course." Cody bit his lip, trying not to pay attention to the way his groin pressed against El's head in this position. Instead, he focused on making lovely circular motions over El's ass, toying with the muscles and watching with awe as the skin moved and formed to his touch.

After getting a good fill, and not wanting to risk getting too excited, Cody moved his hands back up El's spine and then spread them to the sides, working over the rest of El's back. But even if he wasn't touching El's ass, he was certainly getting excited by all the little gasps and moans El made under him. This might have been a bad idea.

Cody finished up working over El's back and then carefully crawled off the bed.

"Oh, do come back," El whined.

"Those patience lessons really do nothing for ya, huh?" Cody smiled at El, who was resting with his eyes closed and a wide smile on his lips. Cody had to quickly struggle out of his pants before the tightness cut off any circulation.

"I guess I just can't be taught," El agreed.

Cody's smile grew and he stepped back up to the bed. If he thought working on El's ass was bad, it was nothing compared to his work on El's thighs. El's legs were properly thick and stocky in all the best ways. Cody allowed himself his own release of a growl as his fingers started musing across one of El's thighs, feeling hard muscles and soft fat creating the perfect blend.

El let out a particularly sultry moan and Cody had to close his eyes and take a beat to calm down.

"Your voice is going to be the death of me, I swear," Cody said as he worked his way down to El's calf.

"I think your hands will be mine first," El said, his voice a rushed whisper. Cody tilted his head and looked at El's hips as he worked. He was trying to imagine just how hard and leaky El's cock was right now. Because lord knows Cody's was just aching with desire, and he wasn't even the one getting touched.

Cody worked his way along, rubbing over El's foot, moving to the other side of the bed, and then working his way up the other leg. By the time he was done with El's second thigh, Cody felt ready to jump out of his own skin with how turned on he was.

"Alright, flip over," he said, wiping the sweat off his brow. The mix of scents did have a relaxing effect, but nothing could relax his libido right now.

"I may need some help," El said. And his voice was so slow and languid.

Cody took a deep breath and then laughed softly. "Full body might have been a bit ambitious, huh?"

El mirrored his laugh. "Half-body works for me," he said. "But only if you get your clothes off and come join me back in bed."

"Deal."

Cody pulled his shirt over his head and eagerly crawled over El, laying down on his back, pressing a kiss to his cheek as their bodies slid together with the still-warm oil between them.

"Ohhh yes," El moaned as he pushed his ass back, pressing into Cody's penis.

"Hang on," Cody mumbled. He reached down and adjusted himself until he was slid deliciously between El's thighs. El in turn squeezed his legs together, creating a hot tension that nearly made Cody come right then and there.

Holding himself up a bit with one hand, Cody then reached around El and grabbed his cock, noting with some surprise and some pride that El had already come, but was still hard. Cody had been so wrapped up in his task that he hadn't noticed El's orgasm.

"Don't wear me out too much now," El warned as Cody started to pump both his hand and his hips.

"No promises," Cody whispered back. He leaned his forehead against the side of El's head and closed his eyes as he slid around between El's thighs. It was honestly a wonder he had lasted so long at all. And once El moaned out in delight, his body shaking slightly as his cock spilled out what little it had left, Cody was quick to follow.

Cody allowed himself a delightful minute in the warmth of El's presence to recover. Then he carefully pulled himself free, earning a disappointed grunt from El.

Cody chuckled and kissed El's cheek before he got up. "Don't worry, I'll be quick. Just gotta get you cleaned up."

"How do you possibly have any energy?" El asked, his words slurred against the pillow.

"You may have endurance for squatting," Cody told him, "but I have it for everything else."

"Oh. Good."

Cody smiled and went to get a washcloth. El was already asleep when he returned, so he was gentle as he cleaned El's skin free of both oil and come. He did have to rouse El a little so he could pull the towel out and get him all settled in the covers, but El was quick to sleep again once he was snuggled up.

Cody blew out the candle and turned the light off before he burrowed his way into bed next to El. In the pale moonlight, his sleeping face really did look angelic. And despite his growing exhaustion, Cody wanted nothing more than to just stare at El for hours on end. But, if he played his cards right, he could hopefully fall asleep and wake up to that face for the rest of his life.

Chapter Twenty-Two
El's Big Moment

Right. This was for all the marbles, so to speak. El took a deep breath and increased his grip on the bat. Two innings in and the score was zero to zero. Which was kind of a good thing, because at least they weren't losing. But if they didn't start winning, they could lose. And El had never actually *wanted* to win a game so badly before. Because for as much as he would enjoy sitting back and watching Cody show off in the finals, he really did look forward to playing against Cody's team in a big showdown. It was the kind of stuff good stories were made of, after all.

But El lived in the real world. And he had to work extra hard to make sure that things like that would work out.

Unfortunately, it didn't seem like El's hard work was going to be of much help here. After striking out, El avoided looking at the stands as he made his way back to the dugout. But El's attempts to hide his shame from his boyfriend were all for naught.

"Refreshing drink?"

El tried not to pout as he took the water handed to him by Cody, standing just outside the dugout. Lawrence had begrudgingly allowed the 'opposition' to hang around since Cody was currently invested in their win as much as everyone on the team.

"Hey, cheer up," Cody said. He stepped over and down, pulling El off to the side as Amy went up to bat. "You guys are going to win, I'm confident."

"I'm glad one of us is," El said. "I might be a nervous wreck by the end of this." He managed a gentle chuckle before taking a sip of his water.

"Well, aren't you lucky your boyfriend knows how to relax you?" Cody stepped closer, placing his hands on El's hip.

"Get a room," Michelle mumbled.

"Later, darling," El promised, placing a hand on Cody's chest and gently putting some distance between them. "I need to stay focused."

"Right, right." Cody nodded and placed his hands in his pockets. Amy made a hit, but it was caught, signaling the end of the inning. "You got this," Cody assured him, before scampering away. But El wasn't so sure.

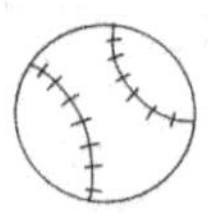

"How is he doing?" Clara asked once Cody returned to his seat.

"A little nervous," Cody said. "But he'll be alright. He's just gotta find his groove."

"El's always so calm and sure of himself, it's a little weird seeing him so wound up."

Cody smiled over at her and nudged her arm. "Don't worry about him. He's gonna do fine. You just watch."

"Oh, I know that." Clara smiled back. Bright and beaming must run in the family. "El can do anything he puts his mind to!"

"That he can," Cody agreed. He leaned back a bit and looked down at the field. He still had to force himself not to think about sex every time he saw El squatted behind home plate. But today there was a worried shake in El's usually sturdy form that distracted Cody.

But he knew that El would pull it out of the bag. He would pull together the defenses and the rest of the team would handle the offense. Even if El didn't get a single hit, it wouldn't matter or reflect badly on him as a player. He was an amazing catcher and that's all that mattered. Cody could see it. Clara could see it. And one day maybe El would come to understand it just as well.

Fifth inning and still no scores for either team. Whether it was just the batters too exhausted to make any hits or that the pitchers were on top form, El couldn't tell. But most people were striking out left and right. And of those that did manage to make hits, Leslie was one of them. He had come dangerously close to getting a run in, foiled by a spectacular dive from Valerie - to much cheer from the outfield triplets in the stadium. It seemed El wasn't the only one trying to show off for a boyfriend. But now Leslie was up to bat with someone else on third. One good hit would be enough to get them on the board. And El could not let that happen.

Time to try out his new material.

El cleared his throat as Leslie took his place. "You have a very nice butt," he whispered.

Leslie startled, looking back at El and missing the first pitch. El hid his smile behind his mask. It wasn't an entirely untrue statement, but it certainly didn't have the intention it had for when El directed it at Cody.

"I'm sorry," Leslie said. "What did you say?"

"You heard me," El said.

Leslie continued to stare at him for a few seconds before shaking his head and getting ready for the next pitch. But he had apparently heard El, as he missed the next two pitches. And thus, the zero-to-zero score was secured for another inning.

"This has got to be some kind of record," Clara said, watching the scoreboard with interest. Bottom of the ninth and not a single score on either side.

"A little odd," Cody said, crossing his arms. The lack of exciting incidents had left him to the devices of his wild imagination. But he had kept himself busy listening to stories from Clara about her and El's childhoods. They all revolved around El being a great big brother who took such great care of Clara. He kind of envied that sort of sibling relationship, but he wouldn't trade a good snarky exchange with Trish for anything. "But not entirely uncommon."

"So, what happens if El's team doesn't score?" Clara asked. "Does it just end in a tie?"

Cody shook his head. "Nah. If they don't score now, they go to another inning and keep playing until someone makes a run."

"So...this could go on for a long time?"

"Only if we're unlucky."

And considering El was the last hitter of this inning, Cody figured their luck wasn't looking too good. And anything that delayed another night spent wrapped up in El's presence was pure torture.

El glanced up at them as he got ready. Cody gave him an encouraging smile as Clara waved. He saw El take a deep breath and then steady his stance as he faced the pitcher. It was hard to tell this far away, but Cody swore he saw a new look of determination in El's face. He knew all too well the impact a watching boyfriend had on one's commitment to a cause.

"C'mon, El," Cody whispered. He leaned forward and placed his elbows on his knees, watching with renewed interest. Making a good hit here would certainly boost his confidence. And, with any luck, end this game on time.

The pitcher made the throw. The bat made contact with the ball. And El seemed genuinely surprised as he just stood there, watching it go off.

Clara stood up and cupped her hands around her mouth. "El, run!"

El startled and headed for first. The ball wasn't far out enough to count as a home run, but the outfielders hadn't expected a strong hit like that, and it would take them a while to get to it.

"Keep going!" Cody called out, joining Clara on his feet as El rounded second.

Cody glanced at the outfield. They grabbed the ball and made a long pass towards third. The ball rolled almost comically between the second baseman and the shortstop. El looked hesitant as he stepped over third base. But Cody waved him on, shouting, "go, go, go!"

El hopped a bit before taking off towards home. It would be close, oh boy would it be close. But Cody knew El could pull it off.

El's foot hit the plate at what looked like the exact same time the catcher's glove swept across his leg. Everyone turned quiet attention to Rafael, who had watched nearby, hands on his legs, leaning over to get a better look.

"Safe!"

Cody and Clara let out a shared cheer. Cody started clapping for his love and Clara bounced up and down excitedly. El smiled up at them, as bright and beaming as ever, doubled over as he panted. The rest of his team flooded out, surrounding El with more cheering and congratulations.

"Told you he could do anything," Clara said.

"He really can."

El couldn't remember the last time he felt so elated. It was a little strange that such elation came from a baseball game, but it was thrilling and wonderful all the same. Cody and Clara had made their way down from the stands, but they were hanging just outside the cloud of players that were currently showering El with praise.

"I knew you could do it if you practiced enough," Lawrence said, patting El on the shoulder.

"Guess my special lessons paid off after all," El said, casting a quick glance at Cody.

"You'd better not let that get in the way of the finals," Lawrence warned, all joy and camaraderie gone from his voice.

El rolled his eyes. "It won't."

"It's El, right?"

El spun around, facing Leslie as he made his way over. El gulped and nodded. "Good game," he said, holding out a hand. He hadn't felt any harm in using his new technique in the moment, not when he was fueled with the desire to win. But now that the danger had passed, he felt a weight of guilt building up in his stomach.

"Erm, yeah." Leslie smiled and shook his hand. "Listen, I'm very flattered." El nodded and tried not to blush too much. "But I'm actually married." Leslie held up his left hand, nodding to the ring now on his finger.

"Oh! Oh, uhm," El let out a nervous chuckle. "Yes, right, of course. N-no worries!"

"I just wouldn't want to lead you on or anything," Leslie said, smiling softly at him.

El nodded again, trying to fight back his rising guilt. Not only had he lied about his tactics, but to such a nice and genuine guy too. If he wasn't so desperately afraid of getting thrown out for cheating (and leaving his team without enough players for the finals), he'd have come clean right then and there. But maybe he could beg for forgiveness after the series was over.

Cody slid up next to him, slipping his arm around El's shoulders as he looked at Leslie with a squint. "Hi, there," he said. "Who are you?"

"Leslie," he said, holding out a hand. Cody just stared at it until Leslie dropped it. "I was just, uh, congratulating El on a game well played."

"Well, I'm sure it doesn't take that long to do so," Cody said. "Off you go, then." He waved Leslie away, and El felt truly horrible watching him leave. He was never going to use that trick again, no matter how dire the circumstances or how effective it was. It really was just a game, after all.

El turned and looked up at Cody. He still had his arm around El's shoulders, but his attention was trained on Leslie, glaring at him until he was out of sight. "Are you alright?" El asked.

"Of course." Cody smiled and looked down, still a hint of a glare as his face softened slightly. "Are you?"

"I'm fine." El wrinkled his eyebrows and looked between Cody and Leslie. He gasped at his realization. "Are you jealous?"

"Of course I'm jealous," Cody half-hissed. "Who does that guy think he is, huh? Hitting on you? Right in front of me!"

El laughed and patted Cody on the arm. "I assure you, dear, you have nothing to worry about. Leslie was not hitting on me."

Cody grumbled and glared after where Leslie had left. "Sure looked like it from where I was standing."

El shook his head. "I promise, it was nothing of the sort. We were just talking about the game. There was a…slight misunderstanding. But nothing romantic or sexual of the nature."

Cody's expression shifted to intrigue. "What kind of misunderstanding?"

"I, erm, used a new heckling tactic," El explained. "It didn't work out." He hoped that would be enough for Cody to drop it, especially since Clara was now making her way over.

Cody released his hold and crossed his arms, scrutinizing El with a playfully raised eyebrow. "What kind of heckling tactic?"

El studied Cody as well, and he knew he wouldn't let it go. Better to just get it over with. "I, uhm, may have told him that he…had a nice butt."

"Oh, oh I see. Uh-huh. Yup." Cody popped his lips and nodded, taking a step back. "I see now. *You* were the one flirting with *him*." El could tell by the tone in Cody's voice and the small smile on his lips that he was only playing around. But he wanted to assure Cody that he really never had anything to worry about.

"I wasn't flirting with him." El stepped closer and grabbed Cody's arms. "It was just a tactic. You don't have to worry about him or anyone else." He looked deep into Cody's eyes, fully meaning every word. "I'm yours."

There was a beat of silence as they looked at each other. Then Cody got the most devilishly handsome smirk on his face. "That's right," he said, his voice soft. He placed a hand on El's chin, a firm yet gentle hold. "You are mine."

And those words sent a jolt of electricity right through El's very core. His knees even buckled, sending him stumbling forward into Cody's arms.

"El!" Clara raced over. "Are you okay?"

El chuckled, holding onto Cody for support as he straightened his legs. "Yes, I'm fine. Must just be a little tired from all the excitement."

"Perhaps we should get you home for some much-deserved rest," Cody suggested.

El nodded. "Yes, that sounds perfect, thank you."

Chapter Twenty-Three
Initial Things

El felt a tizzy in his stomach as he led Cody inside. He was still a little worked up after what Cody had said, what he had done. But for as much as he wanted to just turn around and devour Cody in a most delicious kiss, he knew it was time for the talk.

"Some wine?" El asked, already heading towards the kitchen. "To celebrate?"

"Lots to celebrate," Cody agreed. He wandered into the living room as El poured them out some glasses. He smiled and sat down, watching El with a curious gaze as he took a sip. "You alright?"

"Mhm." El nodded, considered taking a drink, but figured his stomach was too twisted for it. "I just had something I wanted to talk with you about." He set his glass down and sat next to Cody. "About what happened after the game."

Cody cocked an eyebrow and sat up a bit, setting his own glass down. "With that guy?"

"After the guy," El added.

"What happened after the guy?"

El couldn't really tell if Cody genuinely didn't know what he was talking about, or if he was just trying to goad him into saying it out loud. But even if it was just the former, El still wanted to bring it up. Get it out in the open. Move on to the next stage of their relationship.

"When I stumbled," El said.

Cody smiled again, a bit of a twinkle in his eye. He shifted forward and tilted his head. "Ah, yes. Weak leg syndrome. I can have that effect."

"You most certainly can," El agreed. "But I feel like I owe you a further explanation." He could see Cody getting ready to argue the fact, so he held up a hand and rephrased it. "I want to tell you why I reacted so strongly."

"If that's what you really want," Cody said. El nodded and Cody settled down in his seat, waiting patiently.

El took a deep breath and looked down at his lap. It had been a long time since he'd discussed this with someone else in his life. And a boyfriend was very different from a therapist. But Cody was exactly the kind of boyfriend that El knew would understand.

"My first relationship...wasn't very healthy," El started. He really didn't want to get into the specifics, so he would leave it at that. Cody shuffled closer, grabbing El's hand. He didn't even realize it had started to shake.

"We could make it look like an accident," Cody suggested.

El allowed himself a small laugh, already feeling more at ease with every reaction Cody had in this moment. "No, it's alright. It was a long time ago. But the, erm, damage from it is still hanging around, I suppose."

Cody waited patiently, so El took a deep breath and tried to figure out how to formulate his thoughts, and what he wanted to express to Cody.

"I was young," El explained. "And I didn't know much about anything. And it took me an embarrassingly long time to realize that our dynamic wasn't exactly normal or okay." His breath shuddered a bit as he thought about it. He couldn't believe he had been so foolish.

"Hey." Cody placed his free hand on El's back and rubbed it gently. "It's not your fault someone took advantage of you."

El smiled and risked a quick glance at Cody's face. He looked so open and sincere. It settled some of the nerves in El's stomach. "I know," he whispered. "It's just hard to believe it sometimes."

"I get that."

"Anyway." El placed his other hand around Cody's, holding it tight in his own. "The point is, I, uhm, well, I started doing research after we broke up. And I know there are certain...*things*, but I've never really been able to get over it." He closed his eyes and sighed. He wasn't doing as good a job at explaining it as he hoped.

"Things like kinks?" Cody asked.

El bit his lip and nodded. "You see, there were parts of our relationship that I enjoyed a great deal. And, despite all my research, it's still hard to imagine that it's possible to experience those parts without the bad bits." He sighed again. He knew it was an irrational line of thinking and saying it out loud just made him feel even more foolish.

"Trauma is pretty hard to get over," Cody said.

El lifted his head and looked at Cody. He needed to see that love in his gaze if he was going to go through with this. "I just...I've never trusted someone enough to...try." Cody's expression shifted a bit, as if hopeful of what El was trying to imply. But he remained silent, waiting for the implication to be fully realized. El cleared his throat, fighting back the anxiety. "No one's ever treated me as kindly as you have before. And...I feel like I can trust you. I want to trust you." The fear melted away with every word, replaced by a warm, tingling in his nerves. "I'd like to try some things tonight. If you're willing."

"Oh, El." Cody took his hand off El's back and placed it on the side of his face, rubbing his thumb gently over his cheek. "Of course I'm willing. As long as you're sure you're ready for it."

El nodded, leaning into Cody's touch. He had been wanting to be ready for a long time. His first time with Cody had given him some hope. And every moment spent together since had just grown it. He knew Cody would take care of him. "I'm positive."

Cody smiled and leaned in, kissing El softly. "So, what kind of *thing* would you like to try?"

El shifted in his seat, his old excitement returning as he thought about it. "I'd like you to…own me," he said. "But not in a mean way."

Cody nodded. "You want me to prove how much I love you," Cody said. And El was very glad he was sitting, as his legs felt weak again. Cody's voice dipped lower. "You want me to make sure you know that no one else could possibly make you feel as good as I do." El nodded, leaning closer. "You want me to show that no one has a fucking chance with my angel."

El let out an involuntary *whimper* of all things. "Yes, please."

"Anything for you," Cody said. Then he leaned back a bit, putting some much-needed air between them. "But we should have a safe word."

El nodded, glad Cody had thought of that while his mind was too engrossed in the upcoming evening. "How about…foul?"

Cody laughed. "I love it."

"Good." El stood up, picking at his uniform. "Let me just go shower first."

"Of course." Cody hopped to his feet, catching El's arm before he could scamper off. "But," Cody pulled El close and placed that lovely grip on his chin, "you leave the prep work to me, yeah?"

El nodded and Cody gave him a quick kiss before letting him go.

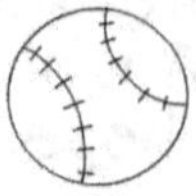

El was a vision of damn beauty. Even standing there in nothing but a thick robe, his hair all wet and tousled, he was the most gorgeous thing Cody had ever laid eyes on. And he couldn't believe his own dumb luck that El was his. And he really couldn't believe his luck that El wanted to be his. And in the most fun way possible.

"All good?" Cody asked. He stood up from his post on El's bed and stepped closer, not wanting to be out of contact for another second. He had nearly asked to share the shower with El, but he figured El wanted the time to prepare, both physically and mentally.

El hummed and nodded. He closed the distance between them, stepping right into Cody's arms and hugging him. "Thank you for being wonderful," El whispered. He gave Cody an extra squeeze then stepped back, his eyes bright and burning. Cody had been a little apprehensive, considering how anxious El looked earlier. But seeing those eyes, that deep desire, he knew without a shadow of a doubt that El really did want to do this. Tonight. With him. Seriously, when did he get so lucky?

"How could I be anything but wonderful to you?" Cody asked, kissing El gently. "My angel?" Another kiss, deeper this time, smiling as El moaned softly into his mouth.

Cody allowed himself a few glorious moments of kissing El's lovely, luscious lips. Then El's hands moved down to Cody's waist, fingers increasing in strength as his foundation seemed to waver a bit.

So, Cody took the initiative to see just how weak he could get those knees. He trailed little kisses along El's jaw, and then gave a satisfied little hum of his own as he started work on a nice little bruise right over where the old one was faded.

"Ah, foul," El said, lightly swatting Cody's back.

Cody popped his head up, looking at El with concern. "What?" He wanted this to continue, of course, but if El backed out at any point, Cody wanted to earn the trust placed in his hands.

El gave him a pointed look. "No hickeys," he reminded him.

"Still!?" Cody sighed and threw his hands in the air with a pout. "What's more possessive than a hickey?"

El shook his head. "I'm sure you can find something else. I still need to be presentable for work."

Cody grumbled. "Fine. No hickeys."

"Good." El pulled him close again. "You may continue."

Cody let out a little growl, placing his own hands on El's waist and spinning him around. "Robe off," he said, gently pushing El towards the bed.

El undid the tie on his belt and maneuvered the robe off his shoulders, the fluffy fabric getting caught around Cody's hands. Cody leaned his head down and pressed open kisses to El's back. His fingers had run over every inch of El's body, and now, it seemed, his lips were keen to mimic the pass.

But El was letting out the most delightful little sighs as Cody worked. And, damn him, those light sounds of his really did Cody in. He shifted from foot to foot, trying to take the edge off. It's like El's voice had a direct line to his dick.

"Alright." Cody leaned back a bit, pulling El's robe all the way off. "On your hands and knees."

El climbed onto the bed and grabbed a few pillows, stuffing them under his hips before laying down. He looked over his shoulder at Cody with a small shimmer in his eyes. "This alright?"

Cody smiled at him. He got up on the bed, kneeling next to El and examining the angle he had set up. "Seems acceptable." He leaned down on one arm, placing his hand on El's head and looking into his eyes. "Comfy down there?"

El closed his eyes and nodded.

"Good." Cody gave him a quick kiss on the cheek and then straightened up again. He positioned himself behind El, his eyes pinned to the world's best view as he reached over and grabbed the bottle of lube. "Fucking gorgeous," he mumbled.

He popped the lid off the lube bottle and held it a bit over El's ass, watching with growing interest as the drop formed near the top. Once it had enough pressure, the lube fell, landing between El's butt cheeks, sending them jiggling a bit as El let out a soft gasp.

"Cold?" Cody asked, tilting his head as he watched the lube slide down towards El's hole.

"Just a bit," El said.

Cody nodded and placed the bottle to the side. He put one hand on El's lower back, the fingers of his other spreading the lube over his entrance. He toyed with him a bit first, pressing gently here and there but not really making an effort to enter. El started to squirm beneath him, then he was pushing back slightly with each pressure.

Cody chuckled softly. "Patience, patience," he crooned.

But he did give in (he would always give in) and slid one finger in, rather smoothly. El let out a shuddering breath and his squirming only increased.

Cody hummed, toying a second finger as El wiggled in place. "Such a wonderful body," he said softly. "So easy and malleable. Perfectly bending to my will." He started sliding the next finger in, El letting out a long moan alongside it. "And with such lovely little sounds to entertain me, too."

Cody shifted forward, letting his one hand run up and down El's back as his fingers worked to loosen him up. "Tell me, angel," he said, leaning down to place a kiss on El's lower back. "How does it feel to have my fingers inside you, hm? Opening you up? Preparing you for me?"

"It feels wonderful." El moaned softly and started wiggling again.

Cody chuckled. "You know, one of these days your impatience is gonna get you in trouble." And oh, how he longed for the day El wanted to try that kink out.

"How can you blame me?" El breathed out. His voice was truly haggard. "How could I possibly want to wait when it comes to the most intense pleasure I've ever felt?"

Cody's smile grew and he tsked a bit as he curled his fingers, pressing against El's prostate, starting to slide a third finger in, a bit more slowly. "Well, don't you know how to stroke a guy's ego?"

"One of my many skills," El said.

Cody nodded, his pants growing increasingly uncomfortably tight as he thought about all of El's other skills. "You are very talented," he said. He gave his fingers a few more seconds of work before he pulled them free, cleaning them off on the towel. "But so am I."

El let out another shuddered breath, an inch away from another whimper. Cody was determined to pull that beautiful sound from his lips again. And Cody thought about that lovely sound as he stood up and maneuvered out of his clothes.

"On your back," he ordered as he put on a condom. "I want you to see me as I fuck you senseless."

El moaned and started shifting about. His penis was already leaking, twitching gently from the new lack of contact.

"Oh, I'll not have you suffering under my watch." Cody climbed back on the bed, cupping El's dick and rubbing as El finished getting settled.

"Cody, please," El moaned. He pulled his knees up, spreading his legs open as he panted under Cody's touches.

"Remind me who owns you," Cody said, getting into position between El's legs. He kept his cloudy gaze on El's flushed face as he rubbed some lube on himself.

"You," El said.

"That's right." Cody grabbed El's hip with one hand, lifting him a bit off the pillows as he pressed the head of his cock in. He took a deep breath, letting it out in a groan as he reveled in the novel feeling of El around him. He kept himself in that tortuous position, running his hands over El's legs before pulling them up and in position. "Now, you look at me," Cody whispered.

El's eyes blinked open, that beautiful shine burning bright within them. Cody smiled, holding that eye contact as he slid himself in further and further, feeling the hot pressure of El accept him eagerly. El's eyes wavered slightly, his breath coming out in delicious moans as Cody worked his way in.

Once fully in, Cody leaned down, keeping his face inches above El's, looking into those bright, wonderful eyes. "Who makes you feel good?" Cody asked. He increased his grip on El's hips, pulling back until he was nearly out.

"Y-you," El said, although it was clearly a challenge for him.

Cody rewarded him with a quick slide back in, making sure to angle his hips and hit his prostate. El panted out Cody's name as he wrapped his arms around him, legs pulsing futility in the air as he tried to get more friction.

Cody chuckled and adjusted his own position, leaning more against El as he moved his hands to the mattress beside him. He gave in a little, making some shallow thrusts as he peppered El's face with kisses. Cody moved his kisses along El's jaw until he was nipping gently at his ear, a motion which made El shiver beneath him.

"You're mine," Cody reminded him in a whisper. He increased his thrusts, grunting as El took him in deep and hard without any hesitation.

"Yes," El agreed. And didn't his voice just sound so heavenly again. "Yours."

"And don't you forget it," Cody said. He continued nibbling on El's ear, since hickeys were apparently still off the table.

With El gasping so beautifully in his ear and squirming so deliciously beneath him, Cody wasn't sure he was going to last much longer. But there was no way he was going to allow himself to finish before El.

"The next time you compliment someone's ass," Cody said, leaning his weight on one hand as he slid the other down to El's butt. "It'll be yours that's in trouble." He gave El an awkward spank that was more like a light swat, but it was enough to send him over the edge, spilling out between them as his hands gripped Cody's shoulders with renewed energy.

"Fucking beautiful," Cody said as he joined his love in completion. He touched his forehead to El's and stilled his movement, taking deep breaths to calm his wildly beating heart.

"Oh, Cody," El said after a few moments of quiet. He laughed softly. "I'll need to stretch out my toes."

Cody laughed as well. He finally mustered the energy to push himself up and pull himself out. "How'd I do?" he asked as he removed the condom.

"Wonderfully," El said with a happy little sigh.

"Yeah?" Cody wanted to indulge his angel, of course, but he didn't want to go too hard too fast right off the bat. He also wanted to just immediately curl up next to El and cuddle. But he had some cleaning up to do.

"Thank you for indulging me," El said, his voice soft and light as Cody cleaned him off with a wet towel.

"Thank you for trusting me with your indulgences," Cody answered.

El smiled and then grunted as he started to sit up. Cody moved the pillows away and helped him, sitting on the edge of the bed by his side. El looked at him as if he had truly hung the stars. "I love you," he said.

Cody rested his head on El's. "I love you, too."

Chapter Twenty-Four
The Gardener's Mischief

El hesitated as he got out of Cody's car, looking out towards the park. There was actually a bit of a crowd, many of the other teams here to see who would win. Well, who would win game one of three. But it wasn't the onlookers that El was currently worried about.

"Everything okay?" Cody asked, already a few steps away. He spun around, rocking a bit on his feet as he looked at El.

"Oh, yes," El said. He smiled at him and nodded. "You go on ahead. I'll catch up."

"Why?" Cody put his hands on his hips and squinted at him. "You hiding some kind of sneaky, cheating device back there?"

El laughed. "Hardly. It's just probably best if we don't go in together."

"You ashamed to be seen with me?"

"Of course not." El sighed and quickly walked up to Cody. He grabbed his hands and gave him a quick kiss. "It'll just be easier to beat you if the others aren't worried about our mingling."

"I believe socializing was the term used to describe us," Cody said. He smiled before pulling El in for a deeper kiss.

And El was so wrapped up in that kiss that he didn't hear Lawrence approaching them until he was clearing his throat. El pulled away quickly and stepped back, giving Lawrence a sheepish look. Cody just laughed at him.

"Don't get your business briefs in a bunch," Cody said. "El is nothing if not ruthless on the field." Cody winked at El and then sauntered off to join his own team.

"Did you two arrive together?" Lawrence asked, looking back at Cody's car.

"Yes," El said. Although he knew his personal life was none of anyone's business, he did want to mitigate the damage and get through the rest of these games with as little incident as possible. "He was kind enough to offer me a ride on his way this morning."

Lawrence nodded, but the squint in his eyes told El he didn't fully believe that lie. Not that it should matter who El had spent the night with. Lawrence walked off to the dugout and El let out a deep sigh. The sooner these games were over, the better. He couldn't wait to just get back to living a normal life.

A normal life with the best boyfriend in the world.

"No napkins today?" Rafael asked as Cody made his way up to bat. El let out a soft chuckle but was otherwise behaving himself.

"Not needed right now," Cody informed them. Then he gave El a suggestive look, saying that they better not be needed.

With El being quiet, Cody could actually focus on the game. He managed a single on the first pitch. Not his best hit, but at least it was something. As Cody stretched a bit on base, he noticed Briney catch his eye with a subtle wave. He raised an eyebrow at them and shook his head as they started waving their hands a bit.

Briney sighed and repeated the motions slower, but Cody still shook his head. It wasn't that he didn't know what they were saying, it's just that trying to steal second right now would be ridiculous. Trying to steal any base with El catching was outright stupid.

Briney growled and gave Cody a menacing look. He rolled his eyes and shrugged. If they wanted him to get out, fine, he'd get out. Maybe then they'd learn not to bother.

During their initial conversation, Cyrus had missed two pitches. Cody took a deep breath and bunched up his pant legs a bit, inching out from first. The light reflected off El's helmet as his gaze shifted slightly, looking at him. Michelle, however, still seemed unaware. It was going to be Cody's running speed against El's throwing power. And he wasn't feeling too confident, truth be told.

Michelle threw the pitch and Cody took off. The small crowd started to cheer as his feet pounded against the ground. Adrenaline coursed hot and stinging through his veins. He could see El in his mind, feel the power of his muscles as he caught the ball and moved to throw it to second in one, swift motion. It had been hot to watch, but now Cody was dreading the outcome.

Once he was within diving distance, Cody lunged forward, stretching his arms out as far as he could. The hit was hard, and Cody's fingers slid up against the plate just as he felt the tip of the baseman's glove grazing over his arm. The world seemed to still for hours as Cody waited for the judgment call.

"Safe!"

"Fuck yeah!" Cody let out a celebratory whoop and rolled onto his back. His left elbow had taken the brunt of his fall, and he rubbed it gently, feeling for anything worse than just a bruise.

"You alright?" a light voice asked.

Cody blinked and looked up. The short-stop, and receptionist, if his memory served him, was holding her hand out, leaning over him with concern.

"Yeah, I'm alright." Cody nodded and took her hand, letting her help him up. "Thanks." He started dusting himself off, purposely not looking at El to let the sting of defeat really sink in.

"Not many people who can outrun that throw," Valerie said.

"Still think he was out," the second baseman mumbled. But there wasn't really room to argue or challenge things in small-time games like this. They were just at the mercy of Raphael.

"Certainly a close call," Cody said. "Imagine he could make a pretty good pitcher, too."

"Enough chatter," the second baseman said, clearly still upset over the call. "Get back in position."

Valerie slipped away and Cody frowned at the second baseman. "Nothing wrong with a little camaraderie among players."

"Shut up."

Cody rolled his eyes and finally looked at El. But from this far away, it was hard to tell how he had reacted to the play. And he was already in position for the next pitch, so Cody couldn't even go by his body language. But he figured El had always been happy for him when he made a good run, so he didn't worry about it too much.

El sighed and tried to ignore the glare from Lawrence at the other end of the dugout. The mood in the air was stifled, everyone silently watching as the coldness from Lawrence's stare settled over them.

"Perhaps you should pay attention to the game?" El finally said, nodding out to the field as Michelle hit a double.

"You were slow on purpose," Lawrence said, accused really.

El rolled his eyes. He had not been slow on purpose. Cody had just outrun him. Which was hardly surprising. He was the fastest player here. Unfortunately for El, that move had allowed Cody to score a run. The Infernals were now leading 1-0.

"It's only the second inning," Valerie offered.

El patted her leg and gave her a small smile as he shook his head. There was no reason for anyone else to get caught in the crossfire. El just hoped this kind of atmosphere didn't continue into the office between games. They had to go a whole week after this game before the final two next weekend. Maybe El would just take an impromptu vacation.

"Just don't let it happen again," Lawrence said. Then he finally looked out at the field and everyone on the team let out a sigh of relief.

El had been unusually quiet all game. Maybe he was just focusing on playing well, but Cody figured he'd try *some* kind of distraction technique. By the sixth inning, Cody was genuinely concerned.

"You alright?" he whispered as he stepped up to the plate. He made a show of stretching to buy them some time.

"Perfectly," El replied. But he sounded a little tense. The game was close, after all, Cody's team leading up until the last inning. Now they were tied 3-3.

Cody let his attention wander over to the opposing dugout. El's boss was staring at him with his arms crossed, murder in his eyes. "They giving you trouble over there?"

"It's alright," El said. "Nothing I can't handle."

Cody hummed. "I could probably make it look like an accident," he whispered. "Just a slightly off-center hit, ya know? Then BOP! Right in his stupid face."

El chuckled, and it warmed Cody's heart to hear him sounding more like himself. "I hardly think that's necessary, but thank you."

Rafael stepped closer. "You gonna be ready anytime soon?"

"Yeah, yeah," Cody said. He shook off his anger at El's team and focused on the game. If he was a better man, he might throw the game on purpose. But he knew El would want an honest win, as would he. They were both going to play their best and just see who came out on top.

Michelle gave Cody a similar icy stare and then readied the pitch. Cody could tell by the tension in her hold that it was going to be a fastball. But he was awfully quick, himself.

Cody made the hit but felt it the second of contact. The ball popped up and behind, a clear fowl. Cody shook the shock from his body and prepared for the next pitch. But there was a noticeable lack of angelic presence behind him.

He turned around just in time to see El standing a few steps back, mitt primed, eyes trained on the sky.

"You can't be serious," Cody muttered.

But El was serious. He caught the fly ball and actually fucking smiled at Cody.

"Oh, you are most definitely out," Rafael said.

"Sorry, dear," El said, stepping back up to the plate. "But we are tied. And I couldn't let you get the chance to make a good hit."

Cody hated how El could both compliment him and pull such a dick move at the same time. Okay, he actually loved it.

"Yeah, well, uh, you tell me how good you think that decision is tonight, hm?" He gave El a knowing look and stalked back to the dugout.

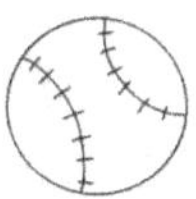

All they had to do was make it through one more inning. One more inning and they would win. El gulped as the teams got ready to swap positions. 5-4. Top of the ninth. If the Infernals couldn't get a run, they would win. And El could breathe easier for the week.

El got into position and smiled at Altan as he stepped up to the plate. Valerie had told El that the two of them decided to wait until after the games were over before going on their first date. It made him happy to know that the two of them would soon feel comfortable being together. He just wished they weren't under all the pressure of rivaling teams.

Altan seemed to surprise even himself as he made a hit.

"That would be your cue to run," El reminded him. He knew all too well the shock that moment came with.

"Oh, right!"

El chuckled softly as Altan made his way to first. If the poor thing hadn't been so surprised, he might have been able to make it to second. But he was safe at first. And Valerie was smiling brightly at him.

"Are those two an item?" Cody asked as he stepped up to bat.

El hadn't expected anyone else to notice, with all their attention so focused on the game and their relationship. But Cody always did surprise him in the best of ways.

"Not yet," El said. "But maybe soon."

"Ah, young love." Cody smirked and then got ready for the first pitch. "Takes me back."

Cody twitched a little when the pitch first left Michelle's hand, but he held himself back, letting the ball pass unquestioned.

"Hard to believe it was only a few weeks ago, hm?" El said. He had committed himself to playing a fair game, but if Cody was going to start it...

Cody made the next hit, but it fouled off to the left, someone in the stands getting a little too excited over catching it. "Feels like a lifetime. A good lifetime, of course."

El hummed in agreement and caught the fastball that Cody just missed. He tossed it back to Michelle and decided he would play a little dirtier. "Hard to imagine what life was like before your di-"

"Alright!" Rafael shouted, stopping Michelle before she let her next pitch go. "That's enough of that." He pointed at El. "Final warning."

"Thank you!" Cody said with relief. "Jeez, finally."

Rafael gave El a scolding look and El tucked his head down a bit. He agreed that was going perhaps a bit too far. "Sorry."

"You're a menace," Cody said with a laugh.

But an effective menace, El figured, as Cody missed the next throw. It was an expert cutter that Cody probably would have missed anyway. But El still felt that mixture of pride and shame for his part he played in the out.

"Oh, you're gonna regret that too," Cody whispered, his voice deep and alluring, before he walked away, leaving the promise of a good time behind.

El's body let out a shudder. He was looking forward to it.

Chapter Twenty-Five
Punishment to Fit the Crime

"I still think you cheated," Cody said, pulling up to El's building. Honestly, if he never went back to his own place, he'd be perfectly happy.

"No cheating," El said, a happy little smile on his face as he got out. "Just better than you."

Cody laughed and followed El up to his door. "It's only the first game," he reminded him. "Next weekend, you'll see. We'll get ya."

"If you say so, dear."

El grabbed Cody by the arm and pulled him inside, immediately pushing him up against the wall next to the door and kissing him deeply. Cody placed his hands on El's face, holding him tight as they kissed. There was no better experience than kissing El.

"One of these days I'm going to give you a real lesson in patience," Cody said as he gasped.

El chuckled and reached over to finally close the door. "And what does that look like, hm?"

"Well, it involves a lot of rope," Cody said, raising an eyebrow as he watched El's expression for reaction.

El's face stayed mainly the same, maybe a glint of mischief hiding behind his eyes. He stepped closer, pinning Cody to the wall as his hands grabbed the front of his jersey. "Oh, it'd take an awful lot of rope to keep me contained around you, you know?"

Cody smirked, his mind already running wild with the image of El all tied up, just forced to wait for Cody, completely at his whims. "Is that so? Good thing I know a bulk rope merchant."

El pulled Cody closer and kissed him again, humming against his lips. It was just a short one, El pulling back away much too quickly. "I don't suppose you have his number on speed dial, do you?" El asked. He licked his lips a bit, adding to the shine that already distracted Cody.

"I'm afraid not," Cody said, noting the slight disappointed look on El's face. "But," he grabbed El's chin and forced him to look into his eyes, "you have a different lesson you need to learn first."

"Oh? And what would that be?"

"A lesson in not heckling players on the field," Cody said, a soft growl in his throat as he thought of the audacity of such an act.

"Ah, that," El said. He tried to hide away, look down in shame. But Cody's hand kept his face held high, only his gaze shifting away. "I suppose I'll have to be punished, then?"

Cody squinted and pulled El's face closer. It was a little hard to tell where he was at right now, whether or not punishment actually was on the table.

"Why don't you tell me," Cody said, dropping his voice to a whisper.

"Well, it wouldn't be entirely uncalled for," El said. But he still wasn't looking at him.

Cody tilted his head and moved his hand, gently caressing El's cheek. "Ah, but which punishment fits the crime, hm?"

El shifted a bit, biting his lip softly. "Perhaps I'll need to be, uhm..." El cleared his throat and then glanced at Cody briefly. "Spanked?"

Cody felt an initial jolt of his energy down below and he had to pinch his leg with his free hand to stop himself from pouncing on El right then and there. "I think a spanking seems like just the perfect lesson for you, angel." He pulled El into a soft kiss. "But let's get cleaned up first."

El nodded and took Cody's hand in his own before leading him up the steps. Cody followed eagerly, more than excited to get the opportunity to indulge El in another one of his fantasies.

"Sharing water, yeah?" Cody asked as he trailed into the bathroom.

El hummed in agreement as he turned on the shower. "Clothes off," he ordered.

Cody laughed and did as he was told. El did the same, shedding his uniform and depositing it in his hamper. He turned to grab Cody's clothes from him and then stopped with a gasp.

"What?" Cody asked. He looked down but couldn't find anything out of the ordinary. Unless El was surprised by how turned on he was already. Which was a little ridiculous because El just *had* to know the effect he had on Cody.

"Your arm!" El hurriedly shoved Cody's uniform in the hamper and then grabbed Cody's left arm, pulling it over and turning it until he was looking at the elbow.

"Ah, that." Cody nodded at the large bruise that was starting to properly form from his dive to second. He hardly even felt it. But it certainly looked like he should.

"Did you put any ice on it?" El asked. He held Cody's arm straight with one hand and gently ran the fingers of his other over the bruise.

"No," Cody said with a shrug. "Doesn't really hurt."

"Just because it doesn't hurt now, doesn't mean it's not a problem." El gave Cody a harsh look. "You need to take care of yourself. Now, go get ice on that." El dropped Cody's arm and pointed to the door, tapping his foot.

Cody looked down at his erection, then over at the shower, then back to the door. "Seriously? Now?"

"Yes, now! The longer you wait, the less effective it'll be." El pouted and crossed his arms.

Cody chuckled at the amazing angel in his life. "What if I promise to ice it after we're done?" Cody stepped up to El and grabbed his waist, kissing the pout off his lips. "Consider it another lesson in patience."

"Wrong kind of lesson to teach," El mumbled against Cody's kisses. But then he sighed and gave in, kissing Cody back. "But you better take care of that."

"Don't worry, I will."

Cody moved his hands around to El's ass, massaging it as he continued kissing the best lips on the planet. And he couldn't tell if the steam filling up the room came from the shower or from them. Not that it mattered; either way it added an extra level of heat to their making out.

For as much as Cody was looking forward to the spanking, he was also really looking forward to the shower. There was something just so sexy about El all lathered up and slippery that did something to him; sent his mind into overdrive. But if he wanted to make it through the spanking, he knew he would have to keep things to a minimum, which was hard when El was just so perfect.

El laughed as they worked their way around each other in the shower. "You're being awfully shy," he commented as Cody turned around while El started washing up.

"Not shy," Cody said, bothering himself by studying the shampoo bottles. "Just strategic."

"Is that so?"

Cody could practically see the little smirk on El's face before he was pressing up against Cody's back, soap making his skin slippery and delicious. His arms wrapped around Cody's waist, one hand grabbing Cody's dick and jerking it off as the other rubbed softly over his thigh.

Cody laughed and leaned back against El. "That's not helping," he said.

"Who said I was going to be helpful?" El asked. Which was exactly the brand of bastard Cody loved the most about him.

"You know, you're just adding to the number of spanks you're about to get, right?" Cody asked.

"Even better," El whispered in his ear. And that idea along with the breath tickling Cody's ear sent a shiver down his spine that sparked a jolt in his hips. He wiggled away from El's embrace as the bastard actually laughed.

"You are in so much trouble," Cody warned, not that El seemed to really mind. "Now you finish up over there so we can get to it, huh?"

El gave him a little look. "Yes, dear."

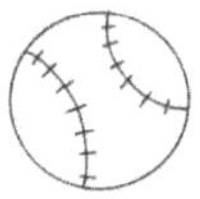

El truly did love Cody. Of that he was never more certain. He loved how easily Cody seemed to slip in and out of his punisher role. He was able to take the reins and control when needed, but in a split instant he could be comforting, and silly, and charming. And he never seemed to have trouble keeping up whenever El changed the mood. He was almost too perfect, like someone had made him in a factory just for El.

"Alright, now, before we begin, you have any aftercare creams or anything?"

El smiled and nodded. He went into his bathroom closet and pulled out his box of goodies, returning with the cream in question.

"Excellent." Cody took it from him with a kiss and then pulled him over to the bed. "Now, this is your punishment, right?" El nodded, not quite sure where Cody was going with this. "So, only you can be the judge of exactly when you've learned your lesson." He placed his forehead to El's. "So, it's up to you to tell me whether you think you're being properly punished or not, got it?"

"Yes, sir," El said.

Cody grabbed his arms, knees seeming to buckle a little as he growled softly. El smiled, happy to know he had a similar weak-leg effect on Cody as he did on El.

"Time to learn your lesson, then."

Cody pulled away and sat down on the bed. He patted his lap and smiled, waiting. El licked his lips and leaned over to give Cody a kiss before he got himself comfortable laying down across Cody's legs. With the way they were positioned, their penises pressed against each other in just the most delightful way, El sighed happily as he got comfortable.

"You good down there?" Cody asked. He was already reaching back for a pillow to place under El's head for added support. "All nice and comfy?"

El nodded and wiggled his hips a bit. "Perfectly."

"Good."

Cody placed one hand on El's lower back and started gently rubbing his other hand across El's ass. El felt all in a tizzy waiting to feel that first, sweet sting. Cody's hand gripped across the skin, pulling at El's muscles and molding his fat to his whims. Then it came, just a little, sharp swat, reminiscent of his first attempt a few nights ago.

Cody hummed as he went back to simple rubbing and grabbing. Then there was a second and a third in quick succession, a little more aggressive than the first. "Oh, beautiful," Cody whispered. "Simply, gorgeous."

"What's that?" El asked.

"This shade of pink," Cody answered. He was back to running his hand over El's ass. "It's adorable on you."

El smiled, feeling himself blush at such a compliment. He did like looking adorable. "I'm glad you like it."

"Oh, I love it," Cody said. Then he went about spreading that shade of pink across El's ass, never focusing his spanks in one spot for too long. A nice, even spread of slaps that made El start to squirm with pleasure. He knew he was supposed to be suffering a punishment, but what a delightful punishment it was.

"Now then," Cody said, ceasing his spanks as he rubbed over El's skin, keeping everything hot and tingly. "Are you feeling like you've learned anything?"

"Oh, perhaps a little," El said, his voice a little breathless. "But I'm sure there's more to learn."

"Yeah?" Cody waited a second and then a rather harsh slap landed, sending a jolt through El's body that pulled a surprised moan from his lips. "Like that?"

El couldn't trust himself to talk, not with the bubble of pleasure building in his chest. So he just nodded. Cody spanked him again, leaving a similar stinging sensation on the same spot on the other cheek. And that was what El appreciated the most about his spanking. He always evened it out.

There were a few more harder spanks that started to really set El's nerves a flame. And just before it became too much, Cody's other hand slid up El's back and grabbed his hair in a gentle tug.

"Learned your lesson yet?" Cody asked, that deep voice back to setting a shiver through El's body.

"Y-yes," El breathed out.

Cody's hand came to a rest on El's ass. "So, what are you *not* gonna do next game?"

"Heckle you," El said. Not that he meant it, of course. Where would be the fun in that?

"Wrong answer," Cody said, a playful hint in his voice as he softly swatted El again. Nothing too strong, just a gentle tap. "Care to try again?"

"Heckle any players on the field," El corrected.

"Good boy," Cody crooned. He shifted slightly, making El squirm to try and get better contact between them. Then he jumped as Cody started to spread the cooling cream over his heated skin.

El continued to squirm as Cody worked, because he was getting much too close, and even all of Cody's radiating love from his soft touches and kind words weren't going to be enough alone to send him over the edge now. He needed some extra contact.

"You alright down there, squirmy?" Cody asked with a chuckle.

"Just a little impatient," El admitted.

Cody laughed and patted down El's hair before sliding his hand between them. It was a little awkward, but El pushed his hips up as best he could to give him some extra room.

"I think someone enjoyed their punishment a little too much," Cody said as his hand laid over El's dick and rubbed him.

"Oh? Was I not supposed to enjoy that?" El asked, knowing perfectly well that he was and that he did.

Cody chuckled softly and pulled back, taking El with him until they were lying down on the bed together, Cody's hand instantly back to rubbing as he hungrily kissed El. El certainly intended to return the gesture, but his stomach tightened, and he was coming before he even knew it.

Cody smiled against his lips as he brought El back down from what could only be described as a heavenly feeling. Every time with Cody felt like the best time, and El couldn't get enough of it.

Cody mumbled something El didn't quite hear, and then he was nuzzling his way to El's ear, nipping gently at his lobe as he moaned, rubbing himself to completion against El's thigh.

"I'll clean up in a second," Cody said, leaning his head against El's shoulder.

Chapter Twenty-Six
Picnic and a Bet

Cody popped his lips and clicked away at his emails. Emails, ugh. He hated emails. And yet he got about a million a day. And heaven forbid he didn't respond to them all in a timely manner. Even if about half of these things had nothing to do with him. He was pretty convinced his actual job title should be switchboard operator, but for emails instead of phone calls.

Cody's phone buzzed in his pocket, saving him from a morning of unending boredom. "Allo!" he answered.

"Hello, dear," El greeted.

Cody smiled, pushing away from his desk and leaning back in his chair. "Well, hey there. Miss me that much, hm?" Cody joked, but they had spent the entire Monday without a text or call or anything, and he really did miss his angel that much. It was probably healthy for them, but he couldn't help just wanting to be around El as much as possible.

El chuckled softly. "I suppose I did, yes. Did you miss me?"

"Of course."

"Good," El said. And Cody laughed. "I was just calling to see what you were up to at work today."

Cody smirked, already envisioning the cute little shy look El would have. Surely he should know by now that he didn't need to pretend to not be interested anymore. "Just answering emails."

"Oh? Anything important?"

"Hardly."

"Are you just saying that to say that, or is it really nothing important?"

"Why do you ask?"

"Just answer the question, please."

Cody tutted and looked at his computer. Technically he probably should get through some of these today. But El clearly wanted him for something else, and he didn't actually care about his job all that much. "Mostly just junk mail," he said. "Nothing interesting today."

"Well, if that's true…" El took a deep breath and Cody furrowed his eyebrows, trying to figure out what could be making him so nervous. "Perhaps you'd like to, erm, play hooky, today? With me?"

Cody's smile widened. "A day spent in bed with the finest man on Earth? Oh, I think I'd love to do that."

"Oh, no," El said quickly. "I was actually thinking about taking a little expedition."

"Where to?"

"Well, as you know, part of my job entails going out to nurseries and doing some facetime with the clients."

"Uh-huh."

"And, well, I have to go meet with a client today. And, well, it's a bit of a drive, but it's really a scenic little place. And I was wondering if maybe you'd like to join me."

"Honestly?" Cody asked.

"Mmhm." He could hear the apprehension in El's voice.

"That sounds even lovelier than my original plan."

"Oh, really?"

"Really, really. What time should I pick you up?"

"In about an hour? Just outside my office?"

"I'll see you then."

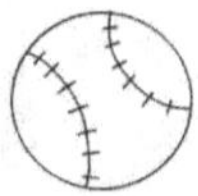

The drive down really was gorgeous. El had spent the time pointing out little landmarks or roads here and there where he had visited or stopped somewhere on his other drives. And the best part was not feeling like they needed to fill the silence in between his little tour sessions. They sat comfortably, just enjoying each other's presence, listening to the radio and watching the scenery pass.

Of course, El worried that Cody might get bored while he was doing his work. But Cody had kept himself very entertained in the nursery. It was one of their larger ones, and the manager had allowed Cody access to their greenhouses, where he apparently entertained the employees with very inaccurate facts about plants delivered with doubtless confidence.

Seeing Cody laughing with a small group of employees made El's heart swell.

"All done?" Cody asked as El approached them.

"Mhm." El smiled and took Cody's hand.

"See ya guys later," Cody said, waving to the employees. El led him back out to the car. It was just after midday, and El was excited for his surprise. "Back home?" Cody asked as he climbed into the car.

"Actually," El said, "I do have one more errand to run. If you don't mind."

Cody leaned over with a smile. "Is this a real errand, or a 'getting milk' errand?"

El gave him an unimpressed look but couldn't stop himself from chuckling anyway. "Somewhere in between," he said.

"Intriguing." Cody leaned back over and dutifully listened to El's instructions as he drove them to the little park on the other side of town. He whistled when they pulled into the nearly empty parking lot. "Gorgeous view."

El knew that Cody was looking out over the hilltop that highlighted the cozy houses below. But El was looking at Cody's bright eyes and wide smile when he said, "Yes, it is."

"We gettin' out?" Cody asked.

El nodded and reached to grab his briefcase before getting out of the car. "Not much of a picnic basket," he explained, leading Cody a few paces out to the perfect spot. "But it does the trick." He sat down and opened his case, pulling out the sandwiches and snacks he had sneakily bought at the cafe next to the nursery.

"And perfect for corporate espionage," Cody said, joining El on the ground. He smiled and took the sandwich that El handed him. "Sneaky, sneaky."

El smiled proudly at his little trick playing off. But then he caught the look in Cody's eye and frowned softly. "You knew, didn't you?"

"Saw you nipping across the street," Cody said with a cute laugh. "But I wasn't going to bring it up."

El sighed softly. "Oh, well. Guess I just can't fool you, hm?"

"No, but you should certainly keep trying."

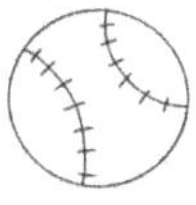

It was the perfect day. And to think, Cody almost had to spend the day reading emails. But instead, he got to drive around with El, listening to his excited chatter, spend some time looking at cool plant stuff, and then go on a great picnic with the love of his life. And they still had the return trip to look forward to as well.

Everything was perfect. Except for the yellow and black menace that seemed intent on ruining the vibes. Cody shifted to the side as the bee dive-bombed him. He bumped into El's shoulder.

"Everything alright, dear?" El asked.

"This damn bee won't leave me alone," Cody said, shifting to the side again, holding his sandwich close to his chest. "You didn't slip a flower into my pocket or anything, did ya?"

El laughed and gently shoo'd the bee away.

"Well, don't piss it off," Cody said. "You ever been stung by a bee? Those li'l guys hurt!"

"It's just a honeybee," El explained. "It's only going to sting you if you threaten it or its hive. They're just curious, is all."

"Curious about me," Cody said, ducking his head as the bee floated back over. "Why not you, hm?"

"Well, perhaps it's because you're so sweet," El said. And he had the cutest, dumbest little smile on his face.

"That was incredibly cheesy," Cody said, briefly distracted from the bug attack.

"Yes," El agreed. "But you loved it."

Cody smiled. "Yeah, I did." He leaned to the side and gave El a kiss, interrupted by the loud buzzing in his ear. "Seriously?" He risked swatting it away.

El chuckled and stood up. "Come on, let's get you away from them, hm?"

"But you went through all the trouble of finding the perfect spot," Cody argued, stubbornly staying seated. Not even a bee sting would get in the way of his appreciation of El's efforts.

"Well, it's clearly not the perfect spot," El argued. He started packing the rest of his sandwich up. "The perfect spot is one we can both enjoy, bug-free."

Cody nodded and looked over his shoulder at the parking lot. It was only a few feet away from the spot and did have a pretty good view as well. "We could just picnic in the car," he suggested.

"Sounds perfect," El said, gracing Cody with another beaming smile. "Let's do just that."

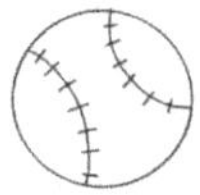

El let out a satisfied sigh as he looked out over the park. The food was gone now, but neither of them seemed intent on moving. Which was just fine by El. He figured the sunset would look very pretty from here.

"Thank you for joining me today," El said. "These little trips are often the highlight of my work, and your company only made it better."

"And thank you for saving me from a day of boring emails," Cody said. He grabbed El's hand and gave him a soft, loving look. One that quickly shifted into a sultry gaze.

"What's that look for?" El asked, feeling his skin heat up at the way Cody looked at him. He did so love to be desired like that.

Cody just licked his lips and glanced quickly at the back seat. El's skin flushed even more. He looked around. There were only two other cars parked here, and they were down on the other side. But there was still no way of knowing whether or not someone else would show up.

El shook his head, noting Cody's overly acted frown. "Sorry, dear. But it's perhaps a bit too public here."

"Fair enough," Cody said. He let go of El's hand and shrugged. "Hate to end the day getting arrested for indecent exposure or whatever it is."

El laughed at his joke, but he could tell that Cody was truly disappointed. "Have you ever done it in a car before?" he asked. "It can't possibly be comfortable."

"Done it three times," Cody said, holding up three fingers. "One for every car I've owned." He dropped his hand and ran it over the steering wheel. "Every single one 'cept this baby. She's special, ya know? Needs the right guy."

El smiled softly. "Glad to know I'm worthy. Perhaps, if we had somewhere private to park it, we could give it a go."

Cody's attention instantly snapped to him, eyes all wide and dilated. "Really?" he asked. El nodded. "You'd do that for me?"

"Of course I would, dear. You indulge my fantasies. Why wouldn't I do the same?"

"It is one of the bigger ones," Cody said, leaning his head back with a wistful sigh and faraway look. "Nothing hotter, I say."

"Only *one* of the bigger ones?" El asked. "What are the others?"

"Eh." Cody shrugged and turned a smile to El. "Nothing all that interesting."

"Oh, come on. You can tell me." He gave Cody his best seducing look. "If you tell me, I might do it."

Cody licked his lips, pulling the bottom one between his teeth as he looked El up and down. Then he tsked and turned his head away rather dramatically. "Nah."

"You're really not going to tell me?" El asked.

"Not yet." Cody said. "See, you really, really want to know. And I think I could have fun with that."

El pouted at him.

"Oh, don't pout. How about, you win the championship, and then I'll tell ya?" Cody smirked, settling comfortably into his seat.

El hummed over that, then shook his head. "No, that's much too big a win for something so simple. How about, if I get a hit, you tell me?"

"Nah, you're too good now for that to be any kind of bet," Cody said. El didn't believe him, but it was cute that he had such confidence in his skills.

"Alright. How about, if I hit a *home run*, you have to tell me?"

Cody sat up, turning a bit in his seat as he studied El's face. "Alright, deal." He held out a hand and El shook it.

Chapter Twenty-Seven
Future Plans

El knew he had nothing to really worry about, not with Cody there. But he couldn't help himself from craning his neck to get a look at what was going on in the kitchen. Clara's place was much too small for the three of them to fit comfortably in there. Still, he hovered around, keeping an eye on things. Waiting to be shoo'd away for being too brotherly.

"Now you keep stirring that," Cody said, handing the spoon over to Clara as he went to the fridge. "Else it'll burn and stick to the bottom of the pan."

"Why?" Clara asked. She took to her duty with care, staring at the saucepan as she stirred. "We don't have to stir the pasta all the time."

"Uh, I don't actually know," Cody said. "Cooking science."

"There's a lot of that," Clara said, earning a soft chuckle from El. "Someone ought to write a book!"

"Oh, I'm sure they have." Cody returned to the stove, measuring out a cup of shredded cheese.

"We should get it!" Clara said. She increased the fervor of her stirring as Cody poured the cheese into the soft. El twitched his hands a bit, resisting the urge to take over. He knew that letting Clara make mistakes was a part of growing up. He just hoped hers weren't nearly as costly as his had been.

"Gently, gently," Cody instructed. Clara slowed her movements back down. El smiled at the two of them and turned his attention back to the window. He really didn't have anything to worry about. Cody had proven himself an excellent chef from his dinners and breakfasts he had made El in the past weeks. Clara was in good hands.

"It smells *so* good," Clara said. And El had to agree. "Is it done yet?"

"Once that gets thick and bubbly," Cody said. The timer went off and he took the pasta off the stove, draining it in the sink. Then he checked the steamer basket full of vegetables, testing a bite of a snap pea.

"Like this?" Clara asked.

Cody leaned over and squinted at the sauce. "Little bit more."

El's stomach let out a soft grumble as the smells filled the air. But he waited patiently as they continued cooking. And it wasn't long before the table was filled with delicious food.

"Oh, this looks divine," El said, already scooping some pasta onto his plate.

"My first, real, official, home cooked meal!" Clara said. She smiled brightly as she took a bite, her eyes widening.

Cody chuckled. "Yeah, you did good."

Clara turned her smile towards him. "I couldn't have done it without your help. Thank you!"

"Anytime."

"Really!?"

Cody shrugged and looked at El. "Sure. Why not?"

El nodded. "A weekly tradition, perhaps?" A good way to keep tabs on Clara without being overbearing, he hoped.

"Yes!" Clara shouted and slammed her hands on the table. "Let's do that!"

El chuckled at her excitement. But he too felt a little giddy at the idea. He loved his sister, and he loved Cody. And he would love nothing more than a regular opportunity for them to spend time together. "Perhaps we should invite Trish as well," he suggested. Afterall, Cody's involvement had helped El and Clara grow closer. Maybe El could help return the favor.

"Oh, well don't go and ruin a good idea," Cody complained.

"Why not?" Clara asked. "Trish is super interesting."

Cody groaned and rolled his head back. "Super annoying, more like."

"We could do a potluck," El continued. And Clara nodded along. "And we can rotate whose place we eat at."

"That sounds perfect!" Clara agreed.

Cody, meanwhile, just stared at El, unamused. El laughed softly and reached over to pat Cody's hand. "Come now, surely dinner once a week with your sister can't be all that bad."

"Give it a month," Cody said. "Then tell me if you think it's still a good idea."

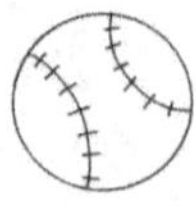

Since Cody and Clara had cooked, El had insisted on cleaning up. But Cody wasn't going to just let him do all that work by himself. He successfully talked his way into drying and putting away as El did the washing.

"Thank you for tonight, dear," El said. "That was the perfect energy boost for our big game tomorrow."

"Mhm," Cody agreed. "Just what I needed to beat you."

El laughed and handed him a plate. "Well, don't tell anyone I told you this, but I kind of hope that you do."

"Oh?" Cody leaned against the counter, raising an eyebrow at El. "Finally realized I'm just too good for your lot?"

"Well, that may be true. But I'm really just looking forward to a big showdown on Sunday. If we win tomorrow, then the championship is over without any real fun."

Cody nodded with a smirk. "Guess I'll just have to do my best."

"El's going to do his best, too!" Clara said, popping up on the other side of the kitchen. "At least, he would, if he took my advice."

El shook his head and rolled his eyes. "Oh, not this again."

Cody's attention perked right up. "What advice?"

"Clara is convinced that I need to paint my fingernails," El told him, sounding already exasperated with the conversation.

"It's true!" Clara said. "The professionals do it all the time! It helps the pitchers see signals more clearly."

"First of all," El said. "We are not professionals. Second of all, Michelle has no problem reading my hand signals."

"All it takes is one time, though," Cody urged.

El sighed. "You're both being ridiculous." But Cody could tell by the look in his eyes and the force of his words that El wasn't as opposed to the idea as he was letting on.

"Maybe I should paint mine," Cody said. He held a hand out, looking over his nails. "Do they make reflective nail polish? I could blind the pitcher instead."

"That would be cheating, dear," El said.

"Takes one to know one," Cody said, with a little bit of a sing-song tune.

"El would never cheat!" Clara insisted.

El's face flushed red, and he gave Cody a look that definitely said *don't you dare*. And Cody certainly didn't. "Yeah, you're right." He leaned over and placed a kiss on El's cheek. "He's much too pure for that."

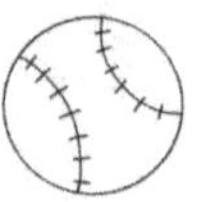

El settled into the bed, resting his head on Cody's shoulder and watching the shadows of the tree branches dance across his ceiling. Cody's arm stretched around him, holding one of El's hands, their fingers mixed up together. They had agreed on no sex that night, but they didn't want to spend the weekend apart either. El knew it was silly, but he had a weird, sinking feeling in his gut that kept trying to convince him that their relationship would fade or disappear once the games were over.

"I think you should go with pink," Cody whispered.

"Hm?" El looked over at Cody, then tracked his attention to their intertwined fingers. He laughed. "Yellow or white is traditional." Not that he had done his research into the matter or anything.

"Yeah, but pink would look really cute." Cody rested his head on El's, placed a soft kiss there.

"Perhaps," El said. It was much too quiet and still in the room. And El couldn't stop his thoughts from ping-ponging around in his head. He'd never get to sleep at this rate. And then he'd be too tired for the game tomorrow.

"You alright?" Cody asked. El wondered how he could tell there was something wrong. But it was almost like a superpower how well Cody could read him.

"Yes," El said. It was only a half lie. True, he was worried about the future of their relationship. But he knew it was just him being silly, so there really wasn't anything wrong at all.

Cody pulled his arm back so he could turn on his side, leaning on an elbow, looking down at El. His face looked so beautiful in the moonlight. El reached up and placed a hand on Cody's cheek. He wanted to keep that beauty in his life.

"Anything you want to talk about?" Cody asked.

"I love you," El said.

Cody smiled softly at him. "I love you, too."

It helped quell the fears a bit, but not for long. "Cody…" El sighed. How did he explain his apprehensions without sounding as ridiculous as he knew he was being. Cody just waited patiently. "How do you feel about going away for a weekend together?"

Cody raised his eyebrows, as if surprised by the question. "I feel extremely excited by the idea."

"Maybe after the games are over," El said. "We could head out to the countryside."

"Sounds romantic," Cody agreed. He leaned down and kissed El. "I kind of wanna go right now and just skip the games."

El chuckled. That was an awfully tempting idea. "We really should play them out," he said. "It wouldn't be fair to our teams."

"Yeah, I guess." Cody sighed and settled back down on the bed. He grabbed El's hand and gave it a squeeze. "Let's make a pact, you and I."

"Okay."

"Next year, no matter how much they beg and plead, we won't give in to peer pressure. No baseball!"

El turned on his side and snuggled up to Cody. He kissed his shoulder. "I don't think I can make that promise," he said.

"Why not?"

"Well, whoever loses this year is going to need a chance at redemption."

Cody hummed. "Good point." Then he sighed again, with a soft grumble. "Alright fine, we'll play again next year."

El smiled and closed his eyes. He still had some unnecessary worries. But hearing Cody talk about the future so definitively made them just a little less worrisome.

Chapter Twenty-Eight
The Penultimate Game

"What's all this?" Cody asked, making his way to the back of the dugout where his team was currently huddled up. He glanced over at El's team, who were all doing a very bad job of pretending not to be interested in the scene.

"We're in trouble, is what this is," Rich said. He grumbled and shook his head.

Cody peeked his head over the crouched-down group, spotting one of the players on the bench, holding a cast arm close to his chest.

"Apparently, he fell while getting ready this morning," Jean added, pulling away from the huddle. "And our backup isn't answering her phone."

"That's a shame," Cody said. And he did sort of mean it. It was a bit of a shame that the championship had to end on a forfeit, but on the plus side, he and El would get an impromptu weekend together, sans baseball.

"We can still play!" Cyrus announced. They had been out on the field talking with Rafael and was now smiling brightly at everyone. "We still have enough players!"

"How?" Cody looked around, counting them all up. "We're still down one."

"Not if you fill in for short-stop," Briney said.

Cody frowned. "No."

"Oh, but you have to!" Anwar said, jumping up to join her sibling. "Else we'll have to quit."

Cody shrugged and turned his head to avoid looking at their pleading faces. He had felt guilty enough about the promotion to fill in as a batter, sure. But he would *not* let them guilt him into playing defense. "Fine by me."

"Is everything alright over here?" El asked. "There seems to be quite the commotion."

Great. Just fantastic. If anyone was going to talk Cody into actually filling in it would be El, of course.

"Everything is fine," Briney said. They stepped to the side to hide the injured player. "Mind your own business."

El made a little face at them and then gestured Cody over. He walked up and leaned against the netting. "Is everything okay?" El whispered.

"Down a man," Cody informed him. "Seems there's no game today."

"Oh dear." El sighed and tutted, looking over at the man. "That is a shame. But, uhm..." he hummed and moved his finger a little. Cody closed his eyes, knowing what was coming next. "Well, you still have enough players, don't you?"

Cody sighed and dropped his head. "Alright, fine," he grumbled. "I'll fill in for...uh..." he snapped his fingers a few times and glanced back at the injured player. He knew he knew the guy's name. Just on the tip of his tongue.

"Seriously?" the short-stop asked.

"Eh, always been bad with names," Cody offered. How was he supposed to remember some random guy from the company he barely talked to?

"We used to work together!" the player said.

"Really?" Cody thought back to his early days in the company, but he didn't really pay attention to anyone back then. Didn't really pay attention to anyone now.

Seriously, how the fuck did he end up getting promoted? "Nope, not ringing any bells."

"It's Farrow!" the player shouted. "We were desk mates!"

"Alright," Cody said. He didn't doubt the guy, just didn't care to remember. "I'll fill in for Farrow then."

The team let out a little hurrah, and Cody turned his attention back to El, who was hiding a smile behind his hand, trying hard not to laugh.

"What?" Cody asked. "Okay, I'm *really* bad with names."

"And faces," El said in a giggle.

"Get back to your own team, chuckles," Cody ordered, pointing over at the opposing dugout. "We got a game to win over here."

"Good luck!"

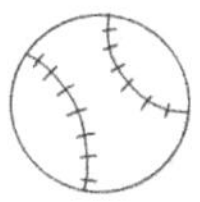

The length of the season was taking its toll on most players. Everyone still had energy, of course. But it was clear that both teams were a little tired. Catches were more easily missed, throws not as far. Only Cody, who hadn't had to play much outside of hitting, was still in his prime.

By the fifth inning it was 7-5, with Cody's team in the lead. And El was a little bit excited for the prospect of him winning. If only so he could crush him tomorrow.

El stood at second, his attention torn between the batter and Cody. It didn't help that Cody was only a few feet away, staring at El with a goading smile. He had been doing quite a good job in his new position, and El didn't think it was very fair that he should be allowed to be talented at both batting and catching.

The next hit was high, certain to go to the outfield. El wasn't the best runner, but he was still pretty confident he could at least make it to third in time. Plus, he'd get to show off a bit in front of Cody.

El took off, and before he knew it, he ran smack dab into Cody, who chuckled a bit as he wrapped his arms around El, a gloved ball touching his back.

El pouted as they detangled. He wasn't sure what was more upsetting, the fact that Cody had tagged him, or the fact that he was so focused on his running that he didn't get the opportunity to see Cody make what was surely an amazing catch.

"Caught it," Cody said, smirking at him.

"I see that."

"Tagged ya," he added. He took the ball from his mitt and tossed it a few times in the air.

"I'm aware."

"Means you're out."

"Mhm."

El knew he should leave the field, but he just continued to stand there and sulk at Cody. It really wasn't fair that he was so talented. Cody laughed at him and leaned forward, kissing him softly. "Don't look so glum," he said. "Gotta keep your spirits up if you want to get that homerun."

El kept frowning as he walked back to the dugout. But El was keeping his spirits up. And if getting an extra kiss from Cody didn't help raise them even higher, he wasn't sure what else would.

"Before you ask," El said, already sensing Lawrence's frustration before even reaching the dugout. "No, I did not *let* him tag me."

Lawrence just grumbled and stared El down. Everyone was performing less than perfectly this game, and El couldn't be blamed for all of it. He sat down and tried not to smile as he caught Cody looking at him. Valerie's hits tended to drift to the right anyway, so it wasn't like he would miss a catch. But still, he should be paying attention to the game instead of staring at El all the time. It was awfully distracting.

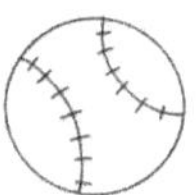

By the seventh inning, Cody's team had extended their lead to 9-5. El's team was thoroughly dejected, but El really didn't mind. He was getting to see Cody's talents shine, after all.

"How do people do this every game?" Cody asked as he walked up to bat. He sighed heavily, shaking his legs out before getting ready. "It's exhausting."

"I thought you had the endurance for everything else," El said. Michelle pitched a wide ball to the side and El had to stretch quite a bit to catch it. He tossed it back, watching Michelle shake her hand. "Just be glad you aren't pitching."

"True." Cody fowled the next pitch. "Hey, wanna have some fun?"

"Depends." El caught the next strike. "What kind of fun."

"Rematch. Your throw against my run." Cody hit another fowl. El suspected he was doing it on purpose.

"It would certainly be close," El said. "But I'm sure I could win."

Cody chuckled, waiting as Michelle switched out for a fresh ball. "Wanna bet?"

"What are the stakes?"

Cody hummed and fowled yet again. That had to be another talent in and of itself. "'Nother hickey?"

El shook his head and rolled his eyes. Michelle slipped a low one, Cody wisely not swinging at it. "Alright. But if I win, you have to invite Trish to the next dinner."

Cody whistled and sighed, almost striking out, but managing to fowl again in the last second. Michelle let out a disgruntled sigh and shook out her arms a bit. El felt a bit bad for her.

"Deal." Cody said. He readied up and then chuckled. "Get ready."

El wasn't entirely sure what Cody's plan was, but he hunkered down, ready to spring into action. Michelle made the pitch, and Cody tilted his bat in and down, bunting the ball into the ground. El gasped as Cody took off running.

"I got it, I got it!" He called to Michelle, waving her back as he raced after the ball. It hadn't gotten too far away, but Cody was already halfway down the line by the time El grabbed it.

El only had time for a half-step, but he was confident it would be enough. He lobbed it to first, feeling it a bit unstable as it left his hand. The first baseman caught it in plenty of time.

"That's an out!" Rafael declared.

El smiled and did a little giddy dance on his way back to his position. Sure, a runner had gotten to third in all of that. But their team was going to lose either way, and this way El got a personal victory.

"Fuuuuuuck," Cody said. He hung his head as he walked past the home plate to make his shameful way to his dugout.

"Don't look so glum," El told him as he went. "You'll need to keep your spirits up if you're going to get through dinner."

Cody gave him a playful glare.

"You guys have a very entertaining relationship," Rafael commented.

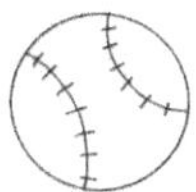

Cody could not wait for this game to be done. It had been kind of fun at first, sure, playing a new position, messing with El a bit. But now he was ready to just get back to El's, have a nice, soapy shower, and curl up together for the rest of the day and all night. His team was already leading by *seven* runs. Why couldn't the other team just give up already?

"One more inning," Cody reminded himself as he settled into his place. "Well, half an inning."

The first batter struck out pretty quick, and Cody let that lull him into a sense of false security. But then the next hitter got a double, and the next two made some solid hits. And before long the bases were loaded and the game was in serious danger of having to go on even longer. He had seen come-backs from even bigger leads before. He just hoped this wouldn't be one of those moments.

But then El was up to bat. And curse his bleeding heart, Cody was really hoping for a good hit from his angel. El deserved it with all the hard work he had put in this season. Cody smiled at him and stood up straight, eager to see him in action.

El looked a little nervous, but he also looked determined. His stance was a bit tense, which meant he was concentrating very hard. Cody looked over his shoulder at the boundaries of the park.

"Oh, come on, angel," he whispered, crouching down a little. "You can do it."

El's first swing was rightfully powerful, but it missed the ball.

"Easy now," Cody continued. "Just focus. Don't think about it too much. You know this."

El missed again and Cody shifted his weight back and forth on his feet, the anticipation building. "Just relax, angel. I got a lot of good desires to tell ya. So, get this one, yeah?"

He saw El take a deep breath. His grip loosened a little, and Cody nodded. "There ya go."

The sound of the bat hitting the ball echoed loudly around the park. Cody jumped in place and turned, tracking the ball as it soared to the outfield. The fence wasn't particularly tall, but Cody held his breath all the same. It would be very, very close.

The ball hit just below the top of the fence, bouncing back into the park as Cyrus chased after it. Cody's heart sank a bit in his chest. That was so close. And he figured El would be crestfallen.

Cyrus tossed the ball to Cody, but things had settled by then. Two runners had made it home and El was safely at second. And he had the biggest smile on his face, looking quite proud of himself. Cody winked at him, just waiting to shower him with praise once the match was over.

The next hitter practically batted the ball right to Cody, who was quick to toss it to third before that runner could make it back. And just like that, the most tiring game was over.

El immediately ran up to Cody, wrapping his arms around Cody's neck and jumping a bit as he hugged him. "Did you see that hit?"

Cody laughed and hugged El back. "It was fantastic, angel."

"That was just about the best hit I've ever made!" El pulled back a bit and Cody wasted no time in kissing him congratulations.

"You were amazing," Cody told him. He kissed him again and again. "Best player on the field."

El laughed and shook his head. "Oh, hardly. There's you, after all."

"Well, alright. Second best player on the field."

"Hmm, now *that* I can accept."

Cody pulled El into another kiss and decided he wouldn't let him go. He may have missed out on his hickey, but he could still enjoy all other forms of kissing. And he had the whole night to enjoy them.

El chuckled into their increasing kiss and then pushed Cody gently away. "Down, boy," he joked. "At least wait until we get home. For goodness sake, my sister is in the stands."

Cody sighed dramatically. "Oh fine. But let's quickly sneak out before they pull me into any kind of celebration."

"Oh? But you deserve a celebration. You did wonderfully, especially filling in for an unfamiliar position."

"Are you saying you *aren't* going to help me celebrate tonight?"

El smiled coyly at him as he started walking back to get his stuff. "I might have something in mind." And Cody couldn't wait.

Chapter Twenty-Nine
A Celebration of Fantasies

"Are you sure you don't want to spend the night at your place?" El asked as he led Cody in.

"Why would I?" Cody closed the door behind them and immediately wrapped his arms around El's waist, kissing over his neck. "Your place is cozy. And closer to the park."

"True," El agreed. He tilted his head and allowed Cody better access, but sure to pay attention unless Cody got any funny ideas about his lost bet. "It's just that we hardly ever go to your place."

Cody stopped kissing and leaned his chin on El's shoulder. "Is that a bad thing?"

El tried to look at him, but it was hard to see his expression at such a weird angle. "Not at all. I just want to make sure you're comfortable."

"Very comfortable," Cody said. Then he kissed El on the cheek and gave him a squeeze.

"Good." El spun around in Cody's arms and smiled at him. "Now, why don't you go pick out a celebratory drink, and I'll meet you upstairs, hm?"

Cody licked his lips and looked El up and down with a raised eyebrow. "I'll be quick."

"Take your time."

El guided Cody towards the kitchen and then raced upstairs. He wouldn't have time to set up everything before Cody finished, but he could at least get a head start. He turned on the water in the bath and dug out his box of candles. He had already pre-picked out some complimentary scents.

"You takin' a bath?" Cody asked, sauntering his way into the bathroom with a bottle of wine and two glasses.

"*We* are," El informed him. He tested the water, finding it a comfortable temperature, and then put in the stopper. "Now, any preference?" He held up the basket of bath bombs.

"Ohhh," Cody leaned forward, looking over the options. "Purple sparkly?"

El nodded and dropped it in the tub, letting out a delighted gasp as it already set to work. "Wonderful."

Cody hummed an agreement and placed the glasses and wine down on the counter. Then he was back to hugging El and kissing his neck again. El laughed and let Cody slowly unbutton his shirt, fingers drifting delicately across his chest. Cody's touches were always so gentle, even when they were meant to be rough. He had a surprisingly delicate air about him that El just loved so much.

"Starting to look like a little galaxy in there," Cody said. The purple had begun to spread out, revealing speckles of gold within.

"It really does," El agreed. "A galaxy all our own."

Cody took a deep breath and let it out in a soft growl. "That is a very intoxicating concept."

El turned around and pulled Cody into a soft kiss. "You get on in, I'll pour the wine."

"Yes, sir." Cody kissed El once more and then took to getting undressed and climbing into the tub. He let out a long hiss as he settled in. "Ahhh, that feels good."

"Does it?" El handed him a glass of wine and then started getting out of the rest of his clothes. "Good temperature?"

"Perfect temperature."

El smiled and poured himself a glass of wine before getting in on the other side of the bath. It was still a bit too warm for his tastes, but it was hardly unbearable. And the bath bomb had left the water feeling particularly silky and smooth, which suited him just fine.

Cody chuckled and took a sip of his wine. He leaned back against the end of the tub and lifted a foot up to El's chest. "Mmm, can't wait to see what you'll do for me when I win the championship."

"*If* you win," El reminded him. He placed a hand on Cody's leg and rubbed it gently.

"You're awfully confident over there," Cody said. "But from where I was standing, your team was hardly in fine form."

"We were just conserving our energy is all," El said. Although he did worry that some of the other players were slipping a bit. Michelle, in particular, seemed quite tired. "Saving up for tomorrow."

"Ah, I see. Uh-huh. Sure." Cody just continued to smirk at him and El knew the argument was worthless.

"Just enjoy the celebration while it lasts," El informed him. "For tomorrow night, it'll be my turn."

Cody laughed and took another sip. "Alright. So," he shifted up a bit, his leg disappearing back under the water. "It's a post-apocalyptic future world, right?"

"Sorry, what?"

Cody shook his head a bit. "My desire," he explained. "Figured you earned one."

"Oh? But I didn't get a home run."

"Close enough, as far as I'm concerned."

"But that wasn't the deal." Sure, El was very interested in hearing what Cody's desires were. But he did want to earn them properly.

"Which is why I'm giving you the impossible fantasy scenario," Cody said.

"Ah, I see." El settled back in the bath, taking a sip of wine. "In that case, do go on."

"Right, so post-apocalyptic future, right?" El nodded. "Humanity on its last legs. And, well, you know, a good top is just *so* hard to find."

El chuckled. "That's true even of today." And he thanked every lucky star he had that he found Cody.

"Oh, but it's so much worse in the future," Cody continued. "Bands of bottoms roam the countryside, looking for whatever piece of action they can get."

El let out another laugh. "I'm sorry," he said, waving his hand and trying to contain his giggles. "I really do not mean to laugh at your fantasy."

"Nah, it's alright," Cody said with a shrug. "It is a bit of a silly one."

"Please, please continue." El reigned in his laughter and bit his lip to prevent any more. He really did not want Cody to think he was making fun of him or anything.

"Right, so. Erm, one of these groups. They, uh, well they capture me, and, uh…" Cody looked to the side, a full blush forming on his face.

El had never seen him so flustered and uncertain. It was enough to sober him up immediately and make him regret every laugh. He quickly put his glass down and slid forward, crossing his legs awkwardly so he could grab a hold of Cody's arm and give it a squeeze. "I really didn't mean to laugh at you, dear."

"Hm?" Cody looked over at him, his stare a little distant. "Oh! No, it's not that." He shook his head and looked El in the eye. "It's just that I've never actually said it out loud before. And I'm only just now realizing how weird it is."

"Well, even if it is weird," El pulled gently on Cody's arm, urging him to sit up and slide closer until they really were in a galaxy all their own, "I would never judge you for it."

"I know," Cody said. He put his wine glass down and placed his hand on El's knee, warming it up from where it stuck out of the water. He looked down at where they touched and took a deep breath. "So, I'm captured. And they...tie me up on this bed." He glanced up at El, who was quick to nod along.

"A nice plush one?" El asked.

Cody smiled softly and nodded back. "Yeah, silk sheets and everything. Tons of pillows."

"Perfect for burrowing," El commented. Cody's smile grew.

"And perfect for sex," Cody added. "Cause, see, they got me tied up, and, well... they just take turns, ya know? One by one, taking their pleasures from me. Sometimes two at a time, but they don't really like to share." He chuckled and then looked back down at his hand. "And, uh, yeah. That's it."

"Oh, Cody." El placed a hand on Cody's cheek and urged him to look up. "I would hardly classify that as a weird fantasy."

"It's a little weird," Cody argued. "I mean, ya know, a top wanting to be tied up like that and *used*."

El ran his thumb over Cody's skin, trying to make that frown go away. "Top and bottom have nothing to do with power dynamics," he explained.

"I *know*," Cody said, once more looking away. "It's just..."

"Hard to believe it sometimes?" El offered.

Cody looked into his eyes again and then let out a soft laugh as he smiled. "Yeah. You get it."

"I do." El smiled back. "And on behalf of bottoms everywhere, I sincerely apologize for anyone who ever made you feel weird for wanting to be submissive."

"Not all the time," Cody clarified. "Just a little, every now and then."

"Well, I can't promise that I would be a very good or convincing dom," El said. "But if ever you were in the mood, I would do my best for you."

Cody chuckled softly, his smile growing more mischievous. "Oh, angel." He maneuvered around until he was practically sitting on El's lap, wrapping his arms around his neck, looking deep into his eyes with that sultry stare of his. "You have the potential to be one of the best doms around. Trust me." He kissed El, tongue doing little flips against his own. And El was very glad for such contact between their groins.

"So much for not having sex over the weekend," El mumbled against Cody's lips.

"Oh, c'mon. A romantic, candle-lit bath where we talk about our fantasies? What did you think was going to happen?"

"I didn't know we were going to talk about our fantasies." Cody pulled back a bit and gave El an unconvinced look. "You can have a romantic bath without it turning sexual."

"Not when the person you're sharing it with is one of the sexiest people alive." Cody smirked and then captured El up in another kiss. Not that El minded, of course. "Plus, we are celebrating."

El chuckled. "Oh, very well." He reached a hand between them and wrapped it around Cody's cock. "But I want to hear more about this fantasy of yours."

"I already told you everything," Cody insisted. He leaned his forehead against El's, moving his hips in time with El rubbing. It created a wonderfully smooth and tantalizing sensation between El's own legs.

"Ah, but I want specifics," El clarified. He dropped his voice to a seductive whisper. "I want to know exactly how they take their pleasure from you."

Cody made a little grunt noise as they moved, the water sloshing gently around them. "Well, there's lots of riding, obviously," he said. "Oh, but there is this pair that get off on blow jobs." He let out a soft laugh. "They like to have competitions over who can do it the best."

El smiled. He was elated that Cody trusted him with his desires. "I bet I could show them a thing or two," he said.

Cody's movements stilled, but his dick twitched excitedly in El's hand. "Oh, you very much could."

"They would be on either side of you," El continued, watching Cody's eyes grow wider, his pupils dilating ever slightly more. "And I'd be in the center, between your spread-out legs." Cody grunted and continued shifting his hips again. "I'd start out by showing them an example of how it's really done, of course. And then I'd guide them as they practiced."

"You'd put your hands on their heads," Cody said, taking over. "Give them praise when they did good. Scold 'em if they were bad." He licked his lips. His breath grew shorter and harsher. His hips moved a bit faster. "And then you'd make them watch. You'd make them all watch as you fucked yourself on me."

"Yes," El agreed. "I'd show them the best way to use you for their ultimate pleasure."

"Oh, fuck." Cody hissed and closed his eyes as he came. El couldn't tear his attention away from how gorgeous Cody looked, how his skin flushed pink all over, his body shaking slightly. "That's gonna make a mess," he whispered.

"We'll shower up soon," El promised. He gently continued to stroke Cody, careful not to overstimulate him too much.

"After you, of course," Cody said. He smiled and leaned back down for a kiss.

"Not tonight," El said. "It's *your* celebration."

"Hey." Cody grabbed El's face between his hands and gave him a playful squint. "No celebration of mine can possibly end until you get off. There is nothing I love more than seeing someone enjoy themselves, hm?"

And after seeing Cody look so handsome and sexy while coming just then, El certainly understood where he was coming from. "Very well, then," he agreed. "But just the once. We need to keep our energies up for the game tomorrow."

Cody smirked at him. "We'll see."

Chapter Thirty
The Family Affair

"Thank you for driving again, dear," El said as he, Cody, and Clara climbed out of the car. "We really should consider that chauffeur outfit for you."

"I would look good in that little hat," Cody agreed. Then his body froze briefly before he ducked around behind the side of the car.

Clara and El looked between him and the stands. But it was hard to tell what had caught his gaze. "Erm, you go on ahead," El told Clara, patting her on the shoulder. "I'll go check on him."

El carefully walked around the car, finding Cody sitting on the ground, back resting on the side of the car, knocking his head softly against the door. "She brought." Thud. "Our parents." Thud.

"Your parents are here?" El peeked back out at the stands. He noticed Trish sitting in one of the front rows. A couple sat on either side of her, but it was hard to tell from looks alone which set belonged to Cody.

"She brought our parents!" Cody repeated. "She's a fucking *psychopath.*"

"Oh dear." El squatted down and placed a comforting hand on Cody's arm. "If you want, I could ask Rafael to throw them out."

Cody looked over at El as if just realizing he was there. Then he sighed and closed his eyes with a soft groan. "Okay, uhm, I haven't told you this yet, but...I'm adopted."

El shifted into a more comfortable seat, his full attention focused on Cody's face. Cody took a deep breath and then stood up, pacing along the length of the car, looking everywhere but at El. "See, the thing is, my childhood? Pretty fucked up. Our birthparents were genuinely just awful people. And Trish and I spent a lot of time in and out and in and out of all these different places, you know? And it was my fault, okay?" At this, Cody finally glanced at El, just briefly, as he placed a hand on his chest. "Cause, like, Trish was older and more mature and probably would have been fine but the stupid agency people insisted that we end up someplace together, which I basically made impossible because I was terrible and kept getting in trouble, you know?"

El wasn't sure if this was the kind of break that required an answer, so he just gave a little nod, letting Cody know he was following along.

"Right, so, anyway, we finally end up with *them*," Cody pointed to the stands and sighed, rolling his head back. "And they were actually really fucking *great*. But I was a dumb kid with a chip on his shoulder who just made their lives miserable, okay? Miserable!" Cody stopped for a moment, standing to the side a bit and breathing heavily. His eyes were a bit red and watery, but El didn't want him to lose his momentum by interrupting.

"So, anyway, uhm, I kind of kept messing up. Like. For a long time. I've got stories, trust me." Cody sighed heavily and sat back down, still not looking at El. "About five years ago I moved here and...I don't know. It's like I somehow figured out a way to get my shit together. And..." his attention wandered over to the stands. "I want to make things right with them." A tear dropped from one eye. "I've wanted to for a long time. But I'm so fucking worried that as soon as they're back in my life I'm just going to fuck everything up again."

Cody hugged his knees close and buried his face in his arms.

El took a deep breath and rubbed Cody's back. "I can understand how you would think that." For the first time in their relationship, he was truly out of the right words to say. "If you want to leave, we can."

Cody gulped and looked up at El. A few more tears had fallen, but he was doing a good job of keeping them in check. "We can't do that to them." Cody nodded over at the teams.

"It's just a game," El reminded him. "It's nothing compared to your mental health."

Cody stared at him for a moment and then laughed softly. "No, I'll be okay. We have to see this through." He straightened up and wiped his eyes on the back of his hand. "Gah, I'm a mess. Sorry."

"There's nothing to apologize for, dear." El gave him a reassuring pat on the back.

"I can't believe Trish would do this to me." Cody growled, all hints of tears leaving his eyes, replaced by anger. "I mean, I always knew she was evil, but this? How the hell am I supposed to focus now?"

"Are we sure she did it on purpose? No offense, but it doesn't seem like the two of you talk about your feelings very much. Maybe she doesn't understand why you're so removed from your parents." Just like El didn't know he was being so overbearing with Clara. Communication truly was key.

Cody pursed his lips at him. "I mean...it's *possible*." He groaned again. "This is going to be spectacularly embarrassing."

El smiled softly at his love. "Would it make you feel any better if I told you an embarrassing thing about me?"

Cody hummed and squinted at him. "Might."

"Well, El is just a nickname," El told him. He wasn't all that embarrassed by his secret, but he figured Cody would get a laugh out of it. And it might help him relax. And he'd have to find out eventually.

"I kind of figured that," Cody said. "But if it's embarrassing, it's probably not Elliot, like I thought, huh?" El shook his head. "Elmer?"

"Oh, I wish," El said.

Cody tilted his head and studied him for a bit. Then he snapped his fingers with a wide grin. "Your parents wanted a girl and named you Eliza!"

El laughed and shook his head again. "Nothing that dramatic."

"Alright, I give. What's El short for?"

El looked down briefly. "Elmo."

Cody laughed and El looked up with a smile. "Elmo?" Cody asked. "Like the little red puppet guy?"

"It's a family name, actually," El said. "Although, I do laugh when someone pokes my tummy."

They shared another few seconds of laughter. "Okay, yeah, that actually did make me feel better," Cody said. "Thanks."

"Happy to help." El patted Cody's arm before standing up. "Now, how about you go introduce me to your parents, and then we play one hell of a game?" He held a hand out to him.

Cody smiled and took El's hand, hoping to his feet. "Oh, they're gonna love you," he whispered as he led El over to the stands.

"Cody, dear, there you are!" The woman sitting next to Trish stood up and rushed up to give Cody a hug. Her husband trailed slowly behind her.

"Hey, Ma," Cody said, hugging her back loosely.

"Son," his father greeted, giving him a side hug.

"Dad," Cody said, patting him on the back with a quick nod. He looked more uncomfortable than El figured possible. "Uh, guys, this is El." He gestured to El and shifted awkwardly on his feet. "My, uhm, boyfriend."

"It's very nice to meet you," El said, holding out a hand.

Cody's mother shook it, and then pulled El into a hug. "It's so good to meet you, too."

"Yeah, should have warned you she's a hugger," Cody whispered.

"One of the reasons I married her," Cody's dad said, shaking El's hand.

"And that's something we didn't need to know," Cody said, shaking a bit.

"I see you've already met my sister," El said, nodding to Clara who was sitting behind Trish.

"Cody, your parents are adorable," Clara said.

"Adorable," Cody whispered. "That's a choice word."

"Well, we'd love to stay and chat more," El said, grabbing Cody's arm. "But we really should be getting to the game. Perhaps we can all go out for dinner tonight?"

"That sounds lovely," Cody's mom said. "Good luck to the both of you. But extra luck to you, of course." She winked at Cody and then went to go sit back down.

"Yeah, thanks."

El chuckled softly and dragged Cody away. "Clara's right. They are adorable."

"Oh, not you, too." Cody groaned.

"Now, I've done some thinking," El added, pulling Cody to a stop before they had to split up. "And I've decided there will be no heckling on my part this game."

Cody studied him with suspicion. "Is that so?"

"Mhm."

"Finally deciding to play by the rules, huh?"

"Well, it's just that I'm sure you're quite shaken up already. And so, it really wouldn't be sporting to add to the mix."

"Uh-huh. And you're always so worried about being sporting, there, are ya?"

"Well, you know. Unless you start doing really well."

Cody laughed and shook his head before pulling El in for a quick kiss. "Go on then, ya hooligan. I've got a game to win."

Chapter Thirty-One
The Final Game

The stands were unnecessarily loud that day. The other teams from the league had all come out to see the grand finale. And of course, friends and family of the players showed up. Including his parents...

Cody sighed and ignored their excessive cheering as he stepped up to bat. They had even made a little sign. No one else had made a sign. Why did they have to make a sign? That was so extra.

"Doing alright?" El asked as Cody got into position.

"Just fine." But his first strike proved him initially wrong. It was only the first inning, so it wasn't like it mattered. Yet. But Cody knew that if he struck out now, he'd be useless all game. God, he really did turn into a screw up around his parents.

"Anything I can do to help?" El asked.

"Nope." Cody didn't like being so short and testy, especially with El. But he had to focus and concentrate on getting a good hit. Which he did.

Cody let out a sigh of relief as the ball sailed away and then started running. He made it to first, but his trek towards second was ruined by the catch made in the outfield. Cody dropped his shoulders and slumped his way back to the dugout. He had popped it too high, but not strong enough to clear the park. That was his bad. And his mom and Clara shouting "you'll get it next time," certainly didn't help.

Cody had no idea how he was going to survive this game. More than that, he didn't know how he was going to pull off a win. He would love nothing more than to win, of course. But even if he lost, he figured he'd still win in the long run. Because a night of spoiling El and loving on him in celebration of his victory would be just as nice.

"Think they're any good?" Rich asked.

Cody turned back to watch as their fill-in for Farrow stepped up to the plate. He was more than thankful she had managed to show up today. He couldn't imagine trying to juggle defense with his parents here as well.

"She looks pretty decent," Cody said. "I bet she's alright."

They watched eagerly as she made her first hit. It rolled between first and second base, and there was a bit of confusion among the catchers as to who would grab it, so she ended up safe on first.

"Not bad," Rich said.

"Should have been playing all season," Cody said. "Then maybe I wouldn't have had to." But then he wouldn't have met El, so that would have been worse overall.

The rest of the inning and the next passed pretty uneventfully. Even the crowd was a little restless by the top of the third. But Jean was on third base, and one of their better hitters was up. Cody watched eagerly as the ball made its way out. It bounced behind the pitcher, jumping right up into the second baseman's glove. He certainly could have gotten it over to first in time for the out, but he tossed it back to El.

Jean didn't even try, and Cody couldn't help but chuckle as he just slowed to a jog and let El tag him. Cyrus hopped up to bat next, and unsurprisingly struck out. And then it was Cody's turn.

He was a little better at ignoring his personal cheer squad as he made his way to bat, but it was still pretty embarrassing. Cody gave El a little glance, but he was so far resolute in his goal to not heckle. It was a nice change of pace, but Cody was also kind of missing it.

But it might have been very good for his game, as Cody hit himself a home run on the first pitch.

"Ah, excellent hit," El told him.

"Thanks." Cody turned and gave El a wink. "Your turn next, hm?"

El laughed but nodded. "I'll do my best."

"Bases," Rafael said. "Run them. Now."

Cody sighed and dropped his bat. "Do I really have to? Can't I just go back?" Normally he would love to do a little celebratory jog for El, but he wasn't interested in doing the whole parade for his family and the crowd. He liked showing off, just not when people were actively waiting for it.

"Either run them or forfeit the hit," Rafael said.

"Fiiiine." Cody sighed and gave El a look before he did his little show.

Things were tense. El was ready for the games to be over so he could go back to his peaceful and relaxing existence. This kind of tension couldn't be good for anyone. Tied in the fourth inning, 3-3. Cody's team had held the early lead, but now things were heating up on both sides.

One of the interesting things about playing in the league was that El had become famous for his inability to be tackled or shaken. Most players had adopted a similar view as Jean of not even trying to take him down. Many had given it a shot at least once, but then they had learned their lesson and decided it wasn't worth it.

And El figured that had lulled him into a false sense of security. So, when the new fill-in came barreling at him, quite unexpectedly, he found himself toppled on the floor, hand loose, and the ball rolling rather dramatically away from his hand.

"Safe!" Rafael called out.

El huffed and frowned at the ball. He should have been more aware. He should have kept his guard up, no matter what. That was a very non-strategic play, and he would certainly hear about it in the dugout.

"El!" Cody's voice called. "You okay?"

El nodded and took Rafael's hand as he stood up.

"I'm fine too, by the way!" the runner called back. "Thanks for asking!"

"Well, I knew *you'd* be fine," Cody said.

El found a small smile at his antics and then got back into position, careful not to look over at the dugout. But then Lawrence called, "Time!" and was running up to him. So, it seemed he couldn't even avoid the lecture for a little bit.

El sighed and stood up, biting the inside of his cheek to stop himself from either crying or yelling in frustration.

"El, you alright?" Lawrence asked, standing too close and dropping his voice to a whisper.

"I'm fine, yes," El said.

Lawrence nodded and looked at the opposing team. "They're starting to play dirty."

"It's hardly an illegal move," El argued. He just wasn't playing at his best.

"Keep a close eye out," Lawrence continued, seemingly unbothered by El's mistake. El eyed him up suspiciously. "They'll probably start trying to steal bases soon. And you know Michelle has tunnel vision up there."

El hummed and nodded along. He was still waiting for the other shoe to drop, but Lawrence just smiled and patted him on the shoulder before returning to their dugout. El still wasn't convinced that he was in the clear yet. And if anything, that worry would probably just put him off his game even more.

He really, really couldn't wait for the game to be over.

Two innings later, Cody's team was managing to keep a hold of their 4-3 lead. It had been really close a few times. El's team had almost scored a double run homer when Amy very nearly got a homerun. But Anwar had made a fantastic jump-catch at the fence that ended the inning in a spectacular way. And that's why the triplets still played despite being incredibly inept at hitting.

But the game was more than half-way over now, and the exhaustion was starting to set in. Cody's team did have the advantage, however, with their sub being more rested. But she was also out of practice and wasn't making as many catches as she should have.

Cody leaned against the edge of the dugout as he watched El step up to bat. He hadn't made a hit yet, but Cody just knew his angel would surprise everyone this game.

El missed the first two pitches, but then fouled the third. "C'mon, El!" Cody called out to him. "Show 'em what's what!"

"Hey!" Briney shouted. "Whose side are you on?"

"The side that gets me laid," Cody answered honestly. It was the last game, after all. It's not like they could kick him out or do anything else about it.

"You're disgusting."

"Thank you."

The sound of the bat making contact pulled Cody's attention back to the field. The ball made its way between second and third, just a bit too quick for the shortstop to grab it. The triplets were all playing closer to the infield, so El wouldn't be able to get a double. But he had gotten a hit and had made it to first without trouble. Cody cheered for him with the crowd, absolutely loving the bright smile that played on his face when he looked up.

"If he ends up tying," Briney warned, "it's your fault."

"And I'm okay with that."

The next batter made an excellent hit wide to right field. They got out at first, but El managed to make it all the way to third. Cody licked his lips and watched with his full, undivided attention. Was this what people who actually enjoyed this sport felt when watching? If so, he could certainly understand the appeal.

"I can't believe you actually want them to win," Briney mumbled.

"Well, obviously I want the *Gardeners* to lose," Cody explained. "I just want El to win. You know, personal victories."

Briney shook their head. "Just focus on your own victories, hm?"

"Oh, I am," Cody assured them. It's just that he had come to appreciate El's victories as an extension of his own. He wanted El to be confident in his abilities, proud of his work, and happy with the results of a game no matter what the score ended up being.

But when the next batter made an ill-timed bunt, Cody knew those hopes for this particular instance were dashed. But as the pitcher grabbed the ball and tossed it back to the catcher, El didn't turn back or slow down. Oh no. He kept running. Much to the surprise of the catcher.

The catcher turned, gloved ball extended to tag El as he passed. But El just dropped to the ground, executing a perfect slide right under the mitt and into home. Everyone seemed shocked and unsure until Raphale called El safe. And then the stands, and Cody, erupted into applause.

"I'm telling everyone that was your fault," Briney said.

Seventh inning, tied 4-4. El was still coming down from the high of his run. He hadn't even expected to avoid the catcher altogether. He just figured he would get back at Cody's team for their early knock-out. But he hadn't even needed to knock the catcher down. Everyone underestimated his offensive abilities. Which seemed to be working in his favor now. Not that he ever expected to get away with it again.

"Nice moves," Cody said as he stepped up to the bat.

El couldn't help but smile behind his mask. Even better than getting a good play was having someone enjoy it with him. "Thank you. I did learn from the best."

Cody laughed at him and managed a nice hit to center field that got him to first. El had been staying good on his promise to not heckle, but he was missing out on some of the fun. And he figured the shock of Cody's family showing up was probably over now. So, if Cody got the opportunity to bat again, El might just have to come up with something to say.

But El would much rather the game finish quickly instead.

The next batter also hit a solid single, putting Cody on second. El watched with a squint as Cody inched his way out from base. He even pulled up his pants a little as he got into running position.

No, El thought. He wouldn't dare try. He had managed to steal second that one time, but third base was closer and in a more direct line to home plate. Cody would have to know that he wouldn't stand a chance.

But, oh, he was going to take it. Michelle threw the ball and Cody took off running. The batter swung and missed, landing the ball right into El's glove. He was up and moving in a second, throwing it to third. It would have been the perfect out, if Louie hadn't been just short of catching it. The ball just touched the top of his glove before bouncing behind them, leaving Cody safe on base. All Louie had to do was jump just a little.

El frowned as Cody did a little celebratory dance. He was happy for him, of course. But he was also a little upset that the play didn't work. And he knew that Louie would probably get an earful from Lawrence about missing the catch. It was too close of a game for anyone to be messing up.

On the next pitch, the batter made a hit to right field. There was no way the ball would get back in time to stop Cody from scoring a run, but they did at least get the out at first. So, they were a little bit closer to preventing any other scores.

"Almost had me there," Cody said with a laugh as he stepped triumphantly on the plate.

"*I* did," El assured him. "It was the baseman who didn't."

Cody laughed and patted El on the shoulder before making his way back to his team. El just huffed at him and got back in position. The heckling was certainly back on the table.

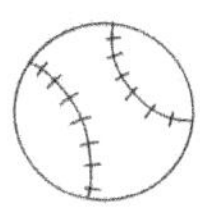

Cody was getting mighty comfortable. The eighth inning had come and gone with a few good hits, but no secured runs. So now his team just had to get through one more inning with their 5-4 lead and they would win.

"Don't get too comfortable," Briney warned as Cody stretched out on the bench. "You're up next, and we need to increase our lead as much as possible to secure this win."

"Yeah, yeah," Cody said. He knew how desperation could make for a surprising comeback. But he really wasn't all that worried about it. El wasn't even likely to bat next inning, so there was already no chance of a nice surprise homerun for his angel.

The batter struck out, but it was only their first out of the inning. So even if Cody fucked up, they still had a chance to get more runs. He felt perfectly content and comfortable as he walked up to the plate. But then Lawrence was calling for a timeout and Cody started feeling a little uneasy.

"Just one moment, dear," El said, before jogging up to the pitcher's mound to get in on the little talk.

Cody sighed and leaned against his bat, trying hard not to look at his family in the stands. But their obnoxious sign waving was a little hard to ignore. He glanced over and gave them a little wave. Overall, it was nice that they were so invested. And he figured being receptive of that would help make up for him being a jerk in the past.

El's raised voice drew Cody's attention to the huddle on the field. El shook his head and pointed at Lawrence while yelling something Cody couldn't make out. Michelle kept trying to interject, but El seemed to cut off her argument every time.

"Wonder what that's all about," Rafael said.

Cody looked over at him with a squint. "Aren't you supposed to be up there keeping an eye on things or whatever?"

"Am I?" Rafael shrugged. "I didn't think so."

Cody just chuckled and shook his head at him. Eventually, Lawrence threw his hands in the air and stalked back to the dugout. Michelle looked down and shook her head. El walked back to the plate looking absolutely flustered. If Cody wasn't so worried about what had happened, he'd be completely overwhelmed with how hot it made El look. What with his chest all puffed out, arms swinging passionately at his side, face flushed, eyes burning bright.

"Everything okay?" Cody asked.

"Perfectly." El gave him a tight little smile and then got himself back into position without another word.

Cody certainly didn't believe him, but he could tell now wasn't the time to discuss that. He'd get the full story after the game, when the two of them were all snuggled up in bed somewhere.

Michelle's first pitch was a curveball that went far out to the right. El huffed loudly as he caught it and waited a minute before tossing it back. Michelle shrugged at him and shook her head.

"Seriously," Cody tried. "What happened?"

"Nothing to worry about," El assured him. But then he whispered, "I hope," as he got ready again.

Cody really wanted to know what happened. Michale made a low cutter pitch that grounded down into El's glove.

"One moment please," El said as he jogged the ball back to the mound.

"Go eavesdrop," Cody told Rafael.

"No, I'm good." Rafael shook his head and looked at El, who was pointing again and speaking very intensely at Michelle. "He's kind of being scary right now."

"I know," Cody said. Then he smiled. "Isn't it hot?"

"Stop that."

Cody chuckled, but his joy died down as El stormed back over. "Are you okay?" he asked.

"I will be," El said. Then he grumbled, "As long as people play the damn game."

Cody wasn't sure he had heard El curse like that before. It was both worrisome and tantalizing. Cody got ready and watched as Michelle shook her arm out. It had been a long game, and it was natural she would be feeling a little worn down. It was a shame they didn't have enough players in their little league to have relief pitchers. They probably would have if the managers treated it like the fun little game it was and not a death match.

Michelle made the pitch and Cody knew it would miss the box as soon as it left her hand. He also knew it was gunning right for him. He did his best to hop out of the way, but the ball still smacked right into his bicep, sending an electric wave of pain up and down his arm.

"Cody!" El was up and holding him in an instant.

"I'm okay," Cody said, although he wasn't sure he could move his arm even if he wanted to. That probably wasn't a good sign.

"Let me see," El ordered. He carefully grabbed Cody's arm and scrunched up his sleeve. He let out a gasp. "That doesn't look good!"

"It's fine," Cody argued. But he had to bite the inside of his cheek to stop from letting out the pain. It was numbing in some places, but mostly throbbing.

"Shit, is he okay?" Michelle asked, jogging up to them. And now Cody's family was making their way onto the field to check on him. Which was the last thing he needed.

"Oh, like you care," El snapped. "You hit him on purpose!"

"What? No, I didn't."

"Please! You wanted to walk him, and I said no, and so you hit him to take him out."

"You wanted to walk me?" Cody asked. "That's not cool."

"I did not hit him on purpose!" Michelle argued. By now both Lawrence and Briney had joined the scene, Cody's family only a few paces away. He had to shut this down fast.

"Look, whatever, okay? Either way, I'm fine. The hit happened. I'll just take the walk and we can all move on with our lives."

"Absolutely not," El declared. "I will not stand here and abide by such immoral play." He pulled his mitt off and threw it dramatically to the ground. "I quit."

"El, you can't quit," Lawrence said. "It's the last inning!"

"I don't care. I'm leaving and taking Cody to a doctor."

Cody chuckled nervously as everyone turned to look at him. One the one hand, seeing El getting so ruffled was incredibly hot. But this really was getting out of hand. "El, it's fine. Really, I'm fine." He turned to his parents and gave them a smile and a nod to quell their worries.

"You are not fine! Look at your arm!" El pulled Cody's arm out, sending a new shockwave of pain that had him wincing and groaning. Already a giant bruise had formed from where the ball had hit him. And Cody was still pretty convinced he couldn't move it if he tried.

"Yeah, alright, sure, it *looks* bad," he said. "But it's really, I mean, all I have to do is run now, right? I don't need my arm for that."

"Exactly," Briney agreed. "That's the spirit."

"That is *not* the spirit," El argued. "Cody is injured and in need of medical attention. And I'm taking him right now!"

He grabbed Cody's good arm and started dragging him away. Cody grabbed El back and pulled them to the side. He gave everyone a warning glare not to follow and then turned to face El's huffy face.

"Look, El, please. Don't do this."

El's shoulders dropped a bit, concern taking over where anger had once been. "You need to get that looked at."

"I know. I know." Cody stepped closer and dropped his voice to a whisper. "Listen, I know this is going to sound incredibly stupid, but if I can do this, i-if I can win this game with them here..." He gulped as tears started to form again. At least he could lie and say it was from his injury. "Maybe there's hope, you know?"

El's body relaxed, his face softening. "Cody..." he closed his eyes and sighed. "Fine. But you have to *promise* that you'll go to a doctor the *second* we're done."

Cody nodded. "I swear. But, El, please, don't throw the game. I need to earn it."

"I swear."

Cody kissed El quickly and then smiled as he led him back to the eagerly waiting crowd.

"Is everything okay?" Cody's mom asked, immediately falling into place and looking over his arm.

"It's fine," Cody told her. "Just a little bruise. I'm okay to keep playing, and El revokes his quitting, right?"

El frowned but nodded.

"See? It's all okay."

"Are you sure you're okay to play?" Cody's mom asked.

"I'm fine. I already promised I'll go see a doctor after we finish. It's only one inning left."

His mom smiled and kissed him on the forehead, smoothing down his hair. He grumbled and shifted about until the crowd finally dispersed. He knew it was silly. This was just a low-stakes company game. But he really did feel like winning would prove he could be around his parents and *not* fuck up. All he had to do was win.

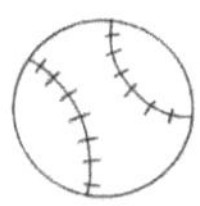

El refused to talk to anyone. He sat in the dugout with his arms crossed as he watched the rest of the game play out. Cody's team hadn't managed to pull a run out, despite their intentional walk, and so the game was still dangerously close. El glanced over at Cody, making sure he was still icing his arm. Cody had even allowed his mom to join him in the dugout, helping him keep his arm properly elevated. Seeing Cody starting to get along with his family did help ease El's anger and worry. But he still wished he could have successfully quit on this whole thing.

El hadn't even been really paying attention to the game, too fueled by his anger. So when he was called up to bat, he was a little surprised to find the bases loaded with two outs. El got into position and looked back at Cody.

It would be easy, he figured. He could strike out with no problem and no one would be the wiser. But Cody had asked him not to do that. And since Cody had proven to be worthy of trust, El knew he needed to be trustworthy himself.

El tightened his grip on his bat and stared down the pitcher. He let his anger inspire his movements. Frustration popped his hips forward as he swung with all his might. He watched, numb and unamused, as the ball cleared the back fence.

The field erupted into cheers. El just turned around and handed his bat to Rafael. "I will not be running the bases."

"Fair enough."

El nodded and hurried away from his teammates, making a quick beeline for Cody's dugout.

"Come on," El said. "Doctor time."

"Hold up! Take a minute to enjoy your win, angel," Cody said with a smile and a laugh. He didn't look upset. But he might just be waiting until they were alone. This whole day had been a disaster, as far as El saw it.

"I will later," El lied. "But first I'm taking you to get that looked at."

"Call me when you're out?" Cody's mom asked.

"I will. Promise."

They smiled at each other and then El grabbed Cody's good arm and dragged him the back way around to the parking lot. Thankfully no one tried to chase after him for the celebration. He was sure he'd snap at anyone who tried, even Valerie.

"Do you even know how to drive?" Cody asked as El all but shoved him into the passenger seat. He probably could have made it with one arm, but no use risking it.

"Of course. I do have a license." El just didn't like driving around in the city if he could avoid it. Too much traffic.

"Like, an active one?" Cody asked.

250

"Yes."

El got settled in the seat and then slowly took off. They crept away from the park, entering more main traffic streets. Cody glanced at the dashboard.

"Okay, the speed limit is, like, 40, here, El."

"I know. But you're injured. We don't want to risk agitating your condition."

Cody laughed a little. "I hardly think driving the appropriate speed is going to cause it to get any worse. It's not even really that bad."

El just hummed a little and continued creeping along down the road. He gripped the steering wheel tight and tried to un-knot his stomach. He glanced over at Cody, who was looking back with worry. "I'm sorry," El whispered. "But you did say not to throw the game."

Cody let out a deep laugh. "That's what you've been worried about? El, I'm so incredibly proud of and happy for you! Are you kidding? You got a fucking grand slam! You should be out there celebrating and going wild, not worrying over me!"

"But I am worried," El said. True, he was proud of his hit, overall. But he wasn't proud that it had come about in such a way.

"I'm okay, El, really. I figured something out while I was sitting there with my mom."

"What's that?"

Cody smirked. "I didn't fuck up. I played a fantastic game and did my damn best despite them being here. Played so damn good your team had to hit me just to take me out."

El's stomach finally loosened, and he smiled at Cody. "Yes, you did. And it was spectacular to watch."

"So, you'll let me shower you with love and affection for making the best play of the entire season?"

El's smile grew. The thought of that sounded lovely. "Only if you let me fuss over your wound properly."

Cody chuckled. "Deal."

El nodded and happily drove along. "You know she didn't do it on purpose," Cody added.

El grumbled for a bit but then eventually sighed. "I know," he said. "I'll apologize tomorrow."

Cody nodded. "Good. Because you're definitely going to be much too busy tending to my wounds tonight for any kind of talking."

Chapter Thirty-Two
Resting and Healing

"I don't see why I have to wear a sling," Cody said, following El inside. "It's not like it's broken."

"It's so you don't move it too much," El explained. He placed Cody's bag down by the door and then turned to give him a kiss. "It needs to rest and heal."

"It's just a really bad bruise," Cody argued. Although he did accept the pain meds they had given him. Because unlike the bruise on his elbow, this one actually hurt.

"And it will only get better if you take care of it." El took Cody's good arm and led him into the living room.

"It is practically like being immobile," Cody said, dropping dramatically to the couch. "I guess I'll need 24/7 constant supervision from a sexy nurse to get through this."

El laughed and sat down next to him. "Just as long as you don't expect me to wear the outfit."

Cody's eyes opened wide at the image in his mind. But wouldn't push El into something he wasn't comfortable with. "What about if your uniform was the lace thing?" he asked instead.

A slow smile crept across El's face. "I suppose. Although, only having *one* uniform might be a problem. I should probably get another one, at least."

Cody leaned his head over, looking at El like he was the most delicious meal in the world. Because he was. "I love you so much," he said.

"I love you, too, dear." El placed a hand on Cody's cheek and kissed him.

"So, how would you like to celebrate?" Cody turned to his side and started kissing along El's jaw. "Big win. Big hit." He nipped a bit, just a gentle graze of teeth. "Deserves a big reward.

El chuckled softly. "Not with a hickey," he said.

Cody frowned against El's skin and let gravity push him down on El's body. "*But I'm injured.*"

"That still doesn't negate the fact that I have to be presentable for work."

Cody huffed, his eyes roaming over El's skin. His lovely, lovely skin that just looked so plump and delicious. He wanted to bite all over it. "Maybe, when we go on our trip, and you don't have to work, I can give you a whole bunch. That should hold me over for a while."

"We're only going for the weekend," El reminded him. "That's not enough time for them to heal."

"Mmm, but if we went for a week…" Cody let his imagination run as he started kissing again. Oh, the things they could get up to for a week. They could have romantic dinners at fancy restaurants. Go for romantic night-time strolls along the quiet streets. Having amazing sex in a big hotel bed, maybe even one of those cute heart-shaped Jacuzzis. He could treat El all kinds of right with a whole week.

"Well, I do have the vacation time," El mused.

Cody's head popped up so fast, he was sure he accidentally gave himself whiplash. "Really? Like, for real? We can do that?"

"Perhaps," El said. He finally looked over at Cody. "Only if you can afford it as well."

"Eh." Cody shrugged. "They'll survive a week without me."

"Honestly, dear. How have you not gotten fired yet?"

"I dunno." Cody sat back a bit and shrugged. "It's not like I'm not trying." He wondered himself how he was still employed there. Somehow, he must accidentally end up doing a good job. Seemed like his earlier years of fucking up were evening out.

El chuckled and turned on his side, placing a hand on Cody's cheek. "You really were meant to be a trophy husband, weren't you?"

"I *really was*," Cody agreed.

El smiled ever so sweetly at him. "Maybe one day," he said. Then he leaned down and placed a gentle kiss to Cody's lips. "But today, we shower."

"Uhhh." Cody let El grab his good arm and pull him up, leading him upstairs. "When you said one day, did you mean us one day?"

"I just mean one day," El said, his voice nonchalant. But the idea of spending the rest of his life with El felt very chalant.

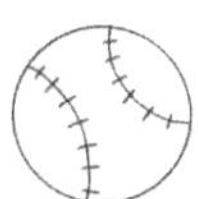

After a steamy make-out session in the shower, during which El had to continuously chastise Cody for using his injured arm too much, El was very much ready for a rest. It was still the early afternoon, but after such an intense morning, he figured a nap was allowed. And Cody had promised to take him out somewhere nice for dinner to properly 'meet the family' as a pre-reward. Although he promised the full reward for winning would come during their trip away. Which he had stubbornly refused to elaborate on.

"Don't forget to put your sling back on," El said as he got out some comfy pajamas.

"Do I gotta?" Cody asked. He had put on one of El's older t-shirts. It just barely covered the tops of his thighs. It was quite an alluring look on him. "I can't sleep with it on like that."

El hummed and dug around in his dresser for his spare sheets. "I suppose I could make you something more comfortable."

He gestured to the bed and Cody dutifully sat down. El stood before him and started wrapping the sheet around his arm and shoulder. The softer material and thicker surface area should surely help provide more comfort.

"Are you sure this is necessary?" Cody asked.

"I can't have you moving this arm now, can I?" El decided to make the whole ordeal a little more in Cody's favor. So, he climbed onto his lap as he finished up, tying the sheet off with a little bow.

Cody's good hand came up to grab his waist. "Nice bow," Cody said. He smirked at him. "Been researching that, have you?"

El smiled proudly back at him. "Oh, just a bit." He ran a hand down Cody's chest. "I could tie you up in all kinds of ways."

Cody's hips bucked underneath him. "Please be serious."

"Don't worry. I am." El smiled and leaned down for a kiss. Cody moaned into the kiss and El chuckled as he felt him struggle against his bonds. "Don't even bother," El informed him. "I'm very good at knots, you know. You will rest. And you will heal."

Cody licked his lips, leaving a delicious shine behind. "How are you so threatening and loving at the same time?"

"It's a practiced skill," El said. He decided he couldn't not kiss those lips after that.

Cody's good hand slid around, grabbing El's butt. Between them, El could feel Cody growing hard again already.

"Ah, dear," he said, pulling away softly. "I'm afraid I really am much too tired. But if you need to, I suppose you could use my legs while I nap."

Cody scoffed. "Wow. You make me sound like some sort of sex-crazed maniac." He laughed and pressed a soft kiss to El's lips. "Which, I mean, when it comes to you, I very clearly am. But I am also civilized and can be tame."

Cody wrapped his arm around El's waist and rolled them backwards, so they were laying on the bed. But he rolled a bit too far to the side. "Ow, ow, ow," he said as he struggled to sit back up.

El chuckled at his antics and stood up. "Here, let me help." He walked to the other side of the bed and pulled down the covers, helping Cody safely crawl underneath. Then he got in on the other side and settled in. "Just ten minutes," he said, already closing his eyes. "Maybe fifteen. But definitely don't let me sleep past twenty."

"You sleep for as long as you need, angel," Cody said in a soft whisper. He snuggled up to El's side, burrowing under the blankets. "We've got time."

And El smiled at that.

Chapter Thirty-Three
Fantasy Into Reality

Meeting up for dinner had become their routine. After work, whoever finished first would find a table somewhere and text the other. They'd enjoy a delightful meal and then decide on whose place to spend the night. Most of the time that place was El's. He had become suspicious that Cody didn't really like his own place all that much, which made sense since the style still didn't seem to match his personality. But after El had moved in a bookshelf, put his spare chair in the living room, and filled a drawer up with clothes, they had been spending more time there than before.

Most nights they spent together. Sure, they had their little fights and squabbles here and there. But the longest they had ever gone without being together was only a week. That was from the 'accidental' mail opening incident that El still didn't buy Cody's story on but wasn't going to let get in the way. They had just celebrated their six-month anniversary, and every day made El more and more glad they had found each other. Even if it had been started by baseball.

"Sorry, I'm late," Cody said. He brought a wave of fresh, cold air with him as he sat down. "Literally no one knows how to drive in the snow."

El smiled and started clearing away the papers before him. "No worries at all. Just glad you got here safe."

Cody studied the papers as he took off his coat and scarf. "What's all that?"

"Oh, just doing some math." El smiled quickly and then picked up his menu. He had been hopeful, but his early calculations were not helping him keep the faith.

"What kind of math?" Cody asked.

El knew that if he told Cody to drop it, he would. But he also knew that Cody would continue to be curious. And they were dating. So, it was okay for him to share his disappointments.

"I have an alert set up in my email," El said, pulling his papers back out. "It lets me know when certain properties are for sale." Cody nodded along. "Well, there's this corner shop not too far away that I've always found to be absolutely charming."

"For your bookshop?" Cody asked.

"Exactly!" El couldn't help but smile as he handed Cody the printed-out listing. "It's perfect! The location. The space. The design. It needs a little bit of work, of course, and the right furnishings, but it could make an amazing bookshop."

"It does look perfect," Cody agreed. He flipped through the pages, a smile forming with every picture.

"Unfortunately," El continued with a heavy sigh, "It's not meant to be."

"What do you mean?"

El gestured to his other notes. "I can just about afford it," he said. "The location, that is. It has living space above it, so I don't need to keep my place. But I would have quite literally nothing left over for fixes and supplies."

"What you need is an investor," Cody said. As if El hadn't already thought of that.

"Easier said than done," El told him. "Not many people are interested in investing in a bookshop, I'm afraid."

"I'm interested in investing in a bookshop," Cody said.

El laughed at him, but Cody just stared at him with a straight face. "Are you serious?"

Cody nodded. "I've got some money saved up. And, I mean, I figured we're about half an inch away from moving in together anyway, so, ya know, we can share that little apartment and I can get rid of my place."

El's mouth fell open slightly. Cody had just admitted to wanting to live together and invest in his business. El had felt they were approaching the 'move-in' discussion himself, but he hadn't expected something big like that.

"Everything okay?" Cody asked. He frowned softly. "Do you...*not* want me to invest in your business?"

El slowly shook his head. "I don't want you to invest in my bookshop." Cody's frown deepened. "I want you to be a full partner in my business." The frown dissolved, forming into a small smile. "If that's what you want, of course."

"I can't think of a single thing I'd want more," Cody said. He leaned forward on the table, his eyes getting a beautiful little shine to them.

"This would be a big step in our relationship," El said. "Are you sure you're ready for that kind of commitment?" Because for as tantalizing the prospect was, El wanted to make sure they were both prepared for that.

"At the risk of sounding too eager, I've been ready for that commitment since the first time you kissed me and then just left me standing there as if I didn't just experience a slice of heaven."

El grabbed Cody's hands and then leaned over the table, meeting him for a kiss.

"Maybe after dinner we can go for a drive past the shop? So you can see it in person before deciding?"

"I've already decided," Cody said. "But I'm not gonna say no to a night-time drive with you."

-

After viewing the property, which looked as magnificent in the night as it did in the day, El decided they had one last trip to make. So, he pulled up a map on his phone and directed Cody down a few backroads leading out of the city.

"Uhhh," Cody looked out at the forest path. "Is this where you're going to stash my body? Was this entire relationship just an elaborate assassination attempt?"

El chuckled and reached over to pat Cody's hand. "Nothing like that. Quite the opposite, actually. I think you're going to enjoy this very much." He pointed to the small side road. "You can pull up over there."

"Alrighty." Cody pulled over and parked the car. "Should I turn the car off?"

"No." El fiddled with the radio controls, flipping through the stations until he found something soft and classical. "I know it's not your normal make-out music," he said. "But I think it fits the mood tonight, no?"

"And what is the mood tonight, angel?" Cody raised an eyebrow and smiled softly.

El tried to keep a straight face, but it was hard when Cody was acting so cute. "Why don't you get into the back seat and tell me?"

Cody's eyes widened, his eyebrow rising even further. "Oh? Is that-I mean, are-are we doing this?"

"If you want to."

Cody's response was to immediately start taking off his shirt as he climbed into the back. El laughed and leaned to the side, avoiding Cody's flailing legs as he crawled through. After he got in and settled, El took a more graceful approach of actually getting out of the car first to pull up the seat.

Cody danced antsy in the seat as El settled in. El worked his way onto Cody's lap, knocking his head softly on the top before bending over enough, and wrapped his arms around Cody's shoulder. Cody's kisses instantly fell to his neck. El laughed, but he knew he had nothing to worry about. Cody had proven to be an expert in kissing, sucking, and biting without leaving any permanent marks behind. And El had learned he didn't need to constantly remind Cody not to give him hickeys. Cody knew what El did and didn't want. He was in good hands.

"It feels like we might be do for another week-long trip," El mused as Cody's lips peppered across his skin.

Cody hummed a note of agreement. "When we own our own business, we can take as many week-long trips as we want."

"Mmm, there is a large book fair in Germany I've always wanted to go to. But it'll probably be a while until we can afford to leave."

"You kidding?" Cody's head popped back up. His eyes were wide, pupils dilated and hungry. "With your charm and my general air of presence, we'll be making a killin' in no time."

"I appreciate your enthusiasm, dear. But we should be realistic. Most new businesses don't usually make a profit until at least year two."

"Most new businesses aren't run by us."

"You're right. Better expect five years to start."

Cody growled and then shifted. His arms wrapped around El's waist as he turned them to the side, pulling out and up so El's body could lay in the back seat, Cody hovering over him. It wasn't entirely comfortable, and half of El was spilling over the edge a bit. But Cody looked so gorgeous with his hair hanging down in soft waves, his eyes lit up by desire, his chest moving high with each rapid breath.

El didn't want to spend any more time joking about the shop. He just wanted to be so completely wrapped up in Cody's presence. He placed his hands on Cody's shoulders and pulled him down until they were kissing again. Cody's body settled like a comfortable weight over El's. And despite how perfectly their groins aligned, there was still much too much in between them.

"How, exactly, does this work?" El asked. His knees were glad to have the rest from straddling Cody's lap, but now his side and hip were starting to hurt a bit. It would have to be quick, whatever it was.

"Yeah," Cody said, looking at the space around them. "My other cars were a bit bigger."

El chuckled and tried to straighten out a bit. "Well, we can make it work, I'm sure."

"Here." Cody reached down, still managing to keep his upper body lifted as his hands grabbed El's waist. He pressed his pelvis down, closing the distance between their groins, rubbing deliciously against El's clothed erection.

"Ah," El said, surprised by the way his voice sounded. "Are you sure that's comfortable?"

Cody just nodded and continued to grind himself around, moving his hips up and down, forward and backward, side to side in a way that sent shivers of delight up and down El's spine.

"Why don't you come back down here and kiss me," El suggested. He worried Cody might pull a muscle in that position.

"Can't get a good angle then," Cody said.

"Well, we'll figure it out." El grabbed Cody's shoulders, pulling him back down. Cody's hands slipped away from El's waist. He kept moving his hips as best he could, but there was much less pressure and sensation.

"See?" Cody said, placing a quick kiss on El's lips. "Not as good."

"Just, wait a moment." El huffed at his impatience and managed to successfully wiggle one leg free. He placed his foot on the floor as best he could, toes just reaching as he bent. Then he shuffled his other leg up and out, pressing his shoe against the frame of the car for support. With his legs open like that, Cody could dig his knees into the seat, using the added pressure to grind them together even better than before.

"Fuck," Cody whispered. His voice was dark and sultry in El's ear.

"I agree," El said.

He wrapped his arms around Cody and held him close as they moved together. It wasn't a very comfortable position, but the lovely rub between their groins was a good distraction. They both knew that this was not maintainable in the long run, so Cody didn't hold back as he moved and pushed and ground down against El. And El did what he could to help things along, running a hand through Cody's hair and whispering sweet words of love against his skin.

Cody came first, a rare feat El had only managed to accomplish twice before. And the wet warmth that spread between them gave El that extra push he needed to chase his own release. Cody was up and moving while El was still coming down. He grabbed El in his arms and helped pull him up, ducking out of the way of his leg. With a little more acrobatic-like moves, they eventually ended up sitting comfortably side by side in the back seat.

"So?" El asked, grabbing Cody's hand and running his thumb over the back of it. "How was it?"

"I'm still not convinced it wasn't a dream," Cody said with a soft laugh.

El knew they would have to move sometime soon, get back to one of their places and clean up. But he was basking in the glow of a future that promised love, joy, and freedom. So, he just laid his head against Cody's shoulder and said, "You know, if we're going to be business partners, we might want to consider being partners in everything else."

"Like crime?"

El chuckled. "Like marriage."

"Oh, thank god you said it!" Cody twisted and pulled El into another hungry kiss. "I've been wanting to bring it up *forever* but didn't want to scare ya off or anything."

El smiled and kissed Cody back. "So that's a yes?"

"That's an abso-fucking-lutely."

El laughed into their kiss and held Cody close. All that time playing a game he didn't really care about was certainly worth it if it meant spending forever with the love of his life.

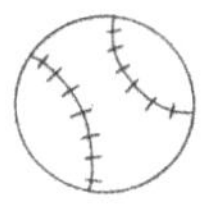

Strike Three: You're In Love

END